Stay in touch through the C. N. Jarrett newsletter!

MISS ABBOTT AND THE SUSPECT LORD

RELUCTANT RECKONINGS
BOOK ONE

C. N. JARRETT

ROGUE
PRESS

To Dee, the truest friend I have ever met.

Your honor knows no bounds.

PROLOGUE

"The rise of the birds in their flight is a sign of an ambush.
Frightened beasts indicate a sudden attack is coming."

Sun Tzu, *L'Art de la Guerre* (*The Art of War*)

JULY 20, 1821, JUST AFTER 6:00 A.M.

The baron is dead.

Brendan Ridley staggered through the gloom of the study, his boots muffled by the thick rug as he sank into an armchair opposite the fireplace. The early morning light strained through the curtains, casting long, pallid rays that mingled with the wavering candlelight to illuminate a scene grotesque in its composition.

Lord Josiah Ridley lay motionless on the carpet, a dark pool of blood seeping beneath his thinning hair. His eyes—glassy and vacant—stared upward into nothing. The silence was thick, punctuated only by the soft flicker of

1

wax-dripped candles and the measured tick of the baron's carriage clock. The once-imposing mahogany desk stood violated, drawers flung wide, their contents ransacked in a hurried search.

Brendan pressed his fingertips to his temples, the weight of realization settling over him like sodden cloak. He had just become Baron of Filminster.

Long live the baron.

The thought landed with the weight of irony and a stab of bitterness. How was he meant to feel? Aggrieved? Hollow? Vindicated?

Perhaps all of those at once.

Josiah Ridley had never been a true father to him. The truth had arrived years earlier, on the eve of Brendan's majority. With clipped formality, he had been banished from Baydon Hall, and the reason had followed swiftly behind. Josiah was not his father but his uncle. The elder Ridley, Brendan's true sire, had died in a fall from a spirited mare mere weeks before his intended wedding. Brendan's mother, already with child, had married Josiah instead. A swift union to preserve reputations and ensure lineage.

Brendan had lived under the man's roof, but never in his affection. They had not spoken in over half a decade, Brendan confined to this London townhouse while the baron brooded in Somerset, tethered to Baydon Hall by fear. A terror of horses had rooted him to the countryside for more than twenty years. And yet, against all expectation, he had come to London. For the coronation.

And now ... this.

Brendan stood slowly, his limbs heavy. He moved to the body, gaze falling upon the twisted sculpture that had been discarded near Josiah's head. Bronze. A horse rearing on its hind legs, nostrils flared in frozen alarm. Blood streaked the muzzle.

The image was obscene. Macabre. Fitting, somehow.

The baron had not left Filminster in two decades, so profound was his mortal dread of horses. That he should now lie dead beside a sculpture of one was not only grotesque, it was unnervingly poetic.

Was it coincidence? Cruel poetry? Or intent?

He swallowed against the lump rising in his throat. A wave of dread built beneath his breastbone.

It would only grow worse from here.

He knew it. *Felt it.*

Brendan rubbed his temples again, more forcefully this time. The gossipmongers would have their whispers before the clocks struck nine. He, the estranged heir. Alone in the house. A quarrel, perhaps. A financial motive. Convenient timing.

He could already hear the murmurs forming in the clubs and drawing rooms.

And Lady Slight—she of the knowing smile and selective allegiance—would not be emerging to offer him an alibi. Of that he was quite certain.

CHAPTER
ONE

"He will win whose army is animated by the same spirit throughout all its ranks."

Sun Tzu, *L'Art de la Guerre* (*The Art of War*)

JULY 19, 1821, ONE DAY EARLIER

"Lily!"

Her heart sank like a stone into a pond. Lily Abbott positioned her silver fork on her plate and, pinning a broad smile to her lips, turned to face her mother. She did not miss her brother pressing his twitching lips together, his chocolate-brown eyes dancing with amusement as he lifted his cup of coffee for a sip.

It was Lily's third Season, a fact that was causing increasing panic in Mama, whose energies were consumed by the imperative of securing her daughter a respectable match.

Lily had hoped that Aidan's recent return from his Grand Tour would divide Lady Moreland's formidable attention. However, it seemed her brother's bachelorhood was far less concerning than her own unmarried state.

"Mama ..." She injected her voice with cheerful enthusiasm, a performance honed through many such encounters. Lily had always been exuberant, but she had honed that quality into a strategic art form, a kind of armor. She had discovered that if she chattered long enough, Mama would become distracted and lose her train of thought, allowing Lily to steer the conversation toward safer ground. "You look lovely! Your gown is immaculate, and the beadwork so intricate. You shall quite eclipse the King's coronation robes in such a glorious ensemble!"

Behind her, Aidan emitted a discreet snort of laughter as Lady Moreland paused to preen, smoothing her hands over her lavish skirts while casting a proud glance down at her coronation finery. Lily's compliment was not without merit. Her mother was striking, her sleek brown hair made luminous by the pearl-studded gold and red velvet coronet that denoted her rank as viscountess.

But the distraction was fleeting. Lady Moreland's sharp gaze returned to her daughter.

"What happened with Lord Ashby?"

"We danced together. It was a waltz, and the music was sublime. I do believe the musicians were quite masterful, and I could have danced until sunrise." Aidan snorted again behind her, clearly stifling laughter as Lily launched into her verbal gambit. Her brother had always seen through her tactics.

"Lily!" her mother interjected, her tone clipped.

Lily clamped her mouth shut and offered an innocent smile. "Yes, Mama?"

Lady Moreland did not appear in the mood to be side-tracked. The grandeur of the coronation had evidently stirred every thought of marriage into a fresh frenzy, and Lily feared this particular interrogation would not be easily evaded.

She cast a subtle glance over her shoulder, a silent appeal to Aidan, who watched the scene with undisguised amusement as he sipped his coffee.

"Lord Ashby was quite taken with you, but after your dance, his mother told me he had abruptly lost interest. What in the world did you say to him?"

Lily lifted a hand to rub the edge of her earlobe, the movement unconscious as she sifted through her memory. Her talent for cheerful misdirection seemed less reliable after a night spent attending a ball until dawn.

"I simply admired the musicians' skill and praised the servants' livery. I may have commented on how splendid the ballroom looked, dressed as it was with hothouse flowers and—"

Her mother groaned aloud. "Did you chatter the entire dance?"

"I suppose I might have," Lily admitted, not quite contrite.

"Oh, Lily! How will you ever make a match if you will not stop blabbering like a fool?"

"Mother," Aidan interrupted with the cool assurance of a man who knew he could take liberties without consequence, "I think we must accept that Lord Ashby and Lily are, regrettably, ill-suited."

Lily's heart leapt with relief when Aidan interrupted. Ever since her cousin Sophia had left their household to marry the Earl of Saunton the year before, Lily had contended with her mother's matchmaking unaided. Now that her brother had returned from his Grand Tour, perhaps she would not have to face Lady Moreland's impatience alone. If they could scheme together, she might yet make a match rooted in love and mutual admiration, like Sophia's, a union of laughter in drawing rooms and quiet understanding at breakfast, not one forged in social obligation and her mother's expectations.

Not that Papa would ever compel her to marry against her inclination, but Mama's relentless ambitions wound through their days like the tightening of a corset at dawn. Subtle, pressing, inexorable.

Lady Moreland frowned, perplexed by her son's bold assertion. "Whatever do you mean?"

"Lord Ashby, if I am not mistaken, is an utter bore who only speaks of horseflesh and hounds. Not to mention he is thirty years her senior and has several children from his previous marriages. Lily and he have no commonalities between them and would have nothing to discuss at the breakfast table."

"Matches have proved successful over less. And Lily's babbling must be reined in."

"I find Lily's conversation delightful and her optimism infectious. She amuses me during even the most melancholy of days. If Lord Ashby cannot appreciate her for the jewel she is and would discard her after a single waltz, then he does not deserve her."

Their mother sighed and leaned back. She appeared unwilling to spar further with her eldest. "You could introduce more of your friends to her, Aidan."

"Perhaps I shall."

Lily had been glancing between them, her head moving slightly as the tension in the air softened. She cast a quick, grateful wink toward Aidan, who returned her look with a small smile, just as his expression changed. His eyes shifted to something beyond her shoulder and widened in astonishment. His jaw fell open.

Startled, Lily twisted to look behind her, one gloved hand flying to her mouth to catch a laugh.

Lady Moreland gave way to laughter—high, musical, and uncontrolled—as her husband entered the morning room. It was a rare sight to see the usually reserved viscountess doubled over, laughter spilling from her as she clutched her waist.

Lord Moreland stood before them, a handsome man in his fifties with silver threading through his brown hair and a build that still commanded a room. But not even his stature could preserve his dignity in the garments required of him.

Thanks to King George IV's whimsical tastes and formal declarations for the coronation, the College of Arms had imposed a sartorial horror upon the peers of the realm. Lord Moreland had been forced into antique dress that had not graced a living man's body since the last century.

He wore a tight-fitting doublet of ivory silk, the buttons glinting like coins in the gaslight. His gold-and-white breeches ballooned absurdly at the thigh, ending high above white silk stockings that clung to his muscular legs like clotted cream. The heeled shoes clicked faintly on the tiled floor. A long cloak of crimson velvet, lined in pristine ermine, swept behind him like a banner, and at his throat, an elaborate ruff framed his face in theatrical absurdity.

"Faugh! I have never been so happy that I am a mere heir and not the holder of the title!" Aidan cried.

Lily's laughter burst free, her chest shaking with mirth as her father turned a rich, mottled red and cast a rueful look at his audience.

"The other options were worse, in my estimation. My tailor insisted this would suit me best."

"That is hard to believe," Lily wheezed, struggling for air.

Lord Moreland's eyes twinkled. "Perhaps he advised me for his own amusement."

At last, Lady Moreland composed herself enough to speak again, smoothing her gown of sapphire silk with both hands as if to re-anchor her dignity. "Aidan, we shall be out late. You must remain home and keep Lily company."

Aidan nodded with exaggerated solemnity. "I promise to keep an eye on my little sister and ensure no harm befalls her, Mother."

Lily's heart warmed. Since his return, Aidan had been constantly in demand by friends and acquaintances, flitting from ball to club as easily as she moved between fittings and musicales. She missed him. She longed to hear the stories he had promised—the rise of the sun over Roman rooftops, the glow of candlelight in Venetian palazzos, and the scent of lavender fields in Provence. But he had been swept up in London society since the moment he had set foot back on English soil.

Their childhood closeness, once unmarred by propriety or separate spheres, had faded like an old watercolor. Now, every shared moment was a small treasure.

"I expect you to keep that promise, young man!" their mother said, her voice sharp with playfulness, her eyes soft.

The entire Abbott household had rejoiced at Aidan's return. For Lily, tonight offered a rare reprieve from social maneuvering, from the artifice of presentation. An evening with her brother, laughing by the pianoforte or reminiscing over slices of currant cake, was a balm to her heart.

BRENDAN DREW A DEEP BREATH, the heaviness of it sitting beneath his ribs, then reached out and opened the door to his rooms. He could put it off no longer.

Lord Filminster had arrived two days earlier—his first visit to London in as much as two decades—and demanded Brendan's presence downstairs today. The baron had sent word of his imminent arrival, but Brendan had been certain he would cancel the trip. He had wagered on the man's cowardice, and so the fact of his arrival, despite the warning, still had the power to surprise him.

Most of Brendan's acquaintances would describe him as an affable young man who always had a friendly word for everyone he met. If he were honest, he caroused too frequently with his friends—not to mention, his days were decidedly idle. But he took the time to lift the spirits of those around him, and he enjoyed visiting his sister and brother-in-law, the Duke of Halmesbury, as well as his nephew, Jasper.

Yet seeing Lord Filminster for the first time in some years had reminded him of the wrenching anxiety that his uncle stirred in the region of his gut, which was currently twisting and writhing as he began his reluctant walk down the hall. That cold tension had never quite gone; it merely slept until roused, and now it stirred with every step.

Fortunately, he had not seen the baron much, but today, he was to meet with him in his study. The *baron's* study.

Deuce it! It is my study!

Brendan had been working out of it since leaving Filminster on his twenty-first birthday, and it was rotten luck that his uncle-father had finally found the courage to leave his estate. The only explanation for showing such fortitude was that the baron was a vainglorious buffoon whose craving to attend the prestigious coronation had finally outweighed his fear of travel.

Lucky me.

With an increasing sense of dread, he began his descent, the worn carpet beneath his boots speaking to how long it had been since the townhouse had been renovated, while the wide wooden boards creaked in protest at his weight.

Why would the old man bother to keep the townhouse properly maintained?

It was a source of irritation to Brendan, one of many. That he was beholden to the baron, a mean-spirited old goat, was galling. Had events transpired as they should have, Brendan's own father would be Lord Filminster, and Brendan himself would be a valued heir. Instead, he was an orphan and obligated to obey his uncle so he could access his allowance.

As he reached the front hall, Brendan's thoughts flittered to the last time he and the baron had corresponded. Three years earlier, Brendan had fancied himself in love with a lovely young woman, until Lord Filminster had written to her father and informed him that Brendan would be cut off if a match was made. The baron had deemed the young woman unsuitable, being from a wealthy but untitled family.

Brendan would have proceeded despite the baron's interference, for he would eventually inherit the title, and it would restore his finances. But her father had abruptly ended their courtship, with a formality that left no opening for hope. Brendan had buried his sorrows in the arms of a friendly widow, who had been flirting with him for some time, and subsequently vowed to never make a match that his uncle approved of. Unfortunately, he feared their conversation today was to address this subject, for he knew of no other reason for the baron to require his presence.

The scent of beeswax and aged plaster lingered in the corridor, faint and dry. Shaking the thoughts from his head, Brendan noticed he had arrived at the study. The carved paneling of the door bore scratches that had not been polished out, and the brass knob was dulled from age and use. He raised a heavy hand to rap his knuckles on the door.

"Come," intoned a disinterested voice.

Brendan entered and closed the door behind him, before finding his uncle standing by the fireplace. The room smelled faintly of lavender water, the sort a valet might splash on linens. He choked back a laugh when he saw how the old man was dressed, raising a hand to cover his mouth as though suppressing a cough.

The baron was in heeled court shoes, which did little to raise his diminutive stature, his spindly legs revealed in white stockings while his white-and-gold striped trunk hose—an antiquated style of short, voluminous breeches—ballooned absurdly around his hips. His doublet was form-fitting, which revealed a potbelly spilling over his codpiece, while a velvet and ermine cape was fitted over his shoulders. A ruff around his neck made him appear to be all shoulders and head, while the gilt circlet on his head did nothing to disguise his thinning hair, which was brushed forward in the style of Napoleon. The baron was at once gaudy resplendent and ridiculous in the unbecoming attire.

Lord Filminster's beady eyes narrowed in suspicion, and he tugged at his doublet with a smugness that belied any awareness of what a humorous figure he cut. But the baron had always had a poor sense of fashion, and no one could accuse him of being a Beau Brummell, so perhaps he thought his attire handsome. Not for the first time, Brendan was grateful that he did not view the world through his uncle-father's eyes. He did not think he would enjoy the perspective.

"There you are, Ridley." Brendan grimaced. Was he going to be addressed as a passing acquaintance, then? "Is it customary for you to leave your rooms so late in the day?"

Brendan once again bit back a laugh. The man probably did not know how to pull on his own stockings, but he was to lecture on tardiness? Forcing a pleasant smile, Brendan walked forward to sprawl into an armchair facing his uncle. From past experience, he knew the old man was like a dog with a bone. If Brendan revealed any reaction to one of his vicious nips, the baron would gnaw at the offending subject with relish, seeking further cracks in the armor.

The trick was to keep a friendly face and steadfast composure. Brendan had not missed these biting conversations in the least, not the hollow remarks nor the grating pretense. Even when he had pined for his half-sister, the only family connection he had ever truly cared for, he had not longed for the baron's company. Fortunately, he and Annabel had reunited after her marriage. Lord Filminster had lost the power to keep them apart once she had gained her autonomy as a duchess.

"While I am in Town, I am arranging for you to meet suitable women."

Brendan kept the smile on his face, though every muscle ached to twitch. Internally, he cursed.

How long is the baron staying?

"My social calendar is currently filled, with engagements with unsuitable women and whatnot."

Lord Filminster clenched his jaw at the supercilious tone, and Brendan squashed a kindling of delight at having raised a reaction from the man who loathed him so. "Those types of engagements will have to wait until you marry."

"You mean I should pursue the type of marriage you were attempting to force on Annabel? Her prospective husband knocking boots on the side while she waits for him in the country?"

The baron's fists balled at his sides, small and pale with liver spots, his rings glinting in the firelight. For a moment, he looked ready to stomp his foot like the imp from the German tale of Rumpelstiltskin. Brendan might have enjoyed the comparison more had it not been his own future the imp meant to unravel.

"It is the way of high society," his uncle responded defensively.

"Not according to the man she actually married—the duke."

"The duke is obsessed with the hoyden for no reason I can fathom. She is a useless girl with no feminine accomplishments."

"I am not sure about that. My friends seem quite impressed with the duchess."

Lord Filminster broke eye contact, his mouth tightening in ire. He was not accustomed to having his heir defy him. The last time they had met in person, Brendan had been little more than a green youth, but the years had lent him something more solid beneath his skin, a quiet defiance that no longer trembled.

"We will meet Miss Hartnett with her family tomorrow night for supper. And you are to meet with me first thing tomorrow morning so I can provide you with a list of engagements we will be attending together."

"Miss Agnes Hartnett? She is seventeen years old!"

Brendan knew he should not react, but the exclamation had slipped out before he could contain it.

"And the daughter of a viscount."

"You mean the *child* of a viscount?"

The baron smirked, his eyes glittering with triumph. He seemed to relish Brendan's discomfort. "All the better for your pursuits with merry widows."

Brendan wanted to roll his eyes, but refrained. He had no intention of pursuing the sort of marriage where he and his wife would live as polite strangers, crossing paths like two guests in a wide hallway. When he married, it would be to a woman with wit, warmth, and steel beneath her stays. A true partner. And he would not stray. But this was not the time to speak of ideals.

He needed to meet with the duke. If anyone could help formulate a plan to rid him of the baron, it would be Halmesbury. Annabel and her husband were among the few people who understood Lord Filminster's particular strain of manipulation. Unfortunately, with coronation obligations consuming them, Brendan would have to endure a few more days of meddling before he could seek their aid.

"When would you like to meet?"

"I expect you to be here at first light."

Brendan forced an affable grin and stood up. "I will see you first thing, then."

The baron waved a hand in a lazy gesture of dismissal, his circlet catching the lamplight. Brendan accepted the wave as his opportunity to escape. And to think.

As he left the study, he nearly collided with Michaels, their London butler, who was stationed directly outside the door. The older man straightened to his full height, several inches shy of Brendan's, and bent his neck back awkwardly to cast a look down his nose with all the theatrical disdain of the little French emperor. With a haughty sniff, Michaels turned and stalked away, the tails of his coat swaying stiffly behind him, leaving Brendan to wonder whether the scornful servant had been eavesdropping.

W HEN L ILY CAME DOWN for supper, she found her brother in the front hall. He was dressed to go out, with a tall-crowned beaver hat perched at a jaunty angle atop his dark hair, a coat slung carelessly over his shoulders, and gloves in hand. The scent of leather and a hint of bay rum clung to him, carried on the faint draft from the opened front door.

Her spirits plummeted in disappointment. "You are not staying in with me?"

Aidan caught her hand in a coaxing manner as he smiled down at her. His cravat was too impeccably tied for a quiet night at home, and the gleam in his eye spoke of mischief and freedom. Lily cursed her height. Her brother towered over her, and all she could do was stand about with the appearance of a child, barely clearing five feet in her satin slippers. If she displayed any anger at being abandoned for the evening, she would simply appear to be throwing a tantrum.

"You do not mind, do you, Lily Billy? It is just that my friends have invited me to enjoy a game of whist at our club, and all the titled nobs are occupied with the coronation, so we will have the run of the place."

"I was looking forward to catching up, Aidan! You have barely spent a moment with me since you returned to London. I am going to be dragged to the country soon for a house party, and Mama will be throwing titled gentlemen at me with every step I take."

"I swear I will stay in tomorrow, but tonight is too unprecedented to pass up. You would not want me to miss out, would you? Not after I distracted Mother from her ideas about Lord Ashby?"

"I did not know that would be an excuse to abandon me!"

"It is not abandonment. It is merely a postponement."

Lily relented. Aidan was clearly committed to his plans, and she did not wish to stand in the way of his fun. She wished she could go with him, to slip past the paneled threshold and out into the lamplit night, where laughter echoed down club-lined streets and gentlemen smoked cheroots beneath the glow of gaslight. But she was a young unwed lady and not permitted to do anything interesting. The rules penned for her gender hemmed her in like the boning in her stays.

If only she could find a gentleman whom she wished to marry. As a married woman, her whole world would open up—an independence of schedule, of conversation, of freedom. But she was unwilling to compromise her standards by settling for an old or inferior gentleman.

"Oh, very well! But I expect you to regale me with stories of your travels tomorrow night."

Aidan lifted a hand to chuck her on the chin. "We will spend the entire evening together in the library, Lily Billy. Thank you for this. You are a dashed fine sister!"

Lily sighed, smiling as she watched him draw on his gloves. The supple leather gleamed softly as he tugged them over his fingers.

"I am holding you to that, Aidan. No begging off tomorrow night."

Once he departed, the house grew still, the echo of the front door fading down the tiled corridor. Lily requested her supper tray be brought to the front drawing room, which overlooked the houses across the street and offered an oblique view of the square. The fire had been lit earlier, and the gentle crackle added warmth to the hushed space. She would feel silly eating alone at the dining table, and the window seat in the drawing room was her favorite reading spot. Cushioned and curved into the bay, it offered a view of flickering streetlamps and the distant glow of lamps in the neighboring houses.

She could not help reflecting that she had been doing far too much reading this past year. It was better than fending off elderly lords at a ball, but still. After three years, it was time she met a genuinely eligible man so she could enter a courtship, but that seemed as likely as sprouting a tail, after her third Season of no success.

Where were the truly intriguing gentlemen? Not on the marriage mart, it would seem.

TWO

"Carefully study the welfare of your men and do not overload them. Focus your energy and build up your strength. Keep your army constantly on the move and make unfathomable plans."

Sun Tzu, *L'Art de la Guerre* (*The Art of War*)

❧

L ily had called for Nancy, her father's former nursemaid, to sit with her while she worked on her embroidery. The dear woman was advanced in years. She was also as deaf as a post, which suited Lily because she could chatter her private thoughts to the servant without any concern for them being heard—or remembered. This was infinitely preferable to being alone or, heaven forfend, chattering to herself like a madwoman. With Sophia gone, Lily had fallen into the habit of jabbering to Nancy far too frequently.

Dash it! She was in desperate need of a suitable gentleman. No debutante was meant to wander the social events for this long.

"It is all rather trying, Nancy. I have discovered that chattering to the gentlemen who are unsuitable has chased them away, as I had planned. The problem is now I babble more than I ever have, so when I meet a gentleman who might be interesting, I become nervous and over-talk more than I would under normal circumstances."

"I thought you already attend formal dances, Miss Lily?" Nancy had looked up from her sewing, confusion on her wizened old face and her mobcap askew in her white hair, which gave her the appearance of having just risen from bed.

Lily hesitated, running her words back through her head before suppressing a giggle. "NORMAL CIRCUM-STANCES, not formal dances."

The old woman nodded without comprehension before lowering her head to continue darning with arthritic fingers. Papa had many times attempted to pension off his beloved childhood servant, but Nancy was adamant that she wanted to remain working in their household, and he had not the heart to reject her wishes. Her duties were minimal, mostly darning and companionship to Lily when she was wont.

"Lord Ashby was scared off, but then later that night, I met his son, Mr. Ashby. The gentleman was quite fine, and I was excited to share a dance with him. But instead of getting to know each other, I babbled like a fool about the flavor of the orgeat, which I thought was exceptional, until Mr. Ashby's eyes glazed over. He hurried me back to Mama and ran off as if his father's hounds were chasing him. How am I to make a meaningful connection when my nerves trip me up so? It was all very disappointing!"

"Mr. Ashby was pointing? Innit rude?" Nancy's raspy voice interjected.

Lily blinked, staring down at her needlework for a second while she tried to think what Nancy thought she had heard. "DISAPPOINTING. MY BABBLING ... is disappointing."

Nancy shrugged. "Yes, miss."

Lily gazed sightlessly at her floss, admitting the truth of it. She had quite been looking forward to meeting Mr. Ashby—a handsome gentleman of a similar age to herself, and one of the very few braving the marriage mart in search of a bride—and she had frightened him off within seconds of meeting him.

Biting her lip, she sighed heavily. She needed to find a match so her life could begin, but she did not want to settle for someone for whom she shared no affinity. Her unfortunate habit of overtalking was a gift when it came to warding off unwanted attentions, a crafty stratagem she had developed after reading the book on military strategy her cousin had given her. But craftiness did not help her be any more measured or composed when she met a man she could genuinely consider marrying, and a certain amount of shyness settled in.

Most men thought she was a silly flibbertigibbet. After three Seasons, she suspected they might be right. She was barely five feet tall, had the general appearance of a young girl dressed in the ridiculous white and pastels Mama insisted she wear despite her being over twenty years on this earth, and being a chatterbox reinforced the impression that she was merely an exuberant child.

"But I shall eventually meet the right gentleman. I could meet my future husband anytime and be betrothed within two weeks. I simply must persevere. Sophia met the earl only twice, and they wed within a week of their second dance, so my luck could change at any moment."

Lily was relieved that her usual optimism had caught up with her. Her thoughts had been taking a cheerless turn, and she did not want to dwell on the passage of time nor her shortcomings. She was bright and friendly. When she wed, she could finally wear the rich colors that would accentuate her brown hair and chocolate eyes. Until then, she would need to persist in her quest to find the gentleman who would find her irrepressibly charming and make an offer to Papa.

"Is someone betrothed?" Nancy's question brought her back to the present.

"No, Nancy! BUT I WISH TO BE. To the right man, of course."

Nancy nodded politely, clearly not understanding.

"Perhaps now that Aidan is home, he could introduce me to some younger gentlemen. I wish to make a match with someone I will spend a lifetime with, not an old man who can barely hold himself up without my assistance, or is as old or older than Papa."

"You wish to eat your supper?"

Lily frowned at the fabric in her hand, trying to work out what Nancy was going on about. "Not supper ... PAPA!"

"Master Hugh is home?" Nancy swung her head round to the door to look for her young—old—charge, causing Lily to burst into a fit of giggles. Aidan could not leave her alone tomorrow night, because if she did not soon have a forthright conversation with someone who could actually hear her, she was sure to be committed to Bedlam before she could meet her match.

Noting the old maid stifling a yawn, Lily took pity and sent Nancy off with an affectionate shooing. She could not formally send her to bed so early in the evening, but she knew Nancy would find a comfortable spot to doze off until bedtime. Anyone who stumbled upon the old maid sleeping would simply turn a blind eye and wander off to a different part of the townhouse.

BRENDAN WAS ENJOYING a snifter of fine French brandy at his club, nestled in a corner armchair with the carved lion feet worn smooth by generations of noble indolence. The soft hum of muted conversation and the faint scent of leather-bound volumes usually provided a peaceful atmosphere. But today, it was shattered.

A horde of young men had descended. With the lords occupied by the coronation, evidently the clubs were being overrun by green fools taking advantage of the usual members' absence to claim the prime seating and avoid the disapproving stares of their elders.

A particularly spirited group of dandies, clad in elegant black coats with gleaming buttons and precisely tied cravats, congregated around the betting book, placing demented wagers about the King's coronation attire. One of the gents claimed inside knowledge, and the others responded with eager, ridiculous bets.

Brendan had come for quiet, to think on how best to free himself from the baron's tiresome attention and to savor a well-earned drink. It had been a solid plan until the lads arrived and unraveled it with their noise and energy. He rubbed his temples in exasperation as the group began squabbling over the cost of the crown hatband on George IV's plumed headpiece.

"Eight thousand pounds! I win!" one crowed, triggering a mild roar of protest from the others.

Brendan recalled making a few foolhardy wagers in his younger days, but the shine of those youthful antics had long since dulled. Reuniting with his sister three years earlier, and observing the quiet devotion that had bloomed between her and the Duke of Halmesbury, had stirred thoughts he had long buried. Thoughts of family. Of belonging.

It had been the arrival of his little nephew, with his mother's brandy-colored eyes and the duke's firm chin, that fully awakened the yearning.

The ennui with his current circumstances had truly set in when one of his closest friends, the Earl of Saunton, had unexpectedly wed Miss Sophia Hayward. Almost immediately, the earl's younger brother, Peregrine Balfour, had dashed willingly into the parson's noose with a young woman from the country, and the pair had disappeared into quiet Somerset life. Brendan could not help but feel the empty space they had left behind.

Genuine friends were thin on the ground these days, with only him and Lord Trafford left from their group to represent the bachelors about Town. Reflecting on this, Brendan supposed he had gained a certain ace of spades from the tangle of romantic changes around him, though not in the way others might think. The widow, Lady Slight, having been deeply offended by Peregrine Balfour's rejection in favor of a country-bred bride, had at last turned her attentions elsewhere and shown Brendan a marked preference that flattered him, after what had been a long, elegant chase.

It had been a pleasant reprieve, he supposed. But even now, the thrill of it was fleeting. As each of his friends had done, he too wished, one day, to find a woman who challenged and inspired him. A woman whose presence lingered long after the wine was gone and the laughter had faded. But today was not that day, and the baron would not be the one to shepherd him toward such a life. Brendan would follow that path when he was good and ready and had found the right woman.

And not a moment earlier.

No one would make such a monumental decision on his behalf.

He finished his brandy and stood, looking about for anyone he knew, but most of the set were a couple of years younger than himself. He might be only seven-and-twenty, but he felt decidedly mature compared to this youthful, unruly crowd.

Drawing out his fob, he checked his timepiece and exhaled in relief. There was a certain vivid-haired beauty in Grosvenor Square who had hinted she would be at home to receive him this evening. Brendan pulled on his gloves and gathered his things, heading for the entrance. He sidestepped with practiced ease when one boy stumbled backward, swearing loudly, oblivious to who might be passing, as only a lad deep in drink could be.

Brendan bit back his irritation. He could still look forward to a peaceful evening—perhaps a warm welcome, a shared glass of wine, a moment of ease before he dealt with the baron in the morning.

Behind him, the boy fell to the ground with a loud thump. Brendan came to a halt. Looking around, he noticed none of the boy's companions were paying the least attention to their friend sprawled on the floor. With a sigh, Brendan stepped back and dropped to one knee to assess the youth's condition.

Oblivious.

Peering at him closely, Brendan squinted, a flicker of recognition dawning. Frowning, he tapped the lad's cheek, prompting him to stir and open bleary blue eyes.

"Ashby, is that you?"

"Sizzme." The boy's speech was slurred and muddled.

"Lad, you are not old enough to be here. How did you get in?"

The boy raised a limp arm to point at the group scribbling wagers in the betting book. "Mabruther."

Brendan whipped his head around and, sure enough, spotted the elder Mr. Ashby howling with laughter a few feet away. Shaking his head, Brendan rose and approached him.

"Ashby, your brother needs to be taken home."

"Bugger off. We are busy."

Brendan clenched his jaw and his fists, but taking in the brother's glassy eyes, he realized the elder Ashby was far too inebriated to know to whom he was speaking, or to do anything at all about his sibling lying on the floor. Or, indeed, to be of any use in any capacity.

Exhaling through his nose and growling in the back of his throat, Brendan turned back and crouched beside the younger Ashby, who was snoring softly against the polished wood floor. The boy looked no older than fourteen, if memory served, despite the recent growth spurt that had added inches to his broad frame. He had no business carousing in clubs with older men. Lord Ashby, it seemed, was too occupied with the coronation festivities to notice his youngest son had been taken out on the Town by his heir. The club staff must have overlooked the much younger boy tailing the university-aged bucks.

Shaking his head in disgust, Brendan reached down

and hauled the lad into a sitting position. He could hardly leave a child passed out in public, sprawled beneath the betting book as though he were a discarded bootjack. If it had been his own family, he would want someone to step in. The elder Ashby was clearly in no condition to care for anyone.

Grunting, Brendan shifted and heaved the boy over his shoulder, the weight of him awkward and unyielding. He rose to his feet with effort, praying that young Ashby would not lose his supper unexpectedly after his excessive indulgence.

Ye Gods, the lad must weigh twelve stone at least.

If the Ashby brothers had not arrived in their own carriage, Brendan would have to forfeit his visit to Lady Slight, or at the very least delay it, so he could make a detour to the Ashby townhouse. With luck, there would be a brawny footman on duty to help settle the boy in bed, and Brendan could leave a firm but polite note for Lord Ashby, apprising him of the evening's escapade.

Lily licked her fingertip to turn the page of her book. The encounter with Mama earlier that day had been a moment of poor preparation on her part, and she was fortunate that Aidan had intervened. The unsettling exchange had compelled her to return to her reading for clarity and reassurance.

Each time she studied *L'Art de la Guerre* by the general Sun Tzu, she gleaned fresh insights into its principles. The military strategies, though ancient and foreign, served her surprisingly well in managing both her mother's ambitions and the more persistent of her suitors. It had become a habit, this practice of rereading the text, not only for knowledge but for calm.

Perhaps I ought to apply the philosophy of winning battles to the task of courtship, rather than the avoidance of such?

It was an intriguing notion.

She was ensconced in the window seat of the drawing room, her knees tucked beneath her as the last hues of daylight dwindled behind the lace curtains. Her parents were out until morning, attending one of the longer routs of the Season. After so many late nights herself, Lily knew she would not sleep until much later. The light from the window had sufficed until the horizon darkened, and she had scarcely noticed the passing time until a footman entered to light the oil lamps, his presence more ghostly than intrusive.

Stretching at last, Lily pressed her hand to the back of her neck, massaging the stiffness that had taken hold during her long reading spell. Outside, the lamplighters had already made their rounds. The street beyond the tall windows glowed in uneven pools of golden light, but the road itself lay empty and hushed.

The ormolu clock on the mantel chimed, each strike crisp and deliberate. Eleven o'clock. As the final chime faded, Lily became aware of the sound of carriage wheels striking the packed dirt beyond the window. Curious, she leaned closer and watched as a well-kept carriage entered the square. A coat of arms was painted on its side—familiar, yet not instantly placeable.

She frowned as it slowed to a halt before the Abbott townhouse.

Who could be calling upon them—upon her—at this hour and without a prior invitation?

A footman scrambled down from the front of the

carriage and came around to open the door, lowering the steps with practiced precision. A polished Hessian boot emerged from the shadows within, followed by the impeccable line of buckskins drawn over muscled thighs. Lily blinked and shook her head in amazement.

Had she wished a gentleman into existence?

As she leaned forward, curiosity piqued, the soft glow of the streetlamps revealed the visitor's face.

"It is Mr. Ridley," she whispered to the empty drawing room, the sound barely louder than the rustle of the curtains behind her. He would have no reason to visit her, of course, however much she might secretly hope otherwise.

Mr. Ridley was tall. Not quite as tall as Aidan or Papa, but certainly more than a head above herself. In memory, his skin had a warm bronze hue, though tonight's shadows gave no hint of it, and the sculpted face of a man born to noble rank. But it was his glorious chestnut curls, casually tousled yet never disordered, that had captured her fancy during the handful of times their paths had crossed.

He had always been kind. Tolerant of her chatter, even amused by it perhaps. But she could not be certain if that kindness stemmed from genuine interest or merely from courtesy. They shared a distant family connection. His sister was married to the Duke of Halmesbury, who was cousin to the Earl of Saunton, now wed to Lily's own cousin, Sophia. Still, such associations meant little in the face of reality.

Mr. Ridley was not on the marriage market. Of that she was sure. He moved in the world of widows, elegant and experienced women with mystery in their smiles and no chaperons at their sides.

Which might well explain his purpose this evening.

The thought left a trace of disappointment, though she tried not to let it linger. Peering down again, Lily saw Mr. Ridley standing alone as his carriage rolled away into the night. Just as she had suspected, he turned and crossed the street with purpose, his long stride taking him directly to Lady Slight's front steps.

She watched as he knocked. The butler answered, and Mr. Ridley stepped inside without hesitation.

Lily sighed and turned slowly back to her book, though the words now blurred before her eyes.

What might it be like to know him better? To discover if his conversation matched the quiet confidence of his bearing? Did he think her merely a young girl with too many opinions, or might he, if he were truly looking, see her as a woman worthy of consideration?

She would probably never know.

Such a waste that a gentleman so affable, so intriguing, should devote his time to a woman like Lady Slight, a viper of the first order, who had once stirred strife between Sophia's brother-in-law, Perry, and the woman he now so happily called his wife.

WHEN BRENDAN finally reached Harriet's townhouse, he was disappointed to learn she had not yet returned as promised. The butler, unperturbed by a gentleman caller at such an hour, accepted Brendan's word that the lady was expecting him and showed him upstairs to the first-floor rooms without comment.

In her private drawing room, Brendan tossed his gloves aside, poured a glass of wine, and settled into a well-cushioned armchair. He stretched his legs out before him, the weight of the day heavy in every muscle. Sipping slowly, he let his gaze drift toward the empty fireplace. The hour was late, and between the early start and the exertion of carrying young Ashby, fatigue wrapped around him like a thick fog.

Setting the half-drunk glass aside, he leaned his head back and let his eyes close. Within moments, sleep overtook him.

When Brendan stirred again, it was to the unmistakable sounds of Lady Harriet Slight returning home in full voice. Her bright instructions to the servants floated upward through the house. Still bleary, Brendan blinked and rubbed his eyes, groaning as he sat up and felt the stiff protest of his shoulders. A clock chimed in the hallway below, and he tried to count the hour, uncertain whether it was four or five. Either would mean it was time he took his leave.

As he rose, Harriet swept into the drawing room in a flourish of silk and perfume, pausing in surprise when she saw him.

For a moment, they both stared.

Lady Slight, widow of a viscount whose life had ended not long after their marriage, was every bit as striking as ever. Her flaming red hair was arranged in careful ringlets that framed her perfect face. Though her gown was cut in the latest daring fashion, it was her animated presence that drew the eye more than anything else.

"Brendan! I completely forgot we had plans," she said with a musical laugh. "After the coronation, I was spirited off to a soirée. Or three, if I am truthful. It was a whirl of introductions and sparkling conversation with all the best of society. I do hope you found a way to keep busy while I was gone?"

Brendan suppressed the flicker of annoyance rising in his chest. Though Harriet was often amusing company, her unreliability wore thinner with each encounter. He could now understand why Perry had left the brief association behind with little ceremony.

Perhaps our time is drawing to a close.

The familiar weight of ennui settled once again across Brendan's shoulders, a heavy cloak dragging at his limbs. He resisted the urge to sit back down on the settee and drift off once more. But he remembered he had to see the baron this morning.

It was time to leave.

Finding a new companion would be an inconvenience at present, and maintaining his current understanding with Lady Harriet was easier for him if he wished to avoid nights alone at his club. The alternative might offer peace and solitude, but it lacked the warmth and comfort of a feminine companion.

"Of course." He stepped forward and pressed a courteous kiss to her cheek, breathing in the gentle scent of rose water lingering on her skin. No man could deny that Harriet was a charming woman—vivacious, confident, with a sparkle in her gaze and graceful curves.

Stepping back, he offered a smile. "Did you enjoy your evening?"

"What a day of marvels!" she declared with a merry laugh. "We shall never again see a coronation so grand. They say it surpassed the one held for that little French tyrant himself. Did you know a tailor went all the way to Paris to study the emperor's robe?"

"I heard a veritable fortune was spent on the festivities," Brendan said dryly. If there was sarcasm in his tone, it was lost on her.

"It was glorious!" she continued, her cheeks pink with either excitement or, perhaps, a touch too much champagne.

Brendan chuckled. "I am glad you enjoyed yourself. It sounds like quite the night."

"Night, darling? I returned at six o'clock in the morning! Proof, if ever there was, of a successful outing."

Brendan blinked. "Six o'clock? I must go!" He snatched his gloves from the side table and muttered a quiet curse. It was not that he feared the baron would cut him off—*forfend such a public embarrassment!*—but Brendan had no desire to worsen their already strained relationship without a clever strategy to send the baron packing back to Somerset.

He made for the door, ignoring Harriet's slightly offended expression as he passed.

There were matters more pressing than morning pleasantries. He needed to get home.

Lily opened her eyes, momentarily disoriented. The familiar hush of early morning filled the drawing room, where the delicate tick of the longcase clock was the only sound beyond her own breathing. Her book had slipped from her hand and now lay open-faced upon the Aubusson carpet, the corner of one page bent as if in protest. She must have dozed off while reading, lulled by the flickering candlelight hours ago.

Sitting upright, she pushed a loose curl behind her ear and blinked away the remnants of sleep. Pale light filtered through the sheer mullioned drapes, just enough to illuminate the high plaster ceiling and gilded frames along the far wall.

The first fragile threads of dawn stretched like silk across the rooftops of Mayfair, turning chimney pots and brick façades into softened silhouettes. A carriage rattled to a stop across the street, its wheels a muted clatter on the cobbles, and drew her attention. Her breath caught slightly as she recognized the familiar crest upon the lacquered panel. It was Lady Slight's barouche.

Several heartbeats passed. Then the widow herself emerged, walking with her customary grace despite the hour. A heavy velvet cape was drawn over her shimmering evening gown, its hem brushing the paving stones as she crossed to her front door. Her stride was measured, though her return at such a time hinted at impropriety.

Lily frowned, a furrow forming between her brows. Had Lady Slight truly left Mr. Ridley waiting through the night? The notion struck her as inconsiderate. Even in an arrangement of questionable propriety, such neglect showed a lack of regard.

She stretched, arms above her head and back arching slightly in a movement that would have earned a stern rebuke from Mama. As she did so, she noted the silence of the household. If she had spent the night in the drawing room, then her parents and brother Aidan must still be at their various engagements. Mama would never have allowed her to remain here, alone and uncovered, if she had returned.

Bending to retrieve her book, Lily's thoughts were disrupted by sudden motion beyond the glass. The door across the street burst open, swinging wide with uncharacteristic force, and Mr. Ridley strode out in haste. His coat flared behind him, and though distance obscured his expression, his urgency was unmistakable.

Had he, like her, fallen asleep and only just awakened?

His manner suggested more than mild alarm. He was not merely late. He seemed almost agitated.

She watched as he disappeared into the lavender-gray shadows at the end of the lane. Hackneys would be difficult to find at this hour. Lily doubted the gentry of Mayfair were stirring yet, and certainly not their drivers.

Clutching the book to her chest, she turned toward the door. It was high time she sought her bed, though she suspected she would not sleep. The image of Mr. Ridley's retreating figure lingered in her mind like the closing line of an unfinished story.

THREE

"Be extremely subtle, even to the point of formlessness. Be extremely mysterious, even to the point of soundlessness. Thereby you can be the director of the opponent's fate."

Sun Tzu, *L'Art de la Guerre* (*The Art of War*)

JULY 20, 1821, THE DAY AFTER

Lily was eager for an outing with her cousin. After a restless night dozing off in the front drawing room, she had finally made her way to bed and awakened refreshed and ready for a visit to Hatchards with Sophia to peruse the latest novels.

After yet another unsuccessful Season, Lily admitted she needed a respite from social events and the endless parade of introductions to gentlemen she scarcely knew.

A morning with Sophia would be a welcome change, a

chance to relax and enjoy each other's company without Mama watching her like a falcon guarding its nest of hatchlings.

She wore a muslin walking dress in the customary white her mother insisted upon. Lily pulled a face at her reflection in the mirror. White was hardly flattering on a pale young lady with brown hair and eyes. Since her marriage, Sophia had enjoyed the privileges of a countess, including a wardrobe of flattering blues and spring hues that perfectly complemented her red-blonde hair and vivid eyes. Even before marrying, Sophia had been allowed greater latitude as Mama's niece than Lily could ever hope for.

How was she to catch the notice of a handsome young gentleman when she looked so washed out and childlike?

Shaking her head in disgust, she drew on a pastel blue Spencer, which did her complexion no more favors than the dress beneath it. Mama, on the other hand, wore rich tones —claret, saffron, and Egyptian brown. They shared similar coloring, and Lily knew well that such shades would lend her vibrancy, but Mama remained unmoved in her conviction that white and pale pastels were the only acceptable attire for a proper debutante.

Not that she was such a young debutante anymore.

Lily grimaced at her reflection. Indeed. After three full Seasons, she could hardly claim youth with any conviction.

She drew on her kid gloves and departed her room, her step lightening slightly. Sophia would collect her on the hour, and Lily could not suppress the flicker of joy at the prospect of escaping the Abbott townhouse without family in attendance.

Reaching the front hall, she glanced at the casement

clock before moving to the window that overlooked the street. She gazed out in hopeful anticipation.

And gazed.

And continued to gaze.

Checking the time again, Lily began to pace. It was not like Sophia to be late. She had even sent a footman two days earlier to confirm their appointment, despite the countess's many obligations surrounding the coronation.

When she checked the time once more, Lily blew out a sigh, her shoulders sagging with disappointment. First Aidan had left her to her own devices the day before, and now Sophia, too, had failed to appear.

Something must have happened.

Lily breathed in and decided that must be the case. Sophia would never deliberately leave her waiting without explanation, so there must be a good reason for the delay.

Just as she reached this conclusion, she heard the rumble of a carriage along the roadway, followed by the shifting shadow it cast across the entrance hall window. Running over, Lily peered outside to find the Saunton carriage drawing to a stop.

Without waiting for a footman to open the door, she pulled it open herself and nearly skipped in her eagerness to reach the carriage.

The Saunton footman stepped forward, opened the carriage door, lowered the steps, and assisted Sophia down. Lily bounded over, calling, "There is no need to come in! I am here—we may leave at once."

But Sophia did not smile in return. Her expression was grim, her complexion pale in the morning light. "I am afraid I cannot go to the bookshop today. There has … something has happened. I only have a moment to inform you of the change in plans."

Lily's spirits plummeted, her stomach tightening. Something had to be terribly wrong. Sophia was a bold soul, a warrior of sorts, unflinching in most situations. For her to appear so somber meant the matter must be grave.

"What is it? Is it the earl?" Then, a far worse thought struck her—Sophia's babe. "Miles?"

Sophia quickly glanced about the square, then took Lily by the arm and guided her into the townhouse. They stepped into the dining room, where Sophia quietly shut the door behind them.

"Richard and Miles are well. It is Richard's friend. Mr. Ridley."

"Mr. Ridley?" Lily's thoughts scrambled, careening in all directions. She had seen him just hours earlier, hurrying away from Lady Slight's home at dawn. Surely, nothing could have happened in so short a time?

"He returned home this morning to find his father had ..." Sophia hesitated, biting her lip. "The baron has been killed."

Lily's eyes flew wide. She took a step back in shock. "What?"

"I hate to tell you such terrible news, but I am on my way to the Ridley townhouse to support the duchess. Richard and the duke are there with her and Mr. Ridley, helping with the authorities. She must be devastated."

Sophia had grown close to the duchess, Mr. Ridley's sister, over the past year. Given the close friendship between the earl and the duke, and the duchess's warm nature, it was unsurprising Sophia would rush to her side. But her eyes now were shadowed with worry.

"I must come with you!"

Sophia turned back, blinking. "What?"

"I can help. Mama expects me to be with you, and your coachman can return me later."

"Oh, Lily. What purpose would that serve?"

Lily drew herself up to her full, if modest, height, placing her hands on her hips. "Do not treat me like a child. I am twenty years old, Sophia Balfour! I am your friend, and I have a good head on my shoulders. The duchess is increasing, and she has her son besides. I might be of some use. I can provide comfort ... or ... or something."

It was not the most articulate of appeals, but Lily was frustrated and sincere. Sophia had always treated her with respect, not as an over-talkative girl but as an equal. If she were denied now, at such a moment, she would feel hopelessly excluded and helpless to offer aid where it was needed.

Sophia's lips curved at last, a hint of her usual mischief returning. "My, my, Lily Billy. Such fire!"

"So I may come?"

The countess sighed, resigned. "Not a word to your mama about where we went, you hear?"

Lily bounced onto her toes, her cheer somewhat restored. "Then we should go quickly before she comes downstairs to break her fast."

BRENDAN SAT SLUMPED, caught in a mild state of shock. They had gathered in the library, as the study was well occupied. A corpse lay there, awaiting the coroner's arrival. The cloying, metallic scent of blood that lingered in that room had quite given him a headache.

His brother-in-law, the Duke of Halmesbury, along with the duke's cousin and Brendan's close friend, Lord Richard

Balfour, the Earl of Saunton, were speaking in hushed tones with the Bow Street Runner who had responded to the summons Brendan had sent via footman.

The three stood a few feet away beneath the muted light of a solitary lamp. The blond duke towered over both men, despite the earl being a tall fellow himself, easily six feet. Yet even Halmesbury's formidable frame was somewhat diminished by the looming bookcases and weighty furnishings of the library. The drapes and armchairs, which might once have been a rich green, had long since faded into a grayed murk. Brendan had always disliked Ridley House. It had been decorated in a previous century, and not with any sense of timelessness.

The earl seemed to know the runner, Briggs. Brendan recalled, with some effort, that Richard had shot a man in his own home the year prior. Perhaps that was the connection.

"So Mr. Ridley ... his lordship ... found his lordship ... the late baron ... when he returned home this morning?"

Brendan winced at the sentence's awkward construction. The runner was a stern, lean man wrapped in a crumpled greatcoat, his battered hat pulled low. He had the look of one who had seen much and grown hard to it, yet his voice was halting, uncertain, as he stumbled over the etiquette of addressing a man who had, mere hours ago, been a baron's son and now stood poised to inherit the title.

Yes. The baron was dead.

And yes, that implied Brendan was now Lord Filminster, though such matters required confirmation by the Committee for Privileges.

The runner, street-born and plainly self-conscious about the particulars, was fumbling to speak with due propriety.

"That is correct," Halmesbury replied. His deep voice carried reassurance, steady and composed. Brendan had yet to fully collect his wits since discovering his father's body, and was grateful that the duke had stepped forward to take charge.

"And where was Mr. Rid—his lordship—the night before?"

The duke cleared his throat into one large gloved hand. A pause followed. Richard intervened smoothly.

"His lordship was staying with a friend overnight. A lady friend."

"Will she be able to confirm his whereabouts?"

Both Halmesbury and Saunton glanced back toward Brendan, still sunk in the armchair, bleary and numb. He shook his head.

"That will not be possible."

"Did any of the household staff witness him arriving this morning?"

All three men turned to look at Brendan. He nodded, then sighed deeply, his voice dull and heavy. "I did not pay attention to who let me in at the front door. I was in a rush. I simply ran inside without noting it, but it must have been the butler or one of the footmen."

Briggs nodded, a lock of lank hair falling away from his brow to reveal a faint scar above it. His face was narrow, dominated by a thick mustache that reminded Brendan of the stable master back in Somerset.

"I shall question the household staff and identify someone to confirm your arrival, milord."

"Will that be sufficient to clear his lordship?" Halmesbury's query made Brendan stiffen. The same thought had haunted him since discovering the baron's body.

Briggs stroked his mustache, expression pensive. "It

might be. But I would advise persuading the lady in question to confirm his whereabouts. 'Tis not my opinion that'll count in the end, but the coroner's."

Brendan grimaced. His arrangement with Lady Slight was not based upon goodwill or discretion. Her allure lay in the pleasures of the bedroom, not her reputation for benevolence. The idea that Harriet would involve herself for his benefit seemed laughable.

As it was, both Halmesbury and Richard had shown visible discomfort when Brendan had reluctantly admitted to spending the night with a woman, though he had withheld her name. He could not fault them, but their thinly veiled superiority, products of their settled domestic bliss, was more irritating now than ever before.

"Is there any suspicion likely to fall on his lordship?" Richard asked, prompting Brendan to lean forward in his chair.

Briggs tugged on his mustache, gaze dropping to his notebook. He hesitated, then finally replied, "The coroner —Arnold Grimes—is new to the post, but he strikes me as a man keen to make his mark. It would be in your lordship's interest to resolve all doubt swiftly. An alibi would strengthen your position."

A heavy silence followed. The only sound was the ticking of the library clock, its surface darkened by age and the tarnish of decades. Its stern, weighty presence lent a near-medieval air to the room.

At last, Richard exhaled. "Thank you for your candor, Briggs."

"The baron has been dead for hours, that much is certain. And it is plain to me that his lordship was out, based on his attire and appearance. If it were my investigation, I would be asking who might have called on the baron last evening."

"But it is not your investigation?" Brendan asked quietly. He had never before dealt with the authorities and found himself uncertain as to the process.

Briggs met his gaze, sympathy flickering across his weathered features. He shook his head. "I'm afraid not. The final say belongs to the coroner."

Brendan rubbed at his temples, then slumped once more into the embrace of the worn library chair.

THE COUNTESS'S footman released Lily's gloved hand after helping her from the carriage, stepping back with practiced politeness as she followed her cousin to the painted front door. A small brass plaque declared the residence to be Ridley House.

It was her first time visiting the townhouse, having never before had occasion to meet the unmarried gentleman in his own home. As a debutante, Lily did not go out much without her mother's chaperonage. She attended social functions with Mama, and on occasion, she accompanied Sophia either to her home or to Hatchards.

A bachelor's residence, even a grand family townhouse, was strictly off-limits. A thrill skittered through her like lightning, sparked by this unexpected deviation from custom. Despite the somber circumstances, it was the most excitement she had known since Sophia had married the year before, following a nefarious kidnapping attempt in the Abbotts' very home.

Lily craned her neck to peer up at the façade of the great house as she came to a halt behind Sophia. It was large, but the drawn drapes prevented her from discerning anything more. The only outward sign that something untoward had occurred within was the air of stillness that hung about the place. Soon, the door opened, and Lily swept in behind her cousin, gazing around the dimly lit hall with open curiosity.

Sophia was eyeing the footman carefully. Since her troubles the previous year, she always paid mind to the servants. It was a heightened awareness Lily could not fault, given how narrowly her cousin had escaped with her life. Chiding herself for being distracted by the furnishings, Lily turned her attention to the conversation unfolding before her.

The young footman was tall, with a pleasant face and a light dusting of freckles across his cheeks that matched the copper-brown of his hair.

"Have we met before?" Sophia asked, though Lily was quite sure her cousin had already determined that she had not.

"No, my lady."

"What is your name, pray?"

"Wesley, my lady. I have worked at Ridley House for several years." His tone was genial, unfazed by the scrutiny.

"Where is the butler, Michaels?"

"He is making arrangements in regard to our household's change in circumstances, my lady."

"Very well. We are here for the duchess."

"Of course, my lady. She awaits you in the red parlor." Wesley bowed and turned to lead the way down a shadowed corridor. Lily scurried after them, nearly trotting to keep pace with the long strides of the countess and the footman. She scarcely had time to notice the worn carpets and faded wallpaper before they came to a halt.

Wesley knocked once, then opened the door and

announced their arrival before retreating. As he stepped back, Lily caught his eye and mouthed a silent apology for Sophia's earlier interrogation. The news of the baron's sudden death had clearly set her on edge, stirring memories of past danger.

The footman offered a small understanding smile before drawing the door closed. Lily exhaled, grateful he had not taken offence.

≈

MICHAELS SHOWED the coroner into the gloomy library, his expression stamped with mild distaste. Brendan growled beneath his breath, his irritation with the servant particularly sharp today.

He had never gotten on with the man, who until now had been the baron's creature. The butler's disdain for the baron's heir was subtle, yet unmistakable. Brendan had never confronted him, but it had long been a source of aggravation during the years he had been forced to reside at Ridley House, after the baron had dispatched him to London.

Once the butler departed, Brendan turned his attention to the coroner—and his heart sank.

Mr. Arnold Grimes was of medium height, with severely cut, receding iron-gray hair and a close-cropped beard that lent him the austere appearance of a Puritan. He wore a black coat and trousers, paired with a stark white linen shirt. The overall effect was one of lifeless neutrality, made worse by the sour expression stamped upon his face.

His cold presence seemed to draw the warmth from the room, and even the runner, Briggs, shifted a few paces away with barely concealed discomfort.

Sniffing with affected gravity, the coroner addressed the duke and the earl. "Your Grace. My lord. I am honored to make your acquaintance."

Brendan rubbed his temple. The words were correct, but the tone betrayed them, the sneering contempt was obvious. Grimes had not even bowed to the noblemen, which was a deliberate slight.

"Mr. Grimes, your reputation precedes you." The duke gave a cool nod, his gray eyes sweeping over the man without flinching. Halmesbury, ever the tactician, was composed and unreadable. Whatever easy candor he had shown with the runner earlier had vanished, making clear to Brendan that his brother-in-law recognized a threat.

Brendan inhaled slowly, gathering his resolve, and then rose from his chair and stepped forward. It would not do to appear weak.

The coroner gave him a fleeting frown, then dismissed him without so much as a greeting.

"Briggs, let me hear the facts."

Briggs cleared his throat and consulted his notebook. "The baron appears to have been killed sometime around midnight. The butler states he returned home for dinner and was still in his attire from the coronation when he apparently encountered someone in the study. He was clubbed over the head with a statuette of a horse, which was found bloodied beside the body. Mr. Ridley returned home just after dawn to meet with his father and discovered the body at approximately twenty minutes past six."

The coroner turned his stony gaze on Brendan, who had to steel himself against the ice revealed there. "And where were you?"

Brendan frowned, drawing himself up and responding in as haughty a tone as he could muster. This man plainly loathed the peerage—or perhaps simply loathed everyone.

"I was out."

"Out?" Grimes repeated, arching a brow.

"Out." Brendan refused to elaborate. He would not cede ground to this man.

Briggs cleared his throat again. "One of the servants should be able to confirm his arrival once I make my inquiries."

"I certainly hope so."

Brendan kept his expression impassive at the coroner's pointed remark, but his stomach twisted with unease. What, he wondered grimly, would it take to convince Harriet to show mercy and offer him the alibi he so badly needed?

 ~

LILY POURED a cup of tea for the duchess, adding a squeeze of lemon before handing Her Grace the cup and saucer. The duchess accepted it with a faint smile of gratitude, her features pale in the dim room. She was an elegant young woman, with a riot of chestnut curls framing her face and brandy-hued eyes that caught the low light, but her eyelids were puffy and red.

Observing the visible signs of Her Grace's grief made Lily feel a twinge of guilt for having, even fleetingly, treated the situation as an escape from the monotony of her day. Lady Halmesbury had just lost her father in a brutal, shocking manner. And despite her usual facility for chatter, Lily could not summon a single word of comfort.

She glanced at Sophia, who stood by the window, staring out as if her thoughts lay a thousand miles away.

The room had remained silent since their arrival. No one had spoken, each woman wrapped in her own thoughts, the terrible events of the morning forming an invisible weight over them all. Lily winced inwardly, remembering that she had talked her way into this gathering on the promise of offering comfort and help. She had to try.

"I ... quite enjoy a cup of exotic tea," she began, her voice soft but steady. "I especially like mine with milk, and one of those dainty biscuits that Cook makes. Do you know the ones I mean, Sophia? They have a hint of lemon, and you can eat them in just two bites ... They are as light as clouds. One day, it would be such a wonder to journey to the Far East and see fields and fields of green tea, stretching out as far as the eye can see."

The duchess tilted her head slightly, her gaze sharpening in surprise at Lily's unexpected monologue. But then her shoulders gave a small almost-imperceptible shift, as though she were easing the weight of her grief just slightly.

"I have often wondered about the lands where tea is grown," Her Grace said quietly. "What would acres of fresh, growing tea smell like, I wonder? We only ever see the fragrant dried leaves sealed in a tea chest after they have traveled months across the sea. This tea"—she lifted her cup gently—"was grown in India, visited Africa in transit, and arrived half a world away in London so that we might drink it while we speak of such terrible things."

Sophia turned back from the window, her curiosity apparent as she looked between the duchess and Lily. Accepting a cup of tea, she murmured, "This tea is a tale from another world. It allows us to journey farther than we may ever travel ourselves."

Lily picked up her own cup and sipped, savoring the

variety of notes while imagining the leaves' voyage. She was content to have offered some comfort, however small. The three of them sat quietly, drinking their tea, until Lily extended the saucer of biscuits. The duchess accepted one, and Lily was pleased to see that Her Grace and Sophia seemed more grounded now, breathing in the fragrant steam as they nibbled on the light confections.

"I wanted to thank you . . . for being here with me," the duchess said softly. "My father and I were never close, but the loss still comes as a shock."

Sophia reached out, placing a steady hand over the duchess's. "Of course, Annabel. We shall always stand beside you when you need us."

"If I am honest, I grieve not so much for what we shared as father and daughter," Annabel murmured, lowering her gaze. "I think ... I mourn what we shall never share. He was a hard man to please, and time spent with him always felt like effort. He never truly appreciated his family."

Lily bit her lip, surprised at such a private admission. It made her feel distinctly grown-up to be included in so intimate a conversation. "I am so sorry. Papa is everything a daughter could ask for. He protects and dotes on us."

Sophia nodded solemnly. "Lord Moreland has been a better father to me than my own ever was. I regret that the baron never recognized how fortunate he was to have such an accomplished daughter."

The duchess offered a faint smile, the corner of her lips quirking up. "Fortunately, I have a wonderful brother."

Lily coughed gently. "I suppose Mr. Ridley is the baron now."

The duchess blinked, sitting straighter. "I had not thought of that. That is a great deal of responsibility to shoulder with so little preparation."

"The duke will guide him through it. And Richard will help, too," Sophia said with quiet conviction. The strength in her tone brought comfort, and Lily felt a swell of satisfaction that her attempt to brighten the mood had succeeded.

Just then, the door opened. Lily turned, her eyes widening as the men entered. Their grim expressions immediately dampened the room's warmth. The duke crossed the space and lowered his long frame beside his wife with a weary sigh.

"Lily Billy," Richard whispered in greeting as he passed, settling beside Sophia. Lily gave him a wink, raising a faint smile from the otherwise solemn earl.

Mr. Ridley entered last, his features drawn. He lowered himself into the chair nearest Lily, and despite the gravity of the moment, a tiny thrill fluttered in her chest at being seated so near such a striking gentleman.

In his upper twenties, he had chestnut curls to match the duchess. They also shared those riveting brandy eyes, but Mr. Ridley was a man through and through, with his lean frame, broad shoulders, and chiseled jaw. He scraped six feet, which meant he towered over her dainty form, and she could not help but wonder what it would be like to waltz with such a fine specimen of manhood rather than the doddery old men she was usually required to dance with.

"That Mr. Grimes is pugnacious and unlikeable," Richard grumbled after several moments.

Sophia frowned at her husband in question.

"I believe he will pursue Ridley for this murder."

"I agree," the duke said gravely. "I spoke privately with Briggs before he left, and he said it is imperative that we find an alibi. Apparently, Grimes has political ambitions and little affection for the aristocracy. Worse still, the little upstart has powerful friends in the House of Commons, so this could turn into a proper fight despite Brendan's connection to me." His tone conveyed his concern as he accepted a cup of tea from his wife and sipped.

"Who is Grimes?" the duchess asked, her voice tinged with alarm.

"The coroner," the duke answered simply.

Mr. Ridley groaned. "Why me?"

Richard puffed in disgust. "Why not you? Grimes sees an opportunity to make a name for himself by bringing the first peer in sixty years to the scaffold. Your father has been absent from Town for two decades, so it is easy for Grimes to claim you are the only man with a motive. The narrative writes itself—estranged heir murders peer in a fit of rage to claim the title and fortune. We must find an alibi to force him to look elsewhere, or we shall have a true battle on our hands."

Lily realized her presence had been forgotten, or perhaps accepted, when the conversation continued openly in front of her. Had she become a confidante in this tight circle of friends? Either way, she would not ruin it by reminding them she was present.

Mr. Ridley sighed heavily. "The lady in question will never agree to come forward, and I cannot name her without her permission."

"Can you speak with her?" Richard asked.

"Not without revealing her identity under the current circumstances. There is a possibility that Grimes will have me under observation."

Lily peeked over at him, noting the pallor of his face. She bit her lip, debating whether to confess that she had witnessed him arriving at and later leaving Lady Slight's home. But what weight would the word of a young debutante carry, especially one who had been up reading until dawn in the drawing room?

"What if someone else saw you arrive … or leave?" Lily almost clapped a hand over her mouth at her own audacity, speaking in a room full of powerful peers. But she held her hands firmly together to resist the urge.

Mr. Ridley tilted his head, glancing at the duke, who shook his head. "It would not resolve the matter. A bystander could not attest that Brendan was there the entire time. It would have to be the lady."

"Or, perhaps, her servants?" the gentleman offered, a flush rising from Mr. Ridley's collar and spreading to the tips of his ears, which turned a fiery red. Lily puzzled at the reaction until she recalled that he had been at Lady Slight's, but the widow had not yet returned. Presumably, he did not wish to admit his paramour had abandoned him all evening, which was why he was now considering the servants instead.

"I suppose the woman in question would need to be agreeable, or her servants will not come forward," the duke replied, his tone marked with pessimism.

Lily stared down at her hands, trying to think of a solution. She knew Mr. Ridley had been at Lady Slight's the entire evening, but young ladies like her were practically invisible until they wed. And she could not attest for certain that Mr. Ridley had not left Lady Slight's in the middle of the night. Only Lady Slight's servants could confirm that, and they would only do so with the widow's permission.

If Lily admitted her knowledge, it was certain her cousin would dissuade her from becoming involved to protect her from a scandal that might affect her eligibility for a good marriage. But if Mr. Ridley could not request help, perhaps Lily could visit Lady Slight and entreat the widow to intervene?

Not, she suspected, if she forewarned the others of her idea. And Mr. Ridley clearly did not wish to reveal the widow's identity. Conferring with him in private would be impossible, and regardless, he would likely decline her offer to assist him.

"So Mr. Grimes means to pursue formal charges against Brendan?" the duchess's voice was even, but thick, and Lily suspected she was on the verge of tears.

"I think it is possible. Briggs is questioning the servants, but so far none of them have confirmed they let Brendan in this morning. Even so, I believe an alibi is the only certain method to have Grimes move on to find the true murderer."

"What happens if he arrests me?" Mr. Ridley sounded haggard with worry.

"You will likely be taken into custody and ..." The duke stopped, looking away with a pained expression.

"And?" Her Grace queried.

Sophia responded reluctantly, stating what each of them was thinking. "In the last century, the Earl of Ferrers was imprisoned in the Tower and then condemned to death by the Lords for killing his agent. If Mr. Ridley is tried and found guilty of murdering a peer of the realm ..." The countess bowed her head, the room descending into silence, with only a low sniffle from the duchess to acknowledge the dire nature of her brother's predicament.

To Lily's right, Mr. Ridley dropped his head into his hands with a groan. "So I am to be arrested, tried, and hanged on the assumption that I am guilty?"

His anguish was palpable. Unlike earlier, Lily did not think her babbling would lighten the mood. She had never been involved in such a grave conversation and felt woefully out of her depth, afraid she had nothing useful to offer. Perhaps she was a silly child, after all.

Her frustration rose to engulf her body, a physical sensation that made her skin itch. She finally had a chance to participate in a mature matter, and she found herself speechless. Even so, if it would help Mr. Ridley out of his predicament, she would stand as a witness.

But the witness they needed was not her.

It was the widow.

I must find a way to help the duchess and her brother!

CHAPTER
FOUR

"Quickness is the essence of the war."

Sun Tzu, *L'Art de la Guerre* (*The Art of War*)

JULY 21, 1821

"Miss Lily, I ain't sure about this. Your mama is going to have words with me." Nancy was plaintive, her voice husky with age as she clutched her shawl more tightly around her shoulders. Her eyes darted over the cobbled street, searching for anyone who might witness them approaching the widow's door. "The talk belowstairs is that Lady Slight is a bit of a fusty luggs!"

"A WHAT?"

Nancy scowled, her wrinkles settling into deep lines as she mumbled under her breath.

Lily frowned in confusion. "FUSTY LUGGS?"

The old nursemaid huffed, her breath fogging in the cool morning air, before replying with obvious reluctance, "A mean-tempered trollop."

Lily's eyes widened in feigned surprise. "Never say there is gossip amongst the servants!"

Nancy leaned toward her, cupping her ear. "Hey?"

Lily tossed her an impish smile and turned back to raise the brass knocker, its lion's head gleaming dully in the pale light. She brought it down with a determined rap, the solid clank echoing behind the grand Georgian façade. She needed to be quick about this before her family noted her absence.

Lady Slight's rake-thin butler opened the door, his dark livery immaculate, though the set of his stooped shoulders suggested disappointment was a daily burden. He swept his gaze over Lily, pausing a fraction too long on her pelisse, then rotated his head with stiff elegance to take in old Nancy, with her wind-frayed hair and drooping mobcap. His lips curled in contempt.

"May I help you, miss?"

Straightening to her full height, Lily adopted the haughty tone she had heard Mama use with tradesmen or minor gentry. She offered him one of her calling cards, holding it as though it carried the weight of Parliament.

"Miss Abbott to see Lady Slight."

The butler's nostrils flared as he read the card, the skin of his jaw twitching ever so slightly. "Lord Moreland's daughter?"

"Indeed. Show me in." Lily kept her chin high. The butler's cold eyes flickered, just for a breath, and she knew she had him.

"Follow me."

Lily grabbed Nancy lightly by the arm and swept in

behind him, ignoring the disapproving sound the older woman made. The black-and-white tiled floor clicked underfoot as the butler's long legs devoured the hall at a pace that forced Lily to half-skip to keep up while simultaneously tugging Nancy along. The house smelled faintly of dried lavender and beeswax, immaculate in fragrance as it was in appearance.

He stopped and opened a door without flourish. "Lord Moreland's daughter, Miss Abbott."

Lily swept in behind him, slightly breathless from attempting to keep up while navigating Nancy, who now stood panting with exertion. Coming to a stop, Lily found herself in a small gilded parlor.

Every surface in the room was an art of embellishment. The walls and furnishings had been overtaken by intricately painted floral patterns and Grecian deities frolicking through clouds and columns. Nymphs and gods leapt across the ceiling medallions, and even the wainscoting bore the delicate brushstrokes of vines and lyres. On the smooth vertical face of the mantelpiece was a frieze of Romans going about their business—one stooped at a market stall, another gestured expansively, while a musician strummed a curved-stringed lyre with a vaguely smug expression. The gold detailing glinted in the candlelight, and Lily caught herself gaping, her eyes tracing the rococo grandeur that marched across every available inch of the space.

She barely registered Lady Slight's presence until a sudden movement drew her gaze down from the frieze. The redheaded viscountess was already seated, perched in a regal armchair of silk damask framed with gilt scrollwork. Her expression was one of clear irritation and her posture one of unrepentant display. Lily's gaze landed, before she could stop it, on the lady's bosom, which was heaving above the edge of a fashionably scandalous bodice.

She forced her eyes upward. *How in the world is she breathing in such tight stays?* The widow's chest was so elevated, it seemed nearly to obstruct her view.

Dropping a curtsy, Lily opened her mouth and forged ahead before her courage deserted her. "I have come to speak to you about Mr. Ridley—Lord Filminster!"

The widow frowned. Her coiffure shifted as she tilted her head, the red curls gleaming like a lacquered wig in the candlelight. "Lord Filminster?"

"The baron is dead. Mr. Ridley is likely to be accused of his murder. You and your servants are the only ones who can clear Mr. Ridley—Lord Filminster. You must inform the authorities that he was here in your home last night before he is arrested and taken to the Tower. The runner says that he must have an alibi as swiftly as possible. You must send for the coroner, who is Mr. Grimes, and he is the one you must inform straightaway of Mr. Ridley's presence here!"

Lady Slight's jaw dropped open in evident amazement. Lily realized she might have said too much, too quickly. Her wretched babbling had struck again, delivered with the velocity of cannon fire when talking to someone who was not familiar with her verbosity. Leaning back on her heels, Lily commanded herself to breathe.

Several moments passed, during which Lady Slight slowly closed her mouth and appeared to be gathering her wits. The ticking of the ornate mantel clock filled the silence, its delicate chime marking time like a judgment.

"Mr. Ridley is to be accused of murder?"

Lily nodded, keeping her lips firmly together.

"And you wish me to speak to the authorities to clear his name?"

Another nod.

"Why on earth would I do that?"

"Because he was here. All night."

The viscountess narrowed her eyes. "How would you know that?"

"I witnessed his arrival and his departure from my window."

Lady Slight rose, walking over to a window, her scarlet silk skirts rustling while a waft of expensive perfume tickled Lily's nose.

"Lord Moreland's daughter? He lives across the street, I suppose." The viscountess leaned to peer outside.

Abruptly turning, she moved to where Lily was standing. Using her superior height, she gazed down her nose at Lily with an expression of distaste. The scent of rose clung to her skin, cloying and deliberate.

"Why should I be concerned about some silly little chit dressed in her silly white lace?" Lady Slight reached out an elegant hand, her rings flashing in the light, to fiddle with the ruffle at Lily's neck. "Mama still dresses you, does she not?"

Lily's heart fell from her chest into the pit of her stomach. It was humiliating to have such dismissive disinterest thrust upon her. The older woman was an alluring Aphrodite, poised and painted, while Lily was … not. The crush of inadequacy pressed like a hand against her throat. Nevertheless, despite the threatening emotions, she was going to hold her ground and convince this viper to do the right thing. At the same time, Lily was afraid she had made the situation much worse with her lack of strategy in visiting. She should have prepared a more compelling argument.

"You know he is innocent! You have a duty to speak!"

Lady Slight lifted a hand to her mouth and tittered, a sound as brittle as glass. But her eyes remained hard and icy, twin chips of polished stone. Lily welcomed the fury that rose through her like a hot tide of righteousness to provide her fortitude.

"Then I shall stand as a witness. I shall inform the coroner where Mr. Ridley—Lord Filminster—was that night!"

The viscountess shrugged gracefully, the motion sending a ripple through the dainty lines of her creamy, naked shoulders. Her gown shimmered as she moved. "I shall deny it."

Lily gritted her teeth. "The coachman who dropped him off will confirm my testimony."

Lady Slight's painted lips twisted into a wintry smile as her eyebrow arched. "The coachman knows nothing about the matter. Ridley promised his carriage would draw up in front of what turns out to be *your* townhouse, not mine, and he would have awaited its departure before crossing the road."

"You do not deny he was here, then!"

"Why would I? Your word is inconsequential, so ..."

"You will not help Mr. Ridley despite his innocence?"

"I think ... not." The reply was callous. Heartless. The viscountess seemed to enjoy toying with her, entertained in the manner of a horrid little boy pulling the wings off an insect. Her voice held a lazy elegance, a studied indifference that curled in the air like perfumed smoke.

Lily clenched her hands lest they fly into the air to slap the shameless hussy across the face. The widow was several inches taller than her and merciless, so an attack seemed ill-advised. Her fingers twitched against the fine stitching of her gloves, and she drew a sharp breath through her nose to steady herself.

"But why? You must care for him? You were to spend the night with him!"

Lady Slight sneered. "Your naïveté is too obvious, dear. If I provide him an alibi, I shall be forced to wed him to save my public reputation. I would never marry a mere baron. I am the widow of a distinguished viscount, with the freedom to conduct any affairs I wish, you ridiculous girl."

Lily stuck out her chin, squaring her shoulders. Her stays tightened with the movement, but she welcomed the discomfort—it bolstered her resolve. "You have no honor, my lady!"

The viscountess froze, her jaw firming. The ormolu clock on one of the side tables ticked in the silence, each tick as deliberate as a footstep. Lily stared Lady Slight in the eye, refusing to yield. Eventually, the older woman blinked and turned away.

"The opinion of an unwed chit carries no weight."

With that, she moved back to her seat, floating through the air like a leaf dancing in the wind. The silk of her gown whispered as she moved, and Lily watched her carefully drape her skirts as she sat down—elegant, composed, and entirely cold. It was a dismissal.

Turning, Lily grabbed Nancy by the arm, who was standing close to the door with wide eyes and craning to hear the exchange.

"We are leaving, Nancy."

"We are grieving?"

"LEAVING!"

Lily stalked through the door, her kid boots striking the polished floor with determined rhythm as thoughts collided in her head. Had she made matters worse? How was she to fix this? Mr. Ridley was innocent, and the dreadful viscountess would not lift a finger to help him.

"YOU MUST INFORM the coroner where you were. It is the only way." The earl's frustration with Brendan was rising, evident in the clipped edge of his voice.

"Who is the lady you were with, Brendan? Perhaps I might visit and persuade her to assist." The duke's tone was even, but his concern was drawn in the lines between his bronzed brows and in the slight narrowing of his eyes.

Brendan shook his head. He could not reveal that without the lady's consent.

Be honest with yourself.

He winced. Wishing to speak to Lady Slight before revealing her identity was part of it. However, the truth was his affair with Lady Slight embarrassed him. Richard despised the woman for her involvement with his brother, Perry. Brendan could not blame him. His behavior from the outset had been despicable, and he knew it.

He knew it had been dishonorable to dally with the widow, taking advantage of the vacancy left by Perry's marriage.

You were thinking with your baser instincts.

This was hard to refute. The bitter self-rebuke settled over him like a wet wool coat.

Lady Slight, while an elegant presence, certainly did not provide scintillating conversation or challenge him as an educated man. She was all artifice and allure, with none of the intellect or warmth that had made Emma—Perry's wife —so singular. There was a reason Perry had fallen in love with a woman who bore no resemblance to the widow.

Richard stood with a grunt of disgust, stalking over to the library windows to gaze sightlessly. His polished boots thudded dully on the worn rug, the hush of the room amplifying the movement. Shaking his head, he turned back to bark the question Brendan had been dreading.

"Who is she? It must be someone we know, or you would not be so reticent! We are your friends—! Your family! We cannot help you unless you tell us all that happened."

Brendan shook his head again. "The lady does not signify."

Lady Slight might be interesting to visit, but he knew without a doubt that the woman was selfish and would never agree to be involved in his troubles at the cost of her reputation. It was one thing for her to engage in affairs privately, and most of polite society was well aware of her behavior. But admitting such formally would be ruinous. The lady would be shunned by the very nobility who had visited her boudoir in secret or had tittered behind their fans with her as they gossiped about their respective liaisons. The hypocrisy of their set was not lost on him.

If he had been more honorable himself, he might now have a legitimate alibi to call on. He could not blame Lady Slight for being in this predicament. There were only his own poor choices at fault.

"We must focus on finding the true culprit."

The earl shook his head in disgust at Brendan's proclamation. "How are we to investigate while the taint of suspicion lies on you?"

The duke sighed, sitting back in his chair and resting his hands on his long, muscled legs. His tailored trousers bore faint creases from the day's wear, and he shifted with the weary elegance of a man who had carried too many burdens.

"I agree. I looked into this Grimes, and he has important supporters, as Briggs asserted. There could be serious repercussions to this if we do not clear your name quickly." He paused, the weight of his words hovering like fog in the stillness between them. "Even now there is talk of your guilt running through the halls of Westminster, which could severely detain your confirmation as baron. Meanwhile, the household and tenants of Baydon Hall, along with the rest of your people, are without representation. There is no lord to sign any documents or to approve any matters. No method to pay any wages." He leaned forward slightly, his voice low and calm, though it carried steel beneath its surface. "We must prevail on this woman to come forward, even if we must offer the proper incentives, discreetly and with honor."

Brendan sat back, rubbing his temples as he tried to think. Two days ago, he had been an heir to a barony, spending his allowance and basking in the indulgences of idle society—dancing, drinking, and casting appreciative glances at widows like Lady Slight. Now he stood on the brink of scandal, facing an accusation of murder and the chilling possibility of confinement in the Tower.

How many men have ever walked free from the Tower once imprisoned?

Brendan shivered at the thought. Cold dread settled between his shoulders like a weight of stone.

"It will not come to that," he said aloud, though mostly to himself. "We simply need to find the actual perpetrator. I am sure having a servant attest to my arrival earlier this morning should stave off any imminent accusation, so we might proceed with hunting for the perpetrator ourselves.

Perhaps we can hire Briggs to look into it further, even if the coroner will not do his duty."

Halmesbury ran his fingers through his hair, his disquiet evident in the way they dragged and stilled at the crown of his head.

"What is it?"

Richard returned to his seat, dropping into it with more force than usual before fiddling with his cravat. Brendan's tension coiled tighter, a dull throb beginning behind his eyes.

"What is it?"

Halmesbury cleared his throat, then leaned forward, resting his wrists on his knees, his boots planted wide. "None of the servants have admitted to opening the door for you this morning."

"What? I came in just past six o'clock, and I certainly was not carrying a key! Someone opened the door when I knocked on it."

Both the earl and the duke were silent.

"You believe me, do you not?"

Halmesbury's head snapped back. "Of course we believe you. The old man was horrible. I wanted to throttle him myself on many occasions for how he diminished Annabel. But you are a civilized man, and we are practically brothers. There have been no thoughts in my head that you did this terrible thing."

Brendan's chest heaved in relief. "Thank you."

Across from him, Richard chuckled. "Personally, I am not so magnanimous. I did briefly wonder whether you may have done it."

A glance of rebuke at the earl only caused him to chuckle harder.

"I appreciated your old man for allowing me to escape

my circumstances at home during my troubled youth. Visiting with you over the holidays saved my sanity. But he did send you to Cambridge, after all."

Brendan gave a half-laugh, amused despite his panic and the burdens he had been carrying since finding the baron in the study. "Cambridge is a fine university, you dolt."

Richard shrugged, his grin wide. "Ah, the defensive lament of all those who did not attend Oxford."

Brendan kneaded his temple with a thumb, chortling at the ridiculous distraction. His entire life might be in crisis, but at least he did not face it alone.

"Is it possible that the truth of my relationship with the baron might come out?"

Halmesbury flinched. "By Jove, I hope not! That would certainly provide further motive for Grimes to pursue the matter."

"Is there anyone other than us who knows the truth?"

Richard fidgeted in his chair, drawing their attention. "The rumors are true, then? The baron is not Brendan's father?"

Brendan slumped, groaning as he collapsed back into his chair and furiously rubbed at his temples.

"You know of the matter?" Halmesbury's question was almost inaudible, denoting his worry.

Richard nodded. "I heard whispers of it while we were at Eton, and again at Lords, when the baron would come up in conversation. It was not my place to question Brendan about it."

Halmesbury shook his head. "I am afraid we might be out of luck."

Tension was boring through Brendan's skull. He half expected to find a hole in his temple, but there was no physical evidence of his torment as he kneaded the spot with growing desperation.

"What is it that Grimes can do? As coroner?" Brendan addressed the question to the duke. He was helplessly out of his element, never having dealt with any criminal matters before.

"If he thought you were a legitimate suspect, he could arrest you while we await a coroner's jury to confirm that the baron was indeed murdered and that you are the primary suspect. It is promising he did not do so today. It suggests that the jury will be called to review the facts of the case, which means there will be more parties involved to advise prudence."

Brendan felt a flood of relief. Perhaps Grimes would continue to investigate until more suspects were found. The man's disapproval of him had been distinct, and Brendan had been fighting off panic since their meeting.

"Unless ..."

Brendan and Halmesbury both turned to Richard, his unease stamped across his features.

"Unless he wanted to confer with his supporters. He could still arrest Brendan once he has secured their approval to proceed."

JULY 22, 1821

Lily paced up and down. She had been doing so since dawn. The patterned rug beneath her feet was worn soft from years of service, and the muted thud of her slippers marked each turn in the still, breathless quiet of the morning.

After leaving Lady Slight the afternoon before, she had

been scrambling for a solution to Mr. Ridley's plight. Somehow, knowing where he had been the night of the murder made her feel personally responsible for his well-being, along with that of his sister, the duchess.

Lady Slight would not do the right thing, and perhaps visiting the widow to beseech her to intervene should have assuaged Lily's conscience.

Yet ... she still felt accountable. Lily knew she should step forward and state what she had witnessed to the authorities, but Lady Slight had thwarted this path. The widow would simply deny it, and then it would be Lily's word against hers. The statement of a widow would hold far more weight than that of an unwed young woman, especially when that widow was a viscountess.

Lily stopped and stomped her feet in frustration, the soft thud muffled against the worn rug, before stalking to her dressing table and glaring down at the news sheet lying upon it. The inky columns trembled ever so slightly in her hands.

Reports of the baron's death were now in circulation, along with lurid mentions of the estrangement between him and his heir. They had not spoken in seven years, according to the article, a detail Lily had not known.

The temerity of the widow still grated on her nerves. The woman had admitted to having Mr. Ridley stop in front of Lily's own home as a decoy for his true destination. Clearly, the viper had no concern for the potential scandal, no hesitation about tainting her or Mama's reputation should a passerby have seen him outside the Abbott townhouse. The utter brazenness of it!

What if ...

Lily raised her head and stared at herself in the looking glass. Brown eyes—eyes she always hoped were the color of chocolate, like Aidan's and Mama's—met her gaze with a flicker of determination. An inkling of an idea formed, but her stomach tightened in dismay. Surely, Mr. Ridley would find a way to address the matter? He had the help of both a duke and an earl at his side.

Except ...

The duchess's quiet sniffles during their recent *tête-à-tête* echoed through Lily's memory. She had seemed genuinely distressed.

Surely, they will come up with a plan to deal with it ...

Lily tried to dismiss the recollection, but another memory intruded—Sophia recounting the tale of the Earl of Ferrers, that infamous nobleman imprisoned at the Tower, tried at Westminster, and hanged. Gooseflesh prickled along her arms.

There must be another way ...

But what if there was not? What if an innocent man were tried and condemned—hanged—because she lacked the courage to act?

It will ruin me ...

Would preserving her reputation be worth the cost of her self-respect? Mr. Ridley was a good man, from an excellent family, and without an alibi, he stood defenseless. Lily believed Lady Slight when she said she would not come forward.

And what of falling in love? Of being wed and having children and gaining the freedoms granted to a married woman?

But what would any of that matter if, in the pursuit of safety, she sacrificed the very part of herself that believed in justice?

No, this was something she could not ask of anyone else. No counsel would do. This was hers to decide.

It was the essence of being an adult.

To do what was right.

To stand on her own two feet.

Lily fell to her knees, the weight of responsibility too much to bear. And she wept, her shoulders shuddering with her despair as she faced the burden of growing up.

For the longest time, she had wished to be an adult, to be treated with respect and behave with maturity. Lily had imagined marrying a man who loved her, as Sophia had done. Bringing her first child into the world, as Sophia had just done.

Now Lily wished she could return to her childhood, where heavy decisions did not weigh upon her. The innocence of those days felt distant, like sunlight glimpsed through a pane of rippled glass.

If she discussed the matter with anyone, even Sophia, she knew she would be dissuaded from doing the right thing. She would hear arguments about how her reputation was paramount. How she must make a successful match. How it was someone else's problem to deal with.

But if she did not do the right thing and protect Mr. Ridley, despite the knowledge she had of his innocence, it would haunt her with guilt.

If she buried the guilt somewhere in the deep recesses of her soul, she would become a heartless hussy like the one who lived across the street, one who welcomed a parade of men through her home, yet possessed no integrity, no humanity, and no true joy. A beautiful but empty shell, seated in an exquisite room where no breath of vitality stirred the air.

Her optimism would die a slow and painful death, and she would no longer be ... Lily—a spirited young woman who may not quite fit in, but who carried cheer in her heart and brightness in her words.

I must do what I know in my heart is right.

She wept for the end of her hopes and dreams and for the beginning of a frightening path into the unknown. Her reputation would be destroyed, she knew. And yet, she could only hope that Mr. Ridley might, in turn, find some way to save her.

Finally, once the tempest of emotion had passed, Lily slowly rose to her feet. She dried her face with trembling fingers and moved to ring the bell.

It was time to leave, before Mama and Papa rose for the day.

CHAPTER
FIVE

"Secret operations are essential in war; upon them the army relies to make its every move."

Sun Tzu, *L'Art de la Guerre* (*The Art of War*)

⁓

"The runner is here to see you." Disapproval dripped from the butler's words, as if to emphasize that Bow Street Runners were not the sort of visitors the late Barons of Filminster would have ever tolerated.

Brendan's temples pulsed at Michaels's dour announcement.

"Where is he?"

Michaels's forehead wrinkled as he peered down his nose at Brendan. "In the entrance hall." The unstated *of course* was practically audible. Evidently, the butler thought it beneath his station to admit such a guest to the baronial library.

Brendan nodded in dismissal. Once the butler's stiff form had departed, he rubbed furiously at his temples. His thoughts had been caught in a punishing loop since Richard's pointed remark, that the coroner might still pursue an arrest, once Grimes had secured support from his powerful allies.

He had not slept. Not a wink. Only stared into the darkness above his bed, his mind scouring possibilities, none of them good.

He stood, intent on finding out what Briggs had to report, but paused mid-motion.

A sick realization crept over him.

They had assumed he would be treated as a peer, with all the deference afforded to the heir of a barony. But the Committee for Privileges had not yet confirmed him. He was not legally a baron.

No title. No protection.

Brendan collapsed back into his chair, his breath coming fast.

What if they take me to Newgate?

Brendan groaned as his headache doubled in intensity. Newgate had a reputation for being filthy, overcrowded, and ridden with parasites. Fingering his hair, he contemplated having to shave it off to rid it of lice. Dropping his face against the table, he groaned again as he knocked his head against the mahogany surface in frustration.

Why could I not have been carousing with friends instead of napping in Harriet's boudoir? A simple life choice which might now get him a turn at the gallows, unless he could find a defense.

Halmesbury was wrong about waiting. We must immediately hire a runner to investigate the matter!

Brendan realized he should have been acting more

swiftly to defend himself. Inking his quill, he jotted out a note to the duke. He sprinkled pounce to dry it, then blew gently before folding it up. Ringing for a footman, he sent it off, praying the duke was at home and able to come. They had been too complacent yesterday. It was time to take matters into his own hands instead of waiting idly for Grimes to do his job.

Finally, he stood at the library door and steeled his nerve. Finding his composure, he strode out to find the runner with feigned composure.

Briggs was waiting near the shadowed staircase, his hat in hand. The runner looked worn in the dim flickering light cast by the hallway sconces, and Brendan found himself wondering what hours the man kept. Did he move from case to case without pause? That seemed likely. Crime had not ceased simply because the Ridleys were in crisis.

"Briggs, how are you this morning?" Brendan's attempt at heartiness rang too loud in the hush of the hall.

"My lor—Mr. Ridley." The correction was awkward, and while Briggs's thick mustache masked much of his expression, the discomfort in his voice was plain.

"What can I do for you?"

"I'm 'fraid the coroner asked me to be present. He's running late."

"Late for what?" Alarm coursed through Brendan's chest as he realized the runner had not come of his own accord.

"To arrest you. I am to wait for the coroner."

Brendan heard the words as if from a great distance. The runner's reluctance was plain, and it underscored what Brendan already feared—even Briggs did not believe this was right. Yet he had known, from the moment he discovered the baron lying lifeless in the study, that this moment was coming.

At only seven and twenty, his entire life could be over.

He reached blindly for the banister, fingers curling around the carved wood as his knees buckled beneath him. Hopes and ambitions flashed through his mind in a painful cascade, like scenes from a tragedy unfolding at Covent Garden.

He could not bear for it to end like this.

He wanted to find a good woman, one who stirred his mind and spirit, and wed her. He wanted to raise children and be the kind of father who read stories and took them walking in the woods, as his mother had once done with him. He wanted to live a life that meant something more than the idle round of social calls and gaming tables.

He wanted to begin his life, not end it.

His breath grew shallow, chest rising and falling with growing desperation. And just as his internal despair crested like a wave crashing upon rock, the illusion shattered.

Michaels interrupted, his steps heavy on the floorboards as he crossed the hall. Brendan barely registered the knock that had preceded the interruption, but his stomach turned as the butler moved to open the front door with his usual blend of disdain and formality.

Heaven help me ... is that the coroner?

But instead of the dreaded figure of authority, Brendan saw the broad shoulders and familiar profiles of Halmesbury and Richard entering the house. Relief hit him with such force that he almost staggered. Color returned to the world in a painful rush. The low murmur of voices, the groan of the door hinges, the brightness of the day streaming through the open entry—all of it struck him at once, too loud and too vivid.

The duke stood near the open doorway, sunlight spilling in behind him like a halo. Brendan squinted up at him, still dazed. The duke's lips were moving, but it took Brendan a few moments to comprehend the words.

"Are you well?" Halmesbury asked again, concern etched between his brows.

Brendan shook his head. "Briggs ... is waiting for the coroner to make an arrest."

Halmesbury's expression darkened. He stepped into the hall without hesitation. "Saunton, see to Briggs. Ridley needs a drink."

Without waiting for Brendan to protest, the duke gripped his arm and guided him into the library. Brendan sank into the worn armchair near the hearth—the same chair he had occupied since the study had been sealed, a silent sentry to his unraveling life.

"I just sent a footman to find you," he muttered. "We need to find an alternate suspect, Halmesbury!"

"I agree," the duke said grimly, striding to the sideboard and pouring a stiff measure of brandy. "That is why Richard and I are here. We realized we wasted too much time lamenting yesterday when we should have acted. This Grimes is worse than we feared. My men say he is more interested in power than in justice. We cannot rely on him to handle this fairly."

Brendan nodded, accepting the glass from Halmesbury with a trembling hand. He tossed back the brandy in one gulp, the burn sharp in his throat but welcome. The shock began to loosen its hold, allowing clarity to return like sunlight piercing fog.

"We need to put as many men on this as we can. I did not do this, I swear it."

The duke settled into the chair beside him, exhaling slowly. "I know you did not do this, and we will do whatever is required to prove it. Annabel and I will not allow such a travesty of justice to proceed, not while this weasel of a coroner pursues his ambitions over his duties. Beyond investigating the murder itself, I have instructed my men to begin looking into Grimes. The man stinks of self-interest. If we can uncover any past dealings, political alignments, questionable alliances, we may be able to discredit him entirely."

Brendan cleared his throat, the movement rough and dry. "Am I to be taken to the Tower or to ... Newgate?"

The duke frowned. "I have not heard that is their intent, but I shall press for you to be taken to the Tower. A matter of this import will not be settled in a lower court. The Lords will insist upon handling it themselves. You may not be confirmed as baron, but your status as the legitimate heir is widely known."

"Even with the rumors about my parentage?" Brendan's voice was low, hoarse with fatigue.

"It does not signify. The law acknowledges you as Josiah Ridley's son. He was wed to your mother at the time of your birth. That makes you legitimate in the eyes of the peerage and the law. The prosecution might raise the matter as motive, but it will not alter your claim."

Brendan nodded, his throat tightening. He sank back into the deep embrace of the armchair and let his head rest against the worn velvet cushion. The ache behind his eyes pulsed with fatigue, but for the first time in hours, his breath slowed. Thank heaven for Halmesbury. The duke would overturn every rock in the kingdom before allowing him to be condemned without cause. And Richard—brash, loyal Richard—would see no sleep until this nightmare ended.

They would find a way. He must believe it.

He would not hang for a crime he did not commit.

LILY WAS the smallest member of the Abbott family, a fact she often used to her advantage. Her diminutive size made it easy to disappear into the background, provided she kept her mouth shut.

But this was no ordinary morning.

"Lily Beatrice Anne Abbott!"

Her heart plummeted. Mama had discovered her absence.

"Where have you been, young lady?"

Lily turned on the stair with exaggerated slowness, mustering the brightest smile she could manage. In most cases, her smile came effortlessly. It was her instinct to greet the world with cheer.

But not today.

Today, she had to summon it like a soldier donning armor.

Today was different.

"Mama! I am so happy to see you. I feel as if we have barely spoken, what with the coronation and everything happening this week. So many late events without me. Did you enjoy ..." Lily's voice faltered. She could not, for the life of her, recall where her parents had been the previous night. "Last night?" she finished, the rising note in her voice betraying her weak delivery. She nearly winced at herself.

Under normal circumstances, she might have chattered

on with deflections and charm, but words were elusive this morning. She had cast off one burden of guilt only to shoulder another. And soon, she would have to summon the courage to confess the dreadful truth to her mama, who lived and breathed for the marriage prospects of her only daughter.

But not yet.

Right now, all she wanted was to reach the haven of her bedchamber, scale the step at the end of her great high bed, and bury her face into her pillows until the world stopped spinning. She would lie there and contemplate her ruination at length. *Ruined!*

All because of that appalling man, Grimes. If he had only done his duty instead of fastening onto Mr. Ridley like a leech!

Lily shook her head minutely and tried to focus. Her mother's expression was thunderous.

"Where were you?" The heat in Lady Moreland's voice was uncharacteristic and made Lily retreat a step. Her slipper caught the edge of the stair, and she had to seize the banister to keep from toppling.

Smile. Keep smiling.

Her lips curved again with effort, trying to present a picture of blithe innocence. "I took a constitutional. With Nancy."

"On your own?" The question rang more like a lament.

"Nothing happened. I am here, all safe and sound." A boldfaced lie, soon to be shredded to ribbons when the truth came out. But Lily needed a moment longer—just a little more time—to collect herself for the inevitable onslaught.

Speaking with Grimes had been an exhausting ordeal, particularly following a sleepless night of tossing beneath her counterpane, the linens twisted about her legs. Lily had dug deep to summon every ounce of insouciant chatter she could muster while enduring the runner's scrutiny. His cold, beady eyes had surveyed her as though she were something foul tracked in from the gutter.

"What if someone had seen you? Of course someone saw you! How are we to explain this? What if it ruins you entirely, young lady?"

Lily restrained the grimace that tugged at her brow. If Mama believed that simply walking with Nancy in the early morning light was enough to tarnish her reputation, she was in for a veritable fit of apoplexy when she learned the full truth.

It pained Lily to know she was about to cause her mother such distress. But she could not carry the guilt of allowing an innocent man to be tried for patricide, not when she possessed the power to stop it. Mama would recover in time—of that, Lily was certain. She would find distraction in arranging Aidan's match or in having the silver polished for the next soirée.

In the grand tapestry of Abbott family legacy, Lily's marriage might have added a stitch or two, but it was not the hem that held the thing together. Viscount Moreland was well connected through generations of strategic unions. One daughter's deviation from the path would not undo it all.

"Mama, I had a chaperon, and I was in a respectable neighborhood, in full daylight." Another untruth, dropped lightly as sugar into tea. Lily just needed this conversation to end. Her limbs ached with the weight of responsibility, and she longed for solitude to contemplate how best to reveal what she had done and why. Someday, she hoped, they would understand. She had done what was right. What was honorable.

Her mother's voice broke, tremulous and wounded. "Oh, Lily! Why would you do this?"

Lily bit her lip as she watched her distraught mother pace and lament her impropriety. A pang of sadness struck her, knowing that life in their household was on the cusp of irrevocable change. Lady Moreland had always been a devoted parent. Yes, a touch suffocating at times and far too concerned with the whispers of high society, but Lily had never doubted her mother's love or the sincerity behind her tireless efforts to shape her future.

They disagreed frequently on what constituted best for Lily, but even now, Lily could not fault her mother's intentions. She swallowed against the knot rising in her throat, the ache of guilt blooming in her chest. She sincerely hoped that, in time, Mama might understand the choice she had made, might see that it had been the only course of action left to her.

"I needed some air," Lily said softly, "because I have been cooped up all week with all the coronation goings-on."

Lady Moreland clutched at her chest, her expression crumpling. "Is this my fault? Have I neglected you?"

Tears welled in Lily's eyes, blurring the silk hangings along the stairwell. She had not anticipated that particular consequence. It had never occurred to her that her mother might blame herself. Hurting her overly watchful but loving parent had never been part of the plan. Then again, it had never been much of a plan at all.

Descending the remaining steps, she stood in front of her mother and reached out to clasp her gently by the arms. Lily lifted onto her tiptoes to press a kiss to her mother's smooth cheek. "You are the very best of mamas," she whispered. "And you have never neglected me."

She stepped back before she could say more, before her resolve crumbled, and turned swiftly, gathering her skirts in both hands. Without waiting for a reply, she dashed up the stairs.

"Do not run! It is not ladylike!" her mother called after her, her voice thick with emotion.

Lily huffed a soft laugh, even as her eyes stung. Running was hardly her greatest crime this morning, not after the defining step she had taken, the step that could cost her everything.

"Grimes is here," Richard intoned from the window.

The earl stood with arms crossed, his handsome features set in stern lines. Once the darling of the *ton*, with a reputation for breaking hearts as swiftly as he won them, he now bore the sober gravity of a reformed man. No smile touched his lips, and the usual warmth in his eye had dulled.

The tension in the room grew taut with that single announcement.

Reluctantly, the duke rose, and Brendan followed suit. His limbs felt as though weighted with lead, the act of standing a monumental task. A dull throb pulsed behind his eyes, and he pressed a thumb against his temple, as though he could dispel the headache mounting there. He summoned every shred of composure and drew it about him like an overcoat, smoothing his features and squaring his shoulders as if dressing for a duel.

Stiff upper lip, Brendan Ridley. Time to face your accusers.

They filed out of the library together, their footsteps muted against the Turkish carpet laid over the polished oak floor. Brendan's thoughts churned as he imagined the grim proceedings to come. Would he be permitted to pack a bag? Could his valet accompany him? The thought of persuading Simmons to step foot in a prison almost made him chuckle, but the laugh caught somewhere near his throat.

No. You must fend for yourself, my lad.

At the base of the staircase, the entrance hall opened before them in a sweep of worn carpeting and dark-paneled walls. There stood Briggs, hat in hand, beside a sour-looking Michaels, whose tight mouth and furrowed brow suggested he had tasted something far more offensive than lemon curd.

Brendan's shoulders dipped ever so slightly. He had gathered every ounce of dignity to meet the coroner face-to-face, and now the man was late. All this poise and principle, and no audience to receive it.

Richard peered up and down the hall and stairs as if expecting the coroner to jump out of the shadows. "Where is Grimes?"

"He has left," Briggs replied. Brendan noted the man's change in demeanor. His earlier reluctance had disappeared. "There will not be an arrest today."

Brendan swayed slightly. The duke caught hold of him, bracing him with his considerable strength and turning to Michaels. "Take Mr. Ridley back to the library!"

Michaels scowled, pursing his lips before stepping forward. Brendan shook his head. "I am all right. I ... shall be in the library."

As soon as he entered the room, he made for the sideboard and poured a short brandy. He had already had one, and being inebriated at this time seemed like a poor idea, but he needed the fortification after so many jolting turns of events. He threw it back quickly, swallowing with difficulty while his thoughts spun like a Catherine wheel.

Why has Grimes changed his mind?

Brendan trudged across the library and dropped into the battered armchair that had become his refuge these past few days. The worn leather creaked under him as he leaned forward, head in his hands, trying to reconstruct his weary mind.

Through the open door, he heard the faint tread of footsteps approaching.

Brendan rose as the duke entered, his questions only half formed.

"The woman you were with stepped forward as an alibi. All charges have been dropped," the duke announced.

Brendan clapped a hand over his mouth in sheer relief as Halmesbury approached. Near the door, he caught sight of Richard speaking in low tones with Briggs.

He sucked air into his constricted lungs. "And here I was hoping to get a tour of the Tower." The quip emerged feebly, nothing more than nerves speaking for him.

Halmesbury shook his head, a slight grin tugging at his lips. His brother-in-law seemed as relieved as he by the sudden turn in fortune.

Presently, the earl finished his conversation with the runner. As soon as the door closed behind Briggs, Richard turned, his face stormy with emotion. He stalked across the room, eyes blazing.

Before Brendan could react, the Earl of Saunton's fist connected with his jaw.

The room swam out of focus. He dimly saw the large duke springing forward, coat-tails flaring as he rushed to intervene.

Darkness swallowed him whole.

"Brendan?"

Slowly, he opened his eyes. Halmesbury loomed above him, his usually unreadable gray eyes revealing a flicker of concern.

Groggy, Brendan tried to recall the past several moments. Or had it been minutes? It was impossible to know. His memory was clouded, the pain in his jaw a steady, pulsing throb.

"Why is Richard angry with me?" His voice came out hoarse, as though it had been scraped with sand.

Halmesbury hesitated, his features tightening. "It came to light why you would not name the woman you were with. We are both rather ... appalled."

Brendan blinked, frowning at the ceiling. His thoughts struggled to order themselves. *Are my wits addled?* He had expected judgment, but *appalled*? That word hit oddly. "About Lady Slight?"

"Nay, you blackguard! About Lily! She is my wife's cousin. An innocent!"

Richard's fury hit the air like a thunderclap. Brendan had never seen the earl so unhinged—his complexion blanched in fury, cheekbones stark, green eyes bright with rage.

"What about Lily?"

"You debauched her, you treacherous lech!"

Brendan turned his head slowly toward Halmesbury, wincing at the movement. "Who is Lily?"

That did it.

Richard surged forward, the air between them charged with violence.

"Hold off, Saunton!" The duke's deep voice rang out as

he blocked the earl's advance, standing firm between the two men. "I think there is more to this."

Brendan raised a hand to rub at his bruised jaw, his mind finally beginning to clear. "I was with Lady Slight that night. I knew if I named her without her consent, she would deny it. And truthfully ... I did not want to admit it aloud. I was embarrassed."

Halmesbury's brows drew together, a flicker of confusion crossing his face. "You are saying ... Moreland's daughter lied about being with you? Why would the young lady destroy her reputation to protect you?"

"I do not know."

"What is this?" Richard's voice cracked with disbelief. "Never say you believe this scoundrel?"

Brendan frowned. "Which one is Lily, exactly?"

Richard let out a growl of disbelief and stalked closer. Brendan tensed, grateful that the duke stood sentinel between them.

"She is my wife's cousin, you deviant!"

Brendan furrowed his brow, trying to remember.

"My word, man! She was with us in this very room two days ago!" Richard gestured wildly toward a nearby chair.

Brendan closed his eyes and searched his memory. "The little one who looks like a fairy?"

The earl took a sharp step forward, rage tightening his features, but the duke's hand shot up again.

"She is lovely," Richard rebuked firmly, warning in his tone.

"The one who never stops talking?" Brendan said, still blinking in confusion.

"She is a lively optimist," the earl snapped. "And she barely spoke the day of the murder. She was heartsick for Annabel."

"I barely know her. I hardly recollect she was here, after all that happened that day."

"You will have plenty of time to correct that—when you wed!"

Brendan's mouth parted. "I cannot marry her!"

"You shall! The young woman has destroyed her reputation to save your neck!"

Brendan sat upright, his hand flying to his throat. A cold chill settled along his spine. He could have hanged. He *would* have hanged. Grimes had nearly arrested him, and without an alibi, there had been no defense. No hope.

The motive had been clear. The means unquestioned. The baron was dead. Brendan would have been tried for patricide.

That the woman—Lily—had sacrificed everything to save him, for reasons he could not fathom, made his stomach clench.

He remembered her now. Tiny, with those wide, expressive eyes and that nervous chatter. She had always seemed like a side character—a child—in the drawing rooms of Town.

And yet, she had just procured his freedom and his life.

Collapsing back to the floor with a slow exhale, Brendan closed his eyes again.

"I suppose," he muttered, "that I shall have to marry her."

"WHAT HAVE YOU DONE?" Her mother's wail cut through the drawing room, a desperate cry that interrupted Papa's calm explanation of Lily's predicament.

Aidan spun away from the fireplace, an ornate creation

of veined marble and carved acanthus leaves, and staggered to a nearby armchair, collapsing into its cushioned depths. His face had turned ashen, his usually rakish expression stripped of all composure. "This is all my fault ... If I had been here as agreed ..."

Lily did not move. She could not. Her gaze remained fixed upon the hearth's blackened grate, now cold and empty. Her hands were clenched in her lap, the tension in her fingers making her knuckles throb. Her family's reactions echoed around her like distant voices muffled by water, her heartbeat roaring in her ears.

"There is no time for regrets," Papa said quietly. His voice, low but unwavering, cut across the disarray in the room. "Lily felt compelled to act, and it is our place to support her."

"But, Hugh, she is ruined!" Mama cried, twisting a handkerchief in her trembling fingers. "Lily will never make a good match now that the peerage believes she was bedded by ... by ... by a murderer!"

Lily winced at the word, her lips pressed together as though to contain the swell of emotion threatening to escape. A wave of cold dread passed through her. Yet still, beneath the mortification, a steady voice within repeated, *You did the right thing. There was no other choice.*

Papa's tone sharpened slightly. "Christiana, Mr. Ridley is not a murderer. Lily has merely reported what she saw. She has done what any decent person ought and provided him with the alibi he so sorely lacked."

"But, Hugh—"

"Our child will be secure," he bellowed, a wall of loud resolve, "because we shall stand with her!"

Lily flinched. She had never heard Papa raise his voice before. He was usually accommodating to her mother's wishes, but there was one subject on which he always stood firm. Family loyalty always came first.

Lily supposed she was fortunate that this was the case. When she had knocked on the door of his study, she had not been certain how he would react to what she had to tell him, but she should have known. Papa had immediately called for the rest of the family to join them so he could break the news. Even now, he stood by her side.

She looked up at her father, towering above her. His face showed the signs of aging, but his square jaw was firm and his expression resolute.

Blowing a deep sigh, Papa relaxed his features before continuing. "I know you wanted Lily to make a good match —the best match—but her conscience dictated that she take action. Now our family must work together to help her forge a new path."

Her mother lifted a hand to cover her mouth, a sob escaping as her chocolate brown eyes glistened. Lily's heart wrenched in her chest. Her own eyes prickled with the threat of tears as she dropped her head to stare at her twisting fingers.

"I am ... so sorry. I ... did not know what else to do."

"Nay, I bear the blame!" Aidan jumped to his feet, pacing back and forth and flinging his hands into the air. "If I had been here that night, I would have seen him myself and been able to step forward as his alibi. It is my fault that Lily was alone. If not for me, she would never have been in this situation in the first place."

"Aidan."

Her brother continued to pace in front of the large fire-place, mumbling about his culpability.

"Aidan!"

He stopped to look at their father, who said, "Lily made

her decision, and there is no undoing it now. News of her spending the night with Ridley will spread through the *ton* shortly, and we must prepare ourselves."

Aidan nodded dully, still pale from the shock of recent revelations.

"Will ... will Mr. Ridley offer for her?" Mama's voice was fretful, and guilt stabbed Lily.

"I shall contact him forthwith to learn his intentions."

"And if he does not?"

Papa firmed his jaw at the question.

Please, Lord. Mr. Ridley must help me!

"We must find a gentleman willing to marry her."

Lily nearly choked at Mama's declaration. What kind of man would be willing to marry her now? Surely not an upstanding one?

Papa shook his head, much to her relief.

"Aidan will take her to the Continent until the scandal dies down?" Her father glanced her way, and Lily nodded in agreement. She had contemplated many alternatives over the course of the night, and that was the only one which appealed.

But Mr. Ridley will do the right thing. He must!

Aidan came to sit by her side, his boyish face gaunt in the morning light. "Whatever you need, Lily Billy. I will pound Ridley until he comes up to scratch, if you wish. Failing that, we will visit the wonders of Europe together."

Lily pulled her lips into a half-hearted smile as she dropped her head against his shoulder. She was grateful that her family would support her over the coming days.

CHAPTER
SIX

"The principle on which to lead an army is to establish a standard of courage that all must achieve."

Sun Tzu, *L'Art de la Guerre* (*The Art of War*)

JULY 23, 1821

Richard's voice was still ringing in his ears as Brendan's carriage came to a halt in front of the Abbotts' home. Through the window, he noticed Lady Slight's townhouse across the street.

Miss Abbott's strange decision made a little more sense now that he could see it was her home where he had disembarked several nights earlier. Practically a stone's throw apart.

A footman opened the door, lowering the steps for him. Brendan descended and then peered up at the modest home of Viscount Moreland. Three bays wide and three stories high, there was no ostentatious display despite the family's wealth. The painted shutters were faded from exposure, and the brass knocker bore the patina of age—pride without pomp. Brendan knew Lady Saunton, the viscount's niece, had boasted a large dowry that had led to all her troubles the year before. The earl had saved her from a dire situation unbeknownst to the Abbotts and had nearly been killed for interceding.

Which reminded him of Richard's agitated admonitions earlier this morning. Butterflies set flight in his stomach as Brendan once again thought about his looming proposal. His lack of sleep, and the shock of the baron's death followed by his near arrest, had his head aching. There were moments when he felt entirely disoriented, as though London had tilted on its axis. The tightness in his chest had not eased since the runner had informed him of his imminent arrest the day before.

Now he was to offer for a young girl he did not know.

Brendan had always promised himself that he would never allow the baron to trap him in an unwanted marriage. When he had learned the truth about his parentage and realized that his mother had married Josiah Ridley out of necessity, to save Brendan from bastardy, he had vowed never to find himself in similar circumstances. His mother had been beauty and grace, and she had deserved better than her marriage to his uncle-father. A compromise for the sake of survival.

Brendan had resolved to one day marry a woman of his own choosing, one he would cherish. Somehow, he would recognize her when he met her, feel it in the marrow of his bones that she was his match. She would make him forget the parade of widows who had warmed his lonely hours and remind him what it was to be cherished unconditionally, in the way his mother had loved him before her untimely death more than ten years earlier.

Yet here he stood, poised to enter the Abbott household and make an offer for a young chit whom he barely knew. A child.

Brendan did not want to be a man who uttered vows only to stray, as so many in the *ton* did without remorse. But how was he to make a life with a veritable stranger who was barely out of the schoolroom? The idea twisted in his chest, an ache blooming behind his sternum.

It was his worst nightmare come to life. He had evaded the baron's influence for years, weaving through traps and expectations, determined to shape his own destiny. The old man would have been ecstatic to learn that Brendan was to marry the daughter of a wealthy and powerful viscount—a step above the two of them in rank. It was galling to contemplate Josiah Ridley's glee had he been present to witness Brendan's descent into propriety and unwelcome ascent in social status.

Several days had passed since he had found the baron sprawled on the study floor, and he had not slept properly since. His temples throbbed with the weight of too many sleepless nights, and his eyes were gritty with exhaustion. His chest remained tight, as though the path ahead had narrowed to a fate he had not chosen.

Bracing himself, he donned his beaver and approached the door, lifting the brass ring with a resolve he did not feel, bringing it down in a decisive knock that echoed on the modest portico.

A tall footman answered, his powdered wig pristine, his livery precise. He accepted Brendan's card with practiced indifference, but upon peering down at the name, his polite expression receded.

"Mr. Ridley."

It was a statement, not a question, and there was no mistaking the hard look the servant threw at him. Brendan had always made a point of getting along with servants. His mother had taught him that kindness was a gentleman's duty, not a choice. But this one was not receptive to the friendly smile Brendan attempted. The staff here were clearly loyal to the household, and it seemed word of Miss Abbott's entanglement with him had made its way belowstairs.

"I will see if Lord Moreland will receive you."

Brendan winced at the servant's clipped tone. Clearly, the man felt no concern that Brendan might lodge a complaint. He cast a scathing glance over his shoulder as he strode away, spine stiff with disapproval.

When Brendan was finally shown into the viscount's study, the shift in atmosphere was immediate. The room exuded quiet wealth. No gilding or ostentation, yet the lines of the furniture were unmistakably Chippendale, each piece balanced in harmony with the dark, polished wood panels cladding the walls. The space spoke of old money and meticulous taste.

Lord Moreland rose from behind his mahogany desk, a figure of solemn authority. He gestured for Brendan to take a seat.

"I confess I am relieved you are here, Ridley. My daughter has taken an extraordinary risk to secure your freedom, and I hope you appreciate her sacrifice."

Brendan nodded. "I am here to discuss terms of marriage."

The older man's brow furrowed. "Marriage? Lily must accept your offer before we can discuss terms."

The throbbing in Brendan's temples had reached a fever

pitch, and it took him a few moments to fully comprehend the viscount's words. "Surely she has no choice, given the circumstances?"

Moreland was a tall man with broad shoulders, dressed in conservative but clearly expensive clothing. His square face bore the sort of calm bred from long-standing authority. But at Brendan's question, his countenance hardened.

"I appreciate you are here and that you are taking steps to correct this situation. However, let me be plain. My daughter has acted with uncommon courage on your behalf, and she has the unwavering support of our entire family. Whether she proceeds with a wedding is entirely her decision."

Brendan raised a hand, pressing his fingertips against his right temple in a vain attempt to ease the pounding ache. As if it were not difficult enough to consider binding himself to a stranger, now he must also contend with a doting father and a household sure to watch his every move.

Perfect. Not only a bride he had never desired, but an interfering family to accompany her.

This was, without question, the worst week of his life. Worse even than the week his mother had died, leaving him and Annabel to the cold charity of the baron's household. In the span of days, he had been accused of murder, narrowly escaped arrest, and was now being ushered into a marriage not of his choosing, with an idolizing family ready to pounce at the first misstep.

"Do I have your permission to speak with her, then?"

"I am in the process of making inquiries into your past, Ridley," the viscount replied with unflinching directness, "and I must confess that what I have learned does not inspire confidence. Your history with your father does not reflect a strong regard for familial duty."

Brendan's breath caught. He forced himself to remain still, to rein in the tide of frustration that rose within him. "That was the baron's choice, my lord. He sent me to London and bade me never return to Somerset."

Lord Moreland's expression shifted slightly, a flicker of understanding softening the hard lines of his mouth. "Your father is the cause of the estrangement?"

Father. Huh.

"Yes, my lord."

"That is something, I suppose." The viscount leaned back slightly, though his eyes remained sharp. "However, any man who maintains an acquaintance with the widow Slight is bound to attract scrutiny. It is not the conduct one expects from a man of serious intention."

Brendan gritted his teeth as the throbbing in his temples ratcheted up. The irony of defending his right to marry a girl he scarcely knew was not lost on him. He searched for an answer that might satisfy a man so clearly invested in virtue. Many fathers of the *ton* would have cared little about such things, as the late baron had made abundantly clear when Brendan's sister had once found her betrothed embracing another woman. But Lord Moreland, it seemed, possessed firmer convictions on the subject of fidelity.

"The actions of an unwed gentleman, I assure you. I have no intention of continuing any acquaintance with Lady Slight if—when—I am wed."

He caught the misstep even as the words left his mouth, but Moreland's narrowed gaze confirmed it had not gone unnoticed. Brendan pressed his lips together. The truth, if he admitted it to himself, was more complicated. Part of him wished he could see Harriet again. She had offered him comfort once—an escape, of sorts. Had she heard of his predicament? Perhaps not. Perhaps, had she known, she might have stepped forward. Unlikely, but maybe.

Moreland stood. "It does not signify. Lily is aware of your prior connection, and the choice is hers. If she chooses to proceed, so be it. I trust my daughter's judgment, and since she has taken such extraordinary steps on your behalf, I will permit you to speak with her to come to terms. Thomas will show you to the drawing room."

The viscount rang a bell. A moment later, the door behind him opened. Brendan rose to his feet, stiff from the weight of expectations now draped across his shoulders like a yoke. He could not help but wonder why an established man such as Moreland would place so much faith in a girl barely out of the schoolroom. How had Miss Abbott even found the courage, or the means, to present herself to the coroner in the first place?

It was with a heady sense of relief that Lily had observed Mr. Ridley's arrival. She had swiftly adjusted the silly lace and muslin gown she had chosen that morning and checked her coiffure in the mirror, her fingers trembling. She had not slept in several nights. Her head ached with the weight of wakeful hours, and her eyes burned from too many unshed tears, but if Mr. Ridley had come up to scratch and was here to offer for her hand, then perhaps this wretched week might yet end with dignity restored.

It was not the manner in which she had envisioned stepping into matrimony. Still, the gentleman was certainly handsome and affable. More importantly, he was courteous and of sound lineage. Given their shared connections, she could do far worse than binding herself to him.

Lily bobbed nervously about the drawing room overlooking the street, unable to still her restless limbs. Excitement shimmered beneath her anxiety. Mr. Ridley might yet salvage her reputation. If he did, perhaps Mama would cease her weeping, which weighed heavily on Lily's already tender conscience. And Aidan, dear Aidan, might stop blaming himself for her predicament.

Some semblance of normalcy would return. Lily would embark on a new chapter as a wife, as a proper member of the *ton*. She might finally make her own decisions—select her own gowns, attend musicales with Sophia, and breathe in the quiet freedom that came from no longer being her mother's ward in every sense. And perhaps she and Mr. Ridley would find common ground. Perhaps, over time, they might come to understand one another. Perhaps, if Providence smiled kindly, love might one day follow.

Checking the clock, she wondered what Papa might be saying to Mr. Ridley.

At last, a knock sounded at the door. Lily hastily rubbed her scratchy eyes and called for the servant to enter. Thomas stepped in, announced Mr. Ridley, bowed with practiced efficiency, and withdrew. Unexpectedly, he shut the door behind him, and the sound echoed like a turning key in Lily's imagination.

This was it. She was alone with a gentleman for the first time. Because he was to propose marriage.

Her eyes sought him at once. Mr. Ridley had come to a halt before the fireplace, his gaze fixed downward. She studied his reflection in the mirror above the mantel, allowing herself a moment's hesitation before turning to face him directly. His tanned complexion looked unusually pale, the tension in his frame unmistakable. Beneath the cut of his impeccable buckskins and green coat, he seemed carved from restraint.

Despite the weariness in his posture, he was striking—handsome in the shifting afternoon light that filtered through the draperies. But it was the hollowness around his eyes that caught her heart. He looked as if he had not slept in days.

Her chest tightened with sympathy. What a terrible week the young man must have endured.

Is he devastated over his father's death? He has not even had time to grieve!

Mr. Ridley cleared his throat. "I wished to thank you, Miss Abbott. Your intervention was most timely. I was moments from arrest when you spoke with the coroner."

"You are welcome, Mr. Ridley! I was quite beside myself over your situation. Lady Slight's decision not to come forward was simply unacceptable, and I could not sit idle. I felt responsible in some way ... and I believed it the only method by which I might assist you."

In the mirror, Lily caught the subtle frown that touched Mr. Ridley's brow at the mention of the widow. Her stomach twisted. Was he still attached to Lady Slight? Did he resent being here, speaking of marriage?

I am afraid I do not care. If he offers me marriage, I will accept.

"Lady Slight likely does not know of my predicament," he said quietly.

Lily bit her lower lip. She hesitated. To confess her ill-advised visit would be unwise, especially now. She still cringed at how she had managed the matter, and this was hardly the moment for such disclosures.

"Nevertheless, I am so very glad you are here!" she burst

out, the words tumbling forth despite her best intentions. "You have come to offer for me, have you not? I lay awake all night reaching my decision, and I must say I am quite worn through, but now, here you are, come to do the honorable thing. I knew you would! You are a gentleman, through and through!"

In a flush of mortification, Lily clapped a hand over her mouth to silence herself. Oh heavens. Her enthusiasm had once again outrun her decorum. Mr. Ridley was unlikely to be accustomed to such effusiveness, and she could not afford to put him off in so delicate a conversation.

Looking back at the mirror, she noticed the gentleman was frowning again. Slowly, he turned to face her fully, his expression incredulous, and Lily's heart skipped a beat. Had she already put him off with her nervous babbling?

"Did you provide me with an alibi"—his voice was quiet, but the disbelief in it rang clear—"to trap me into marriage?"

The words landed like stones.

All the sleepless nights, the strain of consoling her weeping mother, and the quiet burial of her own hopes for a love match, one she had once believed herself destined to find, collapsed within her. The weight of it all surged so suddenly that she raised a hand, half-instinctively, as if to shield herself from an invisible avalanche. But there was no rubble. Only silence. Only the thunder in her chest.

She took a stumbling step backward, nearly colliding with an end table in her haste to retreat.

"Is ... is that what you think of me?" Her voice was scarcely more than a breath.

Mr. Ridley narrowed his eyes, suspicion etched across his features like a line drawn in the sand. "You must admit, Miss Abbott, that your knowledge of my situation was unusually precise. If your aim was to compel a marriage, I can scarcely imagine a more effective means."

Lily felt the sting of those words like a slap. Only moments ago, she had thrilled at the sight of his carriage pulling up to their home. She had believed fervently that her prayers had been answered. That this chapter of humiliation and despair might close with dignity.

But it appeared the nightmare was not yet done with her.

Tears sprang to Lily's eyes as she frantically searched for a resolution. Agreeing to a marriage with a man who mistrusted her so deeply, who believed her capable of fabricating an alibi to ensnare him, was unthinkable. Yet no simple solution presented itself. The air between them was thick with disbelief and judgment.

"Surely you know me better than that, Mr. Ridley? We have several mutual acquaintances, and—"

"Miss Abbott, we do not know each other at all," he interrupted. "I have no knowledge of what you might be capable of, given the right incentive. I could not fathom why a young woman would risk her reputation to defend me, but now ..."

Lily forced down the storm rising within her, her spine straightening as an eerie calm settled over her. She had defended Mr. Ridley of her own volition, and she would not flinch from the consequences.

"Are you here to make an offer, Mr. Ridley?"

She was proud—immeasurably proud—of how steady her voice sounded. She offered no embellishment, no softness, no more explanation. The question now belonged to him.

"What choice do I have?"

Lily inclined her head, her movements sharp and deliberate. "Then I shall respond. I am glad, for your sister's sake and for the sake of our mutual acquaintances, that your name has been cleared. I stand by my actions. I did the honorable thing on your behalf, and I would not change it." Her voice firmed with every word. "As to your offer—no. I will not wed you. Nor do I wish to receive you again. No."

With that, Lily turned. Or at least, she prayed it resembled a turn and not a headlong flight. She kept her shoulders square, though inside her heart fractured like fragile porcelain. Her pride was her last shield against the pain.

Would time on the Continent ease this tempest in her soul? Or would she mourn, always, the marriage she had hoped for—until Mr. Ridley had reawakened that impossible dream, only to dash it in a breath?

She exited without another glance, closing the door on Mr. Ridley and on the past. Her footsteps quickened toward the sanctuary of her room.

She and Nancy would need to pack. There was a journey to prepare for. She must leave as soon as arrangements could be made, if only to spare her mother further sorrow and to give them all space to begin again.

CHAPTER
SEVEN

"Confront them with annihilation, and they will then survive;
plunge them into a deadly situation, and they will then live.
When people fall into danger, they are then able to strive for
victory."

Sun Tzu, *L'Art de la Guerre* (*The Art of War*)

~

Brendan stood in the street, his head reeling. He
suspected that he might have handled the situation with Miss Abbott in a less than exemplary
manner. Raising his hand, he rubbed his temple once again,
attempting to alleviate the tension that had built and built
over the past few days.

The cobblestones beneath his feet seemed unsteady, the
familiar din of London—hoofbeats, hawkers, the creak of
carriage wheels—fading beneath the weight of his own
thoughts. He had barely had time to be relieved that he was
not being arrested before the next crisis had presented

itself. The earl was livid about Miss Abbott, presumably because his countess would be distraught at the news regarding her cousin.

The young lady's act had been so generous, so unprecedented, he simply could not believe it had been altruistic. Unfortunately, revealing his sentiments had brought her to tears, and Brendan was fighting off gut-wrenching shame for mishandling the discussion. Even if she had plotted to trap him, she was just a child. She barely looked old enough to be out of the schoolroom, and perhaps she had harbored grand ideas of marrying a baron.

His head pounded, a stray thought bouncing around his skull. Miss Abbott must be older than she looked, for he seemed to recollect that he had been introduced to her the prior year. In her lacy dress and girlish ringlets, he could have sworn she was not old enough to be having a Season. But if his memory served correctly, the young lady would be on at least her second Season, which simply was not possible. That would make her almost of an age with Lady Saunton, yet she barely came up to his chest. He could not even ascertain if she had curves beneath the flouncy gowns she seemed to favor wearing.

Perhaps Lady Moreland had brought Miss Abbott out early?

He squinted against the bright sunlight, vision blurred by the persistent pain behind his eyes. A horse clopped somewhere behind him, and the scent of dust and hoof oil lingered in the air. He had sent the carriage away, requesting it return after an hour, for he had expected to be negotiating a marriage contract with Lord Moreland.

Now, his options were to walk home or ...

Or to visit Lady Slight until my carriage returns.

Brendan did not think it a wise idea, especially not

within sight of the Abbotts' townhouse, but his composure had grown ragged over the past few days, and the pull toward the widow proved difficult to resist.

Before he had formed a proper decision, his boots were already crossing the street and his hand was lifting the brass ring to knock. Matters felt incomplete with Harriet, and though he could not yet name the nature of what lay unresolved between them, he longed to bring it to a close.

The door opened, revealing the butler, whose eyes flared ever so slightly in surprise. Brendan knew it was improper to call on a widow in broad daylight, yet decorum felt like a fragile concept beneath the weight of his current unrest.

"Lady Slight," he said, his voice low and resolute.

The butler hesitated but acquiesced, opening the door wider to allow him entry. Likely the servant thought it wiser to admit a gentleman quickly than to have him loiter on the front step for all the neighborhood to observe. Once inside, the older man led him toward the painted room. The painted drawing room was Lady Slight's favorite, most likely because it displayed her to full advantage, a striking woman positioned within a striking room.

That observation sparked an unwelcome prickle beneath his collar, reminding him that he had been contemplating ending their arrangement. The viscountess was far too devoted to her own appearance, often arranging herself in postures so artful they seemed borrowed from a portrait. One could easily imagine her practicing such gestures before the gilded mirror that adorned her dressing room wall.

The butler knocked, then entered the drawing room to announce Brendan's arrival. He followed, pausing just inside the threshold to absorb the scene. Harriet sat poised in silk, a cascade of auburn hair spilling over one shoulder, her figure framed by the harmonious tones of the painted walls. To her left, a large oil of Venus cavorted with cherubs in soft, flesh-toned opulence—a tableau of mythic indulgence that echoed, with unsubtle accuracy, the generous display of the painting's mistress.

"Brendan! It is so lovely to see you. I was not sure I would again."

He arched an eyebrow in question.

"I heard you might be arrested," she added lightly.

Brendan frowned. "That little *on-dit* spread rather quickly?"

Harriet waved a graceful hand, her bracelet catching the light. "I heard about it from the oddest little chit who came to call on me. Can you believe she demanded I reveal your whereabouts? She even threatened me!"

His headache vanished in an instant. Brendan took an involuntary step forward.

"Whom do you mean?"

Harriet giggled, fluttering a hand toward the window. "Lord Moreland's daughter ... or niece ... or something or other. From across the street. The little hoyden attempted to intimidate me, but she was scarcely larger than a squirrel. I set her in her place, of course. As if anyone would take the word of a child over that of a well-established widow— of an important viscount, no less."

Miss Abbott had tried to convince Harriet to assist him? What did that mean?

If the girl had been attempting to trap him into marriage, why would she have asked Lady Slight to step forward as a witness to his innocence?

The headache surged anew, sharp and immediate. Brendan lifted a hand to rub at his temple, seeking relief. It never paid for him to be ill-tempered, yet this wretched week had shredded his composure. Now he had accused a selfless young woman of dishonorable motives, and the shame of it struck with stunning force, like a blow to the chest. Dragging in a ragged breath, he turned and sank into a spindly gilded chair, the carved legs creaking beneath his weight.

"Miss Abbott attempted to have you step forward as an alibi?"

"Miss Abbott! That was her name!" Harriet declared with a triumphant little clap. "Hardly a miss—more of a child, muslined up to her chin. I would not leave the house in such a peagoose concoction. So prim, it was nearly ecclesiastical!"

The widow's laughing chatter struck like clashing cymbals against his already frayed nerves. Brendan raised his fingers to his temple again, the effort of restraint pressing down like a vice.

"How did you reply to her request?"

Harriet giggled again. "I put her in her place, I will have you know. I told her that if she made any such accusation, I would deny it entirely. She even had the gall to threaten me with your coachman as a witness, but I pointed out that the only thing he could attest to was that he had delivered you to the residence across the street. I did not need to say it aloud, but it was clear she would imperil her own reputation should she press the matter further."

Brendan bit back a groan. The mystery of Miss Abbott's decision was now resolved. She had concluded that the only way to shield him from suspicion was to imply that he had spent the night in her company rather than in Lady Slight's home. Rather than think her bold, rather than be humbled by her courage, he had accused her of deliberate deceit.

He had not thought the week could descend further into disgrace, but the realization of his own failing struck deep. He had always prided himself on fairness, on weighing character and conduct evenly. And yet ...

"Were you not concerned for me, Harriet? Would you have allowed me to hang?"

The widow, too occupied with her own performance to have noticed his rising dismay, suddenly started at the question. She sprang to her feet and hurried toward him, taking both of his hands in hers. "Of course not, Brendan! I knew you would find a solution. You are an intelligent man with powerful connections."

So, yes. The widow would have continued her untroubled pursuits while he faced trial and execution.

He recalled how he had questioned his choices in the moment he had found the baron's lifeless form. Since then, he had soothed himself with the illusion that Harriet had not known of his situation, that she had cared more deeply than she had ever expressed. But the truth now stood plain.

The one person who had risked her standing—her very future—to aid him had been a young lady who barely knew him at all. Miss Abbott was no schemer. She was a warrior, wrapped in muslin and integrity, acting not for affection, but for what was right. Lord Moreland's willingness to let his daughter govern her own fate now appeared entirely reasonable.

And I am an idiot. A vain, shallow idiot. The sort of man who finds the soulless Harriet alluring.

He had wronged Miss Abbott grievously. And he must make amends.

But how?

LILY HAD BEEN LYING on her bed, staring at the ceiling for several minutes. Her prideful storming from the drawing room had sustained her only until she had crossed the threshold of her bedroom, at which point she had hoisted herself onto the coverlet and collapsed in a state of numbness to consider her future.

The ceiling's plaster roses blurred above her as her eyes welled, but no tears came. Her mind felt like a sodden wool, heavy and slow.

A knock at the door barely registered. "Go away!"

She could not bear another moment of Mama's remonstrations. She knew it came from a place of love, that Mama was distraught over Lily's abrupt change in circumstance, but she had no strength left to absorb her mother's stricken regrets. Her certainty that Mr. Ridley would come up to scratch and rescue her from scandal had come to nothing, and she was hollow with disappointment.

The handle clicked, and a familiar red-blonde head peeked around the edge of the door. "I really would rather come in."

"Sophia!" Lily sat up with a gasp, the tears rushing at last. She burst into sobs at the sight of her best friend.

Her cousin hurried to her side, perching on the edge of the bed and drawing Lily into a warm embrace. The scent of rosewater clung to Sophia's muslin sleeve, and the soft rustle of fabric was the only sound in the room besides Lily's crying.

"Shh, Lily. Everything will work out."

"You heard?"

"Of course! I would have come sooner, but Miles had colic, and I was up with him and the nurse all night."

"I am so happy to see you! Mr. Ridley was here, but he said such awful things, and I sent him away!"

Sophia pulled her closer, tightening the embrace with a gentle comfort that only those bound by childhood bonds could offer.

"Your mother informed me. Apparently, I missed the performance by only a few minutes."

"How would Mama know what happened? Mr. Ridley only just left."

"I am quite sure she was listening at the door. She seemed entirely affronted with the gentleman, muttering about his ingratitude."

Lily pulled back, blinking at her cousin in amazement. "She did?"

Sophia nodded. "She was livid, truly. Pacing like a lioness in a drawing room. She kept repeating that no man ought to treat an Abbott in such a manner."

"Huh! I thought she would blame me for not accepting the offer."

"Nay, Lily. Your mother wants what is best for you. She simply needs time to adjust to all these happenings. Her hopes were pinned to an excellent match, and now she is left clutching broken straws. Just allow her a little time to gather herself together."

"I am ever so glad you are here."

Sophia smiled gently. "What happens now? Are you certain you do not wish to marry Mr. Ridley?"

Lily wailed, burying her face once more in Sophia's shoulder, which was already damp with tears. "I am not certain of anything! I do not wish to be snubbed by good society. Now I must leave London in disgrace and travel to places unknown, merely to show my face in public. Far from everything I am familiar with. How did it all come to this?"

Sophia patted her gently on the shoulder as silence settled between them, thick and still.

"I feel I should warn you," she said at last, "that the gossip rags mentioned you this morning."

Lily groaned into her cousin's sleeve. "My presence in high society has finally been noted."

"I am afraid so."

Lily drew a sharp breath, her chest rising and falling with distress. "What am I to do?"

Sophia turned her head toward Lily, her blue eyes soft with understanding. "Would you ... permit me to speak to Mr. Ridley?"

"Oh, I think that is impossible. It is clear he does not trust me."

"I feel confident we can make this arrangement work. The gentleman has been under great strain these past few days. He has always struck me as a kind-hearted man. He plays with Miles whenever he visits, and he shows genuine fondness for his nephew."

"You believe I should give him another opportunity to make his offer?"

"I believe," Sophia said carefully, "that what we need now is a little patience. Mr. Ridley's belligerence is understandable, if not forgivable. He found his father dead, was accused of murder, and then was compelled to come here and offer marriage. The poor man is reeling. It does not excuse his conduct, but I do believe we ought to try again."

Lily sucked on her lower lip, her gaze drifting toward the bedroom window, where the sunlight slanted across the carpet in golden bars. "I am not sure."

"Mr. Ridley had only Richard to advise him this morning before he came," Sophia added gently. "As much as I love my husband, you and I both know that Richard is still learning how to manage the intricacies of emotional ties. Mr. Ridley is inexperienced in courtship. I am quite certain he is the best solution to your predicament, but he may require a touch of guidance in so trying a time."

Nodding, Lily sank back on the bed, her arms flung out in quiet surrender. "We shall try this one more time."

Sophia settled down beside her, skirts rustling softly against the coverlet, and they both stared up at the ceiling just as they had done as girls. The pattern of shadowed plaster was riveting as they contemplated recent events.

"It was exceedingly brave of you," Sophia said gently.

"I had to do it. Seeing the duchess in such despair ... I had to follow my conscience."

"You gave up much."

Lily sighed, her gaze drifting across the familiar lines of the ceiling. "I shall never have a suitor bring me hothouse flowers or accompany me to Gunter's for ices. I will never have my first dance with a man and realize that he might be my future husband."

Sophia's lips twisted, the expression more wistful than wry. "Neither of us has had an easy time of it, have we?"

"Richard did bring you flowers that day you compromised him!" Lily murmured, her tone tinged with mischief.

Her cousin huffed, though her eyes softened. "And he drove me to Gunter's the day we wed to flaunt our connection in front of the *ton*."

A quiet giggle escaped Lily as she recalled the strange, determined course of Sophia's wedding to the earl. They had battled through the storm and found shelter in each other. The memory, though not hers, warmed her like a hearth on a winter's evening.

Slowly, her high spirits trickled back, buoying her heart

until a fragile optimism stirred to life. "Perhaps it could all work out!"

Sophia reached out to clasp Lily's hand, their fingers curling together with the certainty of family. "I will do everything in my power to make it so."

BRENDAN STEPPED out into the bright, sunlit street just as another man emerged from Lord Moreland's stately townhouse. They both halted at the bottom of the steps, momentarily frozen, assessing one another with narrowed eyes. Brendan realized with a jolt that this must be Moreland's heir. The resemblance was striking—tall, square-jawed, and broad of shoulder. The gentleman bore his father's commanding frame, but the coloring of Miss Abbott. That chocolate-brown hair, those sharply glaring eyes—there could be no mistake.

Before Brendan could step away from the widow's modest door, the younger man strode across the cobbled street, boots striking hard against the stone.

"What are you doing at this ... this ... this harlot's home? Why has Lily turned you down?" he demanded, fury surging in every syllable. Without waiting for a reply, Abbott seized him by the lapels of his coat.

Blazes. Brendan fought a grimace. *I need to visit Gentleman Jackson's. This is the second time I have been manhandled in as many days.*

His lack of rest dulled his reflexes. The pounding in his skull had not abated since morning and now throbbed in rhythm with his rising pulse. "I was here for ten minutes. Nothing happened," he said flatly.

Abbott hesitated, breath hard and uneven. Slowly, he

released his grip. Brendan tugged his waistcoat into place, then smoothed his jacket with deliberate calm, as if dignity could be refastened with sartorial effort alone.

"My sister is ruined, and it is my fault for leaving her alone that night. You have to fix this, Ridley!"

The anguish carved into the young man's features was unmistakable. Despite the ache behind his eyes, Brendan felt a sharp jab of shame strike his chest like the edge of a blade. If it were his sister …

"Miss Abbott refused my offer."

"Why? What did you do?" Abbott's voice cracked on the question. "She hoped you would take care of her after what she did for you!"

Brendan broke eye contact, staring over Abbott's shoulder at the stately line of townhouses across the street. He was hardly going to admit to his own foolish blunder—the cruel accusation flung at Lily, the fumbling, botched proposal.

"It is not what she wants. And what about you? Would you marry a child?"

Abbott's face hardened like carved stone. "She is no child, you scoundrel! What Lily lacks in stature, she makes up for in heart. She is kindness and joy. And, fortunately for you, she is the epitome of honor, or even now you would be imprisoned."

He gestured violently toward the house behind Brendan. "That woman is a vicious viper. Yet you visit her while my sister has retreated, facing certain ruin. I am to take her to the Continent to outrun this scandal. Lily is a young woman with her entire life ahead of her. What is she to do if you will not assist her?"

Brendan winced. His fingers curled into fists at his sides. The more he learned of Miss Abbott—no, Lily—the more deeply ashamed he felt. Her goodness had not only shielded him from disaster, it had been freely offered, with little expectation. And what had he given her in return? Grief. Dismissal. Humiliation.

He had to make amends. But how did one mend something so carelessly shattered?

"She practically threw me out," he muttered. "But I will work something out."

Abbott's eyes narrowed, his gaze raking Brendan from head to toe with measured intensity. Then he stepped back, as if allowing him a last sliver of grace.

"I spoke with some of the chaps this morning," Abbott said quietly, "and they tell me you are a good sort, Ridley. You must wed my sister to save her from this shame. Lily does not deserve this. Everyone she knows will give her the cut direct. It is inconceivable that this should happen to her."

His voice broke then, and his shoulders dipped under the weight of his helpless affection. "She is the very best of sisters. If I could restore her reputation with my own hands, I would. But I cannot. You must help her."

Brendan raised a shaky hand to rake it through his hair. He had not eaten properly in days, and now the sheer weight of this muddle threatened to pull him under.

He had no idea how to repair the damage he had wrought. But he could not walk away from this ... or from her.

"I will try to make it right, Abbott."

It was not much. It was not nearly enough. But in his exhausted, unraveling state, it was all Brendan could summon.

$\sim$

WHEN SOPHIA LEFT, Lily followed her downstairs, trailing one hand lightly along the polished banister for balance. After bidding her cousin goodbye with a soft smile, she turned toward the fateful drawing room, the very room where she had not only seen Mr. Ridley exit Lady Slight's home, but had also awaited his proposal ... and then rejected him.

A chill passed over her shoulders as she entered. Her mother was seated in Lily's favorite spot by the front window, peering through the lace curtains as if she could will propriety back into their lives. At the sound of Lily's approaching footfalls, Mama flinched and turned sharply.

"Lily!" she cried, rising so swiftly the hem of her gown tangled about her slippers. She crossed the room and pulled her daughter into an unexpected embrace. Lily froze, her cheek pressed into her mother's shoulder, her arms stiff at her sides. The floral lavender scent of her mother's toilette enveloped her, and her heart stumbled in confusion. What was happening?

"We shall find a way through this," Mama whispered fiercely. "I cannot believe what Mr. Ridley said to you! I was so relieved when Sophia arrived ... I would have come upstairs, but I did not know what to say. I thought perhaps she might address it better than I."

After a long moment, Lily lifted her arms and returned the embrace, pressing her face into the familiar silk of her mother's bodice as fresh tears prickled at her eyes. The unexpected shift from criticism to comfort was more than welcome. She had feared she would carry this disgrace alone. "Sophia and I had a good talk," she murmured. "Thank you for ... Thank you."

They broke apart awkwardly, neither quite meeting the other's gaze.

"Mama, I would prefer not to attend the Townsend dinner this evening. Perhaps you might inform them I have a headache?"

Something flickered across her mother's face, too swift to read, before she schooled her features. "Our invitation was ... rescinded."

A wave of remorse twisted in Lily's belly. So the whispers had begun. Sophia had warned her how quickly scandal spread among the *ton*. "I am sorry."

Mama shook her head with brisk defiance. "I never liked Lady Townsend that much anyway."

Lily offered a wan smile, unwilling to contradict the claim. Her mother and Lady Townsend had been thick as thieves for as long as she could recall, but truth would do no good here. "Sophia informs me that I was mentioned in the gossip rags."

Mama sighed heavily, blowing out her cheeks. "Sophia was minimizing the truth. There was a drawing of you ... in an inappropriate state ... with Mr. Ridley."

Lily swallowed hard, mortification washing through her in waves. "I am so sorry, Mama."

Her mother's eyes glinted with a mix of grief and steel. "We will prevail. Perhaps Sophia will talk some sense into Mr. Ridley."

"I hope so," Lily said quietly. "I truly do."

"BRIGGS IS HERE."

Michaels's disapproving tone rang out like a cracked bell in the somber stillness of the study. Brendan gritted his teeth. The butler's animosity remained an enigma, a grievance born not of recent events, but present since Brendan's very first night in London. That night, just after his twenty-first birthday, he had arrived fresh from Baydon Hall, dismissed without ceremony by the man who was both his uncle and father.

He ought to be immune to Michaels's disdain by now. And yet, now that he was to inherit the barony, perhaps it was time to consider retiring the supercilious servant altogether.

"Show him in," Brendan said coolly.

The duke shifted in his seat near the hearth, long legs crossed and gray eyes sharp with thought. Across the room, Richard stood beside a towering stack of musty books, his hands clenched behind his back. The earl had been glaring at those tomes since his arrival, his posture a portrait of barely leashed frustration. Though still seething over Miss Abbott's plight, Richard had kept his word and joined the meeting with the Bow Street Runner. With Brendan cleared of all suspicion, the identity of the true killer now demanded swift discovery.

Brendan rubbed his temples with slow, deliberate pressure. Each pulse behind his eyes felt like the toll of a bell. He had not slept. His encounters at the Abbotts' home had drained what little strength remained in him. But this—this inquiry—could not wait. He needed resolution. And soon.

Footsteps sounded in the hallway, and then the runner appeared in the doorway.

"My lord," Briggs said with a brief bow.

Apparently, now that Brendan was no longer in custody, the man had resolved how to address him. That, at least, was something.

"Please, have a seat," Brendan said, gesturing toward a well-worn leather chair across from the library table.

The runner stepped into the room, looking visibly uncomfortable. His eyes darted about before he removed his battered hat and took the proffered seat beside the duke, its leather creaking under his weight.

The duke cleared his throat with quiet command. "We wish to hire you to pursue the matter of the baron's death."

Briggs nodded once, firm. "I was hoping you would, because I have concerns for Lord Filminster's safety."

Brendan had not been listening closely, his thoughts dulled by fatigue, the unrelenting ache at his temples acting like a vise about his skull, but the runner's words cut through the fog. He sat up straighter, pulse flickering.

"What?"

"Before I raise my concerns, I must ask … Would your father have answered the door himself?"

Frowning, Brendan gave his head a weary shake. "Never. The baron would not lower himself to fulfill the duties of a servant. He was … a vain man."

Briggs exhaled slowly. "I was afraid of that."

From his armchair, Halmesbury leaned forward, forearms braced against his knees. "What are you thinking, Briggs?"

"Lord Filminster"—the runner inclined his head respectfully toward Brendan for clarity—"spoke of being let in early in the morning. None of the servants admitted to being the one who opened the door for him. That is suspicious in itself, but …"

Brendan's nerves, already frayed to threads, snapped taut. Sleep deprivation and mounting dread had stripped away his tolerance. His voice emerged clipped, roughened at the edges.

"But?"

Briggs tugged thoughtfully at his mustache, the motion

slow and deliberate, betraying his reluctance to speak aloud the conclusion. "The baron was murdered by one of the servants, or a servant knows who killed him, because they provided the killer access to your home."

Brendan groaned and dropped his face into his hands, pressing his fingertips against his eyelids as if physical pressure might forestall the rising tide of dread. Of course. He had been so consumed by scandal, guilt, and exhaustion, he had failed to apply the most basic logic. Yes, the murder had to be solved, but he had not considered that the guilty party might still be under his roof. Or worse, that betrayal had flourished among those who served him.

"Blazes," Richard muttered under his breath, jaw clenched. "We have been contending with family pressures, so we did not stop to think about the implications."

The duke sighed, long and measured, steepling his fingers beneath his chin. "I, on the other hand, have had time to consider it. That is why I insisted we meet with Briggs. Annabel reached the same conclusion. The baron would never deign to open the front door himself. Michaels also confirmed that the door had been locked and checked, given recent reports of break-ins in the area."

Briggs nodded. "I do not wish to cause panic, but I believe it is imperative that the servants be questioned again. With Grimes overseeing the investigation, I was not free to act independently. However, now that he is preoccupied with the inquest and displeased with how things have unfolded, I may proceed without his supervision. I wish to interview the household quietly and compile a list of suspects."

Brendan drew a slow breath, his hands falling back to his lap, palms open in surrender. "What of Grimes? Is he likely to pursue me further?"

Halmesbury shook his head slowly. "Fortunately, since Miss Abbott has provided you with an alibi, I was able to persuade the Home Secretary to intercede with Grimes about pursuing proper lines of inquiry."

A breath Brendan had not realized he was holding escaped him in a rush. The anxious knot in his chest began to loosen, and for the first time in days, a flicker of control returned to him. "Briggs, you may have whatever you need. The safety of my household must be secured."

He made swift arrangements with the runner, offering him double his usual fee along with a generous bonus so he might turn over his other cases. The matter of the baron's murder could no longer be deferred or shared. It required singular focus.

Once Michaels returned and escorted Briggs away to see to his needs, Brendan found himself once again alone with the duke and the earl. Silence fell like a weight across the room. It was an expectant hush, the air thick with the shift in subject, the unspoken name hanging there between them.

Miss Abbott.

Brendan resumed his seat with a low sigh, rubbing at his burning eyes. He waited, knowing what must come next.

"When is the wedding?" Richard's voice cut through the quiet like a whipcrack—sharp, accusing.

"There is not to be one."

The earl's expression darkened instantly, his features twisting into a scowl. A low growl escaped him, primal and dangerous. Brendan rose, moving behind his chair, bracing as if for a second attack, though this time it would be made with words, not fists.

"What happened?" The voice came not from the storm, but from its calm center.

Brendan turned, startled anew by the duke's quiet interjection. He had nearly forgotten Halmesbury's presence, so focused had he been on Richard's fury. But the steadiness of the duke's tone was a balm, cooling, stabilizing.

"There was a misunderstanding. I ... may have ... accused the young woman of deliberately trapping me," Brendan admitted, voice low, eyes trained on a knot in the wall paneling.

Silence followed. A silence broken only by the unmistakable sound of a snarl from Richard's direction.

Halmesbury sighed deeply, long-suffering but not without sympathy. "What do you plan to do?"

"I do not know. Miss Abbott refused my offer." Brendan hesitated, shame curling like smoke in his lungs. "I must confess I was relieved. I am not ready to marry a child."

"You are the child, Ridley! And it is time for you to grow up!" The words were thunder as Richard's voice rose with fury.

At that moment, a knock sounded at the door.

Michaels stepped inside, impassive as ever. "Lady Saunton is here."

Richard froze, startled, his eyes cutting to the entrance.

Sophia entered with quiet elegance, gliding into the room like moonlight through heavy curtains. Her eyes settled on her husband, and the anger drained from him.

"Sophia! What are you doing here?" he asked, his voice a shade of the tempest it had been.

The countess tilted her head, offering him a serene smile that belied the steel beneath it. "I am here to speak with Mr. Ridley about Lily, of course."

CHAPTER

EIGHT

"There has never been a protracted war from which a country has benefited."

Sun Tzu, *L'Art de la Guerre* (*The Art of War*)

JULY 24, 1821

S heer exhaustion from several days of insomnia had at last carried Lily off to the land of sleep. Her dreams were mercifully blank, a welcome balm after so many nights haunted by doubt and disgrace. It was the first true rest she had known since the night of the baron's murder, and the relief of it seemed stitched into her very bones.

By the time her eyes fluttered open, it was midmorning. Pale sunlight filtered through the curtains, casting softened stripes across the coverlet. Sitting up slowly, she stretched her arms overhead and inhaled deeply, her limbs loose and unburdened for the first time in days. Her toes wiggled beneath the linens, and a small smile pulled at the corners of her mouth. The dull aches and tight muscles brought on by fatigue had disappeared, replaced by a buoyancy of spirit. Her usual optimism crept back in—quietly, cautiously—filling her thoughts with possibility.

"Lily! You have a visitor!"

Spinning toward the door, now fully open, Lily blinked in surprise. There stood Mama, smiling broadly, her cheeks tinged with unmistakable delight.

"My abigail is here to assist you in dressing."

Lily's gaze shifted to the hallway, where her lady's maid stood behind her mother.

What on earth?

The last few days replayed in Lily's mind with sudden clarity. When news of her ruination had first broken, Mama had wept bitterly, her tone despairing as she lamented the death of Lily's future. Then, after Mr. Ridley's appalling accusation—dressed as a proposal—Mama had burned with indignation, storming about the drawing room in a fit of moral fury over the poor conduct of young men in modern society. Dinner afterward had been an ordeal, with Lily's brother seated like a statue, shoulders rigid, eyes fixed on his untouched plate, lost in guilt. Papa had not even returned, summoned away on urgent business.

And now ... joy?

She stared at her mother, bewildered.

Now she is joyful?

What could cause such a drastic shift in mood? "Who is it?"

"It is not for me to say. Quickly, we must get you ready." Mama clapped her hands together, and her lady's maid bustled into the room.

Lily was still groggy from sleep, her thoughts thick and sluggish, but she reluctantly slipped from the warm cocoon of her bed. She had hoped to rise at her leisure and perhaps enjoy a cup of tea before facing the world, but clearly, that was not to be.

Mama swept toward the wardrobe, rifling through the gowns and muttering under her breath. At last, she emerged with a creamy confection of lace and cotton. Lily pulled a face. It was the most unflattering choice for her complexion, but Mama had always insisted it was perfection.

With its profusion of bows and flounces, the gown made Lily feel like a child about to sit for a formal portrait, the sort where wealthy families donned antiquated costumes for the sake of posterity. Perhaps, if Sophia failed to bring Mr. Ridley up to scratch and Lily was indeed sent abroad, Aidan might help her replace the entirety of her wardrobe, well away from Mama's discerning eye.

Lawks, these clothes are hideous for me!

Her whispered prayer was cut short as the maid descended upon her with a hairbrush and vigorous purpose, drawing tears with each sharp stroke.

Twenty minutes later, she was ready, her hair arranged in the dreaded ringlets, and Mama was already pulling her by the hand into the hallway. Lily stumbled slightly, catching up with her mother's longer stride.

"Mama, I am short!"

Her mother barely paused. "We must hurry. It has been an age."

Lily nodded, gathering up her skirts in one hand as she quickened her steps. As they neared the first floor, her nose gave a warning twitch. She pinched it between her fingers to fend off a sneeze, nearly tripping on the final stair. Mama's arm shot out to steady her.

Achoo!

Mama ignored her, charging toward the drawing-room door and flinging it wide.

Achoo!

Lily sniffled once, then stepped into the sunlit room and gasped in surprise.

On every surface stood vases overflowing with lilies. They adorned the tables, the mantelpiece, even the broad windowsills—beautiful, fragrant lilies in every shade and variety. Lily had never seen so many flowers outside the Covent Garden market.

Achoo! Achoo! Achoo!

And there, across the room, stood Mr. Ridley, bathed in sunlight. His expression was relaxed, his skin returned to its usual golden hue. He looked ever so handsome, rejuvenated, almost boyish. Mr. Ridley must have finally taken proper rest.

Achoo! Achoo! Achoo! Achoo! Achoo! Achoo!

Lily swiped her fingertips beneath her stinging eyes, blinking furiously even as her heart brimmed with feeling. Flowers! He had brought her flowers. Dozens—no, hundreds—of them.

Achoo! Achoo! Achoo!

"Oh, Lily! I forgot!" Mama's voice rose in dismay, her hands fluttering like startled doves. "I completely forgot!"

Mr. Ridley had stepped forward, alarm tightening his brow. "Are you quite well, Miss Abbott?"

Achoo! Achoo! Achoo! Achoo!

"She is not, Mr. Ridley," Mama said, wringing her gloved hands. "I forgot that Lily suffers from a sensitivity to lilies. We must quit the room at once!"

"Of course," he said promptly. "I shall take her for a drive in my carriage, as we discussed. I believe your maid is already waiting outside."

Achoo! Achoo! Achoo!

Mama took a firm hold of Lily's elbow, swiftly ushering her from the drawing room and along the corridor to the staircase. Down to the lower hall they went, where Lily inhaled deeply, her lungs at last spared the perfumed assault.

A handkerchief appeared before her face.

"I am so sorry," Mama said, breathless with regret. "I quite forgot. The flowers will be gone when you return."

Lily dabbed at her streaming eyes, then blew delicately into the handkerchief. There was no denying the inelegance of the moment, but even so, she could not suppress the radiant grin blooming across her face.

She had a suitor! And he had brought her flowers! So many, many, many flowers!

Everything will work out for the best!

Mr. Ridley appeared beside her. "My apologies, Miss Abbott. It was meant as a thoughtful gesture, but I fear it has gone rather awry."

Lily shook her head and tilted her chin to smile up at the tall gentleman. "Not at all, Mr. Ridley. I would not have missed it for the world!"

He looked down at her in astonishment, the light catching in his brandy-colored eyes, illuminating the flecks of gold threaded through the warm amber depths. Shaking his head, he gave a low, bemused chuckle. "I do believe you are telling the truth."

Lily wrinkled her brow in mock severity. "I always tell the truth, Mr. Ridley." Then she winced. "Except when I exaggerated to the coroner, that is. But I felt it justified, as I knew your whereabouts."

Mama groaned quietly from her other side, visibly restraining herself from scolding.

"Shall we?" Mr. Ridley offered his arm.

With a thrill of delight, Lily slipped her hand through the crook of his elbow. In step, they moved toward the front door, which Thomas now held open in solemn silence.

The past few days may have been a nightmare, but now she had awakened into a lovely dream, and the joy of it was so powerful, it bubbled through her veins like spring water over sunlit stones.

Mr. Ridley led her to the waiting carriage and assisted her up the steps with practiced ease. Inside, she found Nancy huddled in a corner, wearing the expression of one unimpressed at being conscripted into a courtship ritual. Lily settled beside her while Mr. Ridley took the bench opposite.

Turning toward the still-open door, Lily blinked in astonishment. Mama stood in the entrance hall, composed and unmoving. Her mother was permitting her to depart with only Nancy for propriety?

Mr. Ridley's footman closed the door with a firm click, and Lily blinked in shock. Her famously overprotective mama was truly allowing her to drive away with Mr. Ridley, chaperoned only by the old nursemaid.

Her heart thudded wildly in her chest.

When she looked back to Mr. Ridley, she found him smiling at her, the expression warm and assured.

"Where are we off to?" she asked.

"It is to be a surprise," he replied. "You shall have to wait and see."

Lily bit her lip, unable to help the delighted flutter in

her stomach. She shifted toward the window, peering out as the carriage lurched into motion, the world beyond slipping past in a soft blur.

"I should like to apologize, Miss Abbott," Mr. Ridley said quietly. "Yesterday ... was an aberration. The baron interfered with my marital prospects once before, and so it has long been a sore subject. Coupled with recent events ... well, I ought not to have displaced my umbrage onto you. You have been extraordinarily generous to me, and I am afraid I behaved quite reprehensibly."

Lily turned her head to study him. "It was reprehensible, but I can understand that you have been under considerable strain. With everything that has occurred and the sheer shock of it all, any person might behave poorly when faced with so many challenges at once."

"You are too kind."

Her lips curved into an impish grin, and she gave a light shrug. "The alternative is to be cruel. Where is the amusement in that?"

Mr. Ridley chuckled, revealing a flash of even white teeth, which Lily observed with no small amount of fascination. He truly was a perfect physical specimen of manhood. It remained something of a marvel that he was not already married.

"I must apologize that we are confined to my carriage," Mr. Ridley said, gesturing toward the corner where Nancy sat, unbothered and slightly slumped. "It requires the presence of a chaperon. My curricle is undergoing repairs."

"Nancy? Do not concern yourself. She hears nothing," she replied, then turned to the servant and added rather loudly, "CAN YOU HEAR US, NANCY?"

"I think the footman's name was Beasley, not Yancy."

Lily's lips twitched with amusement. "She will be

asleep before we pass the first milestone. Nancy cannot remain awake in moving vehicles."

"Ah. Your mother and Lord Moreland exchanged words when she suggested Nancy as your companion. He was of the opinion someone else ought to attend you."

Lily's brows rose. "Then I suppose Mama wished for us to have an opportunity to speak freely."

So her mother had taken measures—subtle, but deliberate—to tip the balance in her daughter's favor, even if it came at the cost of strict propriety. Lily could only imagine her father's disapproval at the notion of his daughter being sent out with anything less than a dragon as chaperon.

"What was it you wished to say?" she asked. If Mr. Ridley had gone to such trouble to ensure they had privacy, there must be something of consequence to discuss.

Mr. Ridley shook his head, and his chestnut curls shifted with the motion. Lily caught herself reaching and promptly sat on her hands. Sometimes they acted with a will of their own.

"In time," he said with a faint smile. "There is something we must do first before we speak of the future."

Lily's heart leapt in her chest. The gentleman was going to renew his offer just as Sophia had predicted!

A dizzying rush of relief swept through her. Traveling might prove an adventure, but how much finer it would be to do so with a husband beside her and not under a cloud of scandal, where every acquaintance whispered that she was a ruined girl.

Turning back to the window, she leaned slightly to study the shops and homes flashing past. She tried to calculate their destination by the direction they traveled, but after several minutes of watching the ebb and flow of

London's traffic, she still could not determine where they were headed.

Until the carriage turned gently onto a broad, fashionable street.

"Berkeley Square!"

"Indeed."

"We are visiting Gunter's for ices?"

"Your cousin assured me you would appreciate it."

Lily's eyes widened. "Was it her idea, the lilies?"

Mr. Ridley grimaced ever so slightly. "Not precisely. She mentioned hothouse flowers might not go amiss, but I fear I rather overdid it, given your sensitivity."

Lily clapped her hands and leaned back with a sigh of delight. "I have never been! The other debutantes speak of it endlessly. Mama visits with her friends, of course, but we seldom go out in public except for the theater or fittings at the mantua-maker's."

"And I have never escorted a young lady to Gunter's," Mr. Ridley replied, a hint of amusement in his tone. "So I believe we are on equal footing."

The carriage pulled to a halt beneath the shade of the leafy trees. Lily peeked out to see gentlemen lounging along the wrought-iron railings and young ladies perched atop high curricles, fanning themselves with elegant languor. White-aproned servers from Gunter's moved smartly between carriages, delivering ices in delicate glass goblets.

Mr. Ridley's footman—Wesley, the same one Sophia had interrogated on the day of the baron's death—appeared at the door and lowered the steps. A moment later, one of the liveried Gunter's servers approached and leaned through the doorway.

"May I inquire after your preferences today, miss?" he asked with a deferential bow.

Lily's thoughts scattered. This was it. A moment she had imagined on countless nights. But now that it had arrived, it felt suddenly monumental. What if she chose poorly? What if her first taste was disappointing?

Mr. Ridley opened the opposite door to allow a breeze to cross through the carriage. The air stirred gently, carrying with it the fragrance of crushed grass, warm stone, and the oak trees that framed the square.

The server listed the options in an efficient monotone: "Chocolate, lavender, maple, Parmesan cheese, Gruyère, and bergamot."

Her mind reeled. She had not expected cheeses.

"Um ... lavender?"

"It is an excellent choice, miss."

"Agreed," Mr. Ridley said from across the carriage. "I will have the same."

Lily turned back to find him watching her with a quietly bemused expression.

"Would Nancy like one?" he added, bobbing his head in the direction of the old woman.

Nancy had slumped at an angle so alarming that Lily half-feared she might topple. Her mouth hung open, and a loud, wheezing snore filled the small space.

Lily pressed her lips together to keep from laughing and gave Mr. Ridley a look that clearly said, *I told you so.*

He chuckled and dismissed the server with a nod.

Brendan watched Miss Abbott as she relished her lavender ice, her expression as radiant as a child at a fair. He and his valet had locked themselves in his chambers the previous evening to guard against any further nocturnal intrusions, which had granted him the rare luxury of uninterrupted sleep. Now that his general outlook had markedly improved, he was forced to concede that the Countess of Saunton had been correct.

Miss Abbott was an exuberant creature—spirited, artless, and wholly alive to the pleasures of the world. She embraced existence with a wholeheartedness that was most disarming.

He supposed he was exceedingly fortunate. She had stepped into the role of his scandalous paramour with such verve that even Grimes was utterly convinced he was a licentious debaucher of gently bred virgins. Under ordinary circumstances, the mere thought that society might deem him a scoundrel of the highest order would have horrified him. But given the alternative, being charged with patricide, he supposed he could endure whispers about his depravity.

Soon enough, their marriage would reshape the narrative. The scandal of seduction would become the tale of a grand, tempestuous passion.

It was, unquestionably, the only honorable path forward. They would have to make the best of it.

And yet, hang it all, she was of such tender years.

Even now, she scooped her ice with the wide-eyed focus of a child devouring cake at a fête. There was not the slightest trace of flirtation in her enjoyment. Her laughter was unguarded. He could detect no suggestion of a bosom beneath that avalanche of frothy lace and flounces. If the young woman possessed curves, they were obscured with such diligence that it was a wonder she had received any attention from suitors at all.

It remained an enduring mystery why debutantes chose to dress in a manner least calculated to attract male notice, particularly when their entire Season revolved around ensnaring a husband.

But it did not signify. This marriage must proceed, for both their reputations. It was a matter of honor.

Miss Abbott had taken an extraordinary risk to spare him the ordeal of arrest and trial. Even had he been declared innocent, the stain of suspicion would have clung to him for years, rumors of murder whispered behind fans and snorted into brandy glasses. But thanks to her bold intervention, the conversation had pivoted. Now, society's tongues wagged not over death, but seduction. And once their betrothal was made official, even that would soften into speculation about a love match.

Despite her unmistakable youth, Miss Abbott's zeal and her integrity were steadily growing on him. He began to believe that forging a true partnership might not be impossible.

If only I found her physically appealing.

There lay the rub. Brendan understood that once he married, dalliances would be dishonorable. He had observed too many marriages within the *beau monde* decay into bitterness and estrangement—husbands and wives who could scarce endure one another's company, each conducting affairs with a studied lack of discretion. It was not a future he intended to emulate.

And so, he must somehow reconcile himself to sharing a bed with this spirited but undeniably immature girl within the sanctity of marriage.

The thought unsettled him more than he liked to admit.

When they had finished their ices and Nancy still slumbered soundly in the corner of the opposing bench, the Gunter's server returned to collect their goblets. The carriage doors were closed once more, but the vehicle did not lurch into motion. This was it. It was time to do the honorable thing.

"Miss Abbott?"

She turned those large brown eyes upon him, and for a fleeting moment, Brendan wondered how she might look in the deeper hues favored by Lady Moreland, colors that flattered her rich complexion and dark eyes so handsomely. Miss Abbott had the same luxurious brown hair, softly framing an elfin face of remarkable delicacy. Her eyes were extraordinary—lively, alert, and full of spirit. Yet the pale, lacy confections she habitually wore were quite abysmal. He could only hope she would adopt a more becoming wardrobe once they were wed.

"I am deeply ashamed of my conduct yesterday," he began. "And after speaking with Lady Slight, I now understand how grievously I misjudged your character. It must have taken considerable courage to confront her ... to demand she speak in my defense."

Miss Abbott's eyes widened in astonishment. "She confessed to our conversation?"

Brendan inclined his head. "She did. And I wish you to know that it would be a great honor for me to wed a courageous young woman such as yourself. If you would do me the honor of becoming my wife, I vow to spend every day of our union striving to show you the depth of my esteem. Your actions were not only bold—they were noble. I was an innocent man, and you risked your own reputation to shield me."

She tilted her head, studying him with gentle thoughtfulness. "What if I still wish to visit the Continent?"

"Then we shall plan a journey," he replied. "I could take you to Florence, if that is your desire."

Her eyes widened again, this time with wonder. "You would truly do that?"

"If we are to wed, I would consider our marriage a partnership. Your wishes shall be as weighty as my own."

She sighed then, a sound full of wistfulness. "That does sound lovely. And I suppose I have little choice. I always hoped for a love match, but now ... it appears a marriage of convenience is our only course."

Brendan hesitated, then offered gently, "Perhaps it would be more fitting to think of it as a marriage of friendship? What you did for me ... my late mother would have called it a selfless act. An act born of compassion. I cannot repay such kindness, but I can strive to honor it. Offering you the protection of my name is but the beginning. Beyond that, I hope we shall build something strong and enduring."

Her gaze lingered on his, her expression unreadable for a long moment.

"Is it to be ... a faithful marriage?"

Brendan puffed a quiet breath of surprise at Miss Abbott's forthrightness. She truly was an unusual girl.

"I assure you," he said, "that Lord Saunton would tear me limb from limb were I to entertain even a passing thought of infidelity. There shall be no risk of dalliance if we wed."

Miss Abbott nodded solemnly. "A marriage of friendship, then." She extended her gloved hand between them and held it there, waiting. Brendan looked at the offered appendage, momentarily baffled. "Friends shake hands, do they not?"

His lips curved into a reluctant smile. Reaching forward, he took her small hand and gave it a brief, proper shake, only to find himself surprised by the strength of her grip. She might be so slight that a gust of wind could carry her aloft, but it was abundantly clear that her backbone was forged of iron. "It is a bargain."

At his knock on the ceiling, the carriage began to move. Brendan leaned back against the squabs of his bench while Miss Abbott returned her attention to the window, watching the passing streets with avid curiosity.

It was done. The match was made. He was to marry this peculiar, principled young woman in order to protect her reputation, and to his surprise, he did not regret it.

But the thought pricked at his conscience and curled somewhere dark in his mind.

Confound it. What if I get her killed?

A fresh wave of unease rolled through him at the reminder. The baron's death remained unresolved. There might yet be a murderer concealed within his household. Perhaps the wedding ought to be delayed until the investigation is complete?

CHAPTER
NINE

"Victorious warriors win first and then go to war, while defeated warriors go to war first and then seek to win."

Sun Tzu, *L'Art de la Guerre* (*The Art of War*)

~

JULY 25, 1821

L ily examined herself in the mirror. Soon she was to take her vows, yet her critical eye insisted that she still possessed the air of a child. The flouncy gown she wore, though finely made, did little to lend her the dignity or poise of a woman about to be wed. It certainly would not cause any gentleman's pulse to quicken, least of all her intended. Not that she desired to appear wanton or garish, but still ... did she look like someone worthy of longing?

Her mind drifted, unbidden, to the widow. That lady was always so composed in her bold silk gowns,

commanding attention with her daring neckline and confident manner. Lily's own figure was modest in comparison,
her gown innocent and pale, her demeanor demure. She felt
painfully invisible in contrast.

A sigh escaped her lips as she stepped back and leaned
lightly against the carved foot of her tall bedstead, the cool
wood grounding her.

This would not do. She could not walk down the aisle
appearing no more than a schoolroom miss. She wanted to
be seen as a woman. To inspire admiration, yes, but more
than that, to be truly noticed by Mr. Ridley. For him to look
at her and feel something stir that went beyond friendship.
That warm gleam in his eyes, could she ever rouse it?

Sophia and the duchess were effortlessly elegant. Each
wore colors that seemed chosen by the heavens themselves.
The duchess, with her rich chestnut hair and eyes the color
of aged brandy, always looked perfectly adorned. Sophia,
her stormy blue eyes offset by her reddish-gold locks,
selected gowns with a confidence that Lily deeply admired
and she suspected that the rich tones her mother wore
would suit her far better than these pale pastels.

Most brides simply wore an existing gown. It was sensible, traditional. But Lily did not feel sensible just now. She
felt … determined.

"Bah! I need a new gown for my wedding."

"I agree," Sophia said, stepping beside her. "And I know
just where to get one."

"What do I say to Mama?"

"You say you are a grown woman who requires a
wardrobe fit for matrimony and that you will not take no
for an answer."

"And then?"

"Then we hike up our skirts and make a dash for the

front door, where my carriage is waiting, before your mother can descend and scold us into submission."

"We should call to her from across the hall," Lily said with a wry smile, "so we gain a bit of a lead."

"I think we wait at the foot of the stairs," Sophia replied with equal mischief. "Then, as soon as she appears at the top, we inform her where we are going. That will give us more of a head start."

Lily nodded slowly. "We must go to a proper modiste. Mama's mantua-maker fashions gowns for matrons. I need something more … compelling. Mr. Ridley is a fine-looking man, and I do not wish to appear lacking in comparison. It must seem, especially to Society, that what passed between us sprang from deep feeling, not mere circumstance."

"I made an appointment with Signora Ricci for this morning," Sophia replied with a knowing smile.

"You knew?"

"Of course I knew. No self-respecting woman permits her mother to select her wedding gown, not when she is to marry a man who should see her in her best light." She bobbed her head subtly toward Lily's bodice.

Lily looked down. Her gown was embellished with tiny bows across the front, a detail that had once seemed charming but now felt juvenile. She resembled nothing so much as a Twelfth Night cake, the kind confectioners displayed in their windows, adorned with sugared roses and fondant flourishes. Decorative. Delightful. But not desirable.

She wanted to be more than a cheerful display. She wished to be seen—by him. She wanted Mr. Ridley's heart to stir when he looked at her, to feel fortunate in his choice of bride. Not to glance back at what had once been.

"There is not much time," she murmured. "Papa insists

we wed swiftly to still the gossip. Mr. Ridley has already applied for a Common License."

"Signora Ricci will manage. She is a miracle worker. Now that your wedding is set, we must ensure Mr. Ridley sees you for what you are—a woman worthy of admiration and devotion. You deserve far more than polite companionship."

Lily drew in a slow breath, then released it, her fingers tightening at her sides. "Mama will descend shortly. We should position ourselves if we mean to catch her on the steps."

Sophia's eyes lit with mischief. "I do so enjoy a good caper!"

As they turned toward the door, Lily paused. The question that had been gnawing at her could not be silenced.

"How bad is it?" Her voice was soft, laced with uncertainty.

Sophia's smile faded. She glanced away for a moment, then back. "The gossip?"

Lily gave a small nod.

Sophia hesitated only a beat. "Let us say … it is very fortunate that your wedding is near."

"You need to apply to the Home Secretary for a writ of summons."

The duke's announcement halted Brendan mid-stride.

He had secured Miss Abbott's agreement to marry, thus easing the burden on his conscience. Now his thoughts were consumed with ensuring her safety once she entered his household. Briggs was to brief him later that day regarding the servants' interviews. Thus far, no one had burst into the library bearing grim news, which at least suggested that if the Bow Street Runner had uncovered anything, it was not urgent enough to herald his immediate demise.

"For what?" Brendan's tone was not defensive, merely bewildered. He could not imagine what Halmesbury was referring to.

"To take your seat in the House of Lords." The duke's tone was pragmatic, his gray eyes trained steadily on Brendan, who blinked at him, trying to comprehend the significance of the statement.

"I do not think this is the time for politics!"

Richard, standing at the window, gave a derisive snort. "Dunderhead! This is not about politics. At this moment, hundreds of tenants and servants are without a landlord. Thousands of constituents lack representation. There is more at stake than your own affairs."

He stepped forward, his expression stern. "You are a peer now … or will be once the Committee for Privileges confirms your succession. You must authorize funds, sign documents, manage households and lands. Even your own household's operations are affected. Or do you imagine that your late … benefactor … arranged for the coffers to open from beyond the grave?"

The pressure at his temples pulsed with a dull insistence. Brendan slumped into an ancient damask-covered sofa, its cushions long past their prime, and cast his gaze upward to the faded crown moldings that framed the ceiling. Once cream, they had darkened with age.

"Lawks! We only just buried the baron."

Across from him, the duke's lips pinched into a taut line. He began to drum his long fingers —slow, deliberate— against the worn mahogany arm of his chair.

"Annabel wished to attend, but ..."

"But women do not attend funerals," Brendan supplied, voice heavy.

Halmesbury nodded once. And in that pause, Brendan realized how selfishly inward he had turned. The strain upon his brother-in-law had barely registered amid the chaos of his own thoughts. He looked again at the duke's face and saw the exhaustion etched around his eyes, faint shadows betraying sleepless nights, a weight carried quietly.

"I told her I did not care about convention," Halmesbury said at last, his voice low. "She should attend if she wished. But she woke this morning unwell. The tension of the past days has done her no good, and she is well along now. She chose rest over the condemnation of men who would stare and judge. I wished her to have an opportunity to say goodbye, but she said her health and our child's must come first."

Guilt stirred in Brendan's chest. He had not asked after his sister. Not once. His mind had been wholly consumed by threat, inheritance, scandal.

"I should pay her a visit," he murmured.

Richard stepped away from the window, his boots whispering against the polished floorboards, and settled into a nearby chair. "Perhaps we might dine together. Talk a little. Perhaps reminisce about the baron. It might allow her to close this chapter."

Halmesbury tilted his head slightly, considering. "I would like that. The five of us, then? You and the countess, Brendan, and ourselves?"

Richard nodded. "Yes. I shall cancel our other plans."

"I appreciate it. A quiet supper among family ... more fitting than the posturing dandies the baron kept company with." Brendan's fingers traced the embroidery of the sofa arm. "We can speak of old anecdotes. Give her chance to air her memories."

"Sophia will be glad to assist the duchess," the earl replied, his tone soft.

Brendan closed his eyes. The filtered light through the mullioned windows pressed too sharply against his temples. Everything ached with new gravity.

A few short days ago, he had been a carefree heir, drinking in the laughter of Town, dancing through life with no thought for consequence. Now, he was a man weighted with responsibility. Not just a wife. An estate. Lives dependent upon his steadiness. Tenants. Servants. The people of his district.

He had never been tutored for this. His estrangement from the baron meant he had learned nothing of stewardship. The steward was a name, the solicitors mere acquaintances.

He rubbed his brow, voice low. "Let us not forget, we have a murder yet unsolved."

Halmesbury exhaled heavily, the sound weighted with fatigue. "Thunder an' turf! This is a grim week."

Richard leaned back in his chair, fingers tugging absently at the folds of his cravat. The motion was agitated, though his voice remained dry. "Which part? The grotesque crime, the unexpected death in the family, the averted arrest, or the betrothal born of scandal?"

Brendan let out a disbelieving laugh, short and incredulous. "All of it. Every last bit of it."

The silence that followed was companionable, each man seated with his own disquiet, the room echoing faintly with the creak of ancient floorboards and the distant tick of a longcase clock.

At length, the duke spoke. "I would advise you to remain vigilant. Take precautions. Until the matter is resolved, you are still very much a target."

Brendan nodded slowly, fingers splayed against his knee, then pressed together as if in prayer. "I am. But the thought of bringing a bride into this chaos ... it weighs heavily."

"There is no avoiding it," Halmesbury replied. "The so-called tryst between a diabolical seducer and a highborn debutante is all that is being talked about. I have spread word of your impending nuptials far and wide. The sooner it becomes fact, the sooner the outrage fades."

Brendan gave a low, strangled sound and leaned back, thudding his head lightly against the chair's curved backrest. "I feel as if I am attempting to douse house fires using a mere teaspoon."

Richard gave a humorless chuckle, eyes glinting. "It will pass. Just see the wedding through. Once that has occurred, Society will find something else to wag their tongues about. Some new travesty of judgment to replace yours."

CHAPTER
TEN

"All men can see these tactics whereby I conquer, but what none can see is the strategy out of which victory is evolved."

Sun Tzu, *L'Art de la Guerre* (*The Art of War*)

JULY 29, 1821

"Hugh! It is not suitable attire! You must tell Lily to change."

"I think Lily looks lovely."

"But ... but ... it is red!"

"More of a burgundy, I think."

"And gold!"

"What is your issue with gold? She wore gold ribbons with her ball gown last week."

"It is not the same!"

Lily peered down at her dress. The deep burgundy silk

gleamed softly in the daylight filtering through the tall sash windows, its folds catching subtle highlights of claret and plum. Despite Mama's distress, she could not contain the huge grin of joy that had her cheeks stretched so widely the muscles in her face were aching.

Signora Ricci had not disappointed. The talented modiste had created a gown that was utter perfection for Lily. The elegant cut, the delicate gold embroidery about the cuffs and hem, and the way the fabric flowed like poured wine conspired to make her feel radiant. She had never felt more beautiful.

"It is clearly not meant for wearing during the day!"

"It is her wedding, Christiana. It is customary for a young woman to wear one of her best gowns for such an occasion."

"And her hair! It is far too inappropriate!"

"She has beautiful hair. Quite like yours, wife."

Lady Moreland stamped her foot in outrage. "I forbid this! Lily shall not leave our home wearing such a frock! She must change and do her hair in a manner appropriate to a debutante."

Lily paid no mind, still stunned by how mature she appeared. The gown was better than even she had envisioned when Signora Ricci first described it a few days earlier.

"Aunt." Sophia's voice was calming amid the family chaos. Her cousin had always been calculating in her approach to life, clear in her goals and acting with decisiveness. Since her marriage, Sophia's confidence had flourished, lending her the poise and authority of a formidable countess of the realm. "Lily has selected a gown that is appropriate for her complexion. She is no longer a debutante."

Lily ran her hands over the fine tulle overskirt in reverence, the fabric whispering beneath her fingertips.

"She is a bride."

The occupants of the entry hall froze, the moment suspended like the hush before a church bell tolls. Then all eyes turned toward Lily. She looked up in amazement, catching Sophia's gaze. She was smiling gently at her, composed as always.

"I am a bride," Lily murmured.

"And a bride should choose what she wants to wear." Lord Moreland's deep voice cut cleanly through the silence that followed. His tone held no room for argument. "Now, I believe it is time to leave. We have a wedding to attend."

Lady Moreland was still wailing her distress as they bundled into their carriage. The butler oversaw the loading of bags and boxes while footmen swung open the heavy lacquered door to admit the family into the waiting barouche. Sophia joined them, taking a seat next to Lily. She had promised to accompany her so she could dissuade Mama from interfering with the day's proceedings.

Outside, the early light gilded the street with a sheen of soft amber. Inside the carriage, Lily smoothed her skirts once more, feeling the luxurious weight of the silks settle around her like a shield. She had every intention of forging a happy marriage, one rooted in mutual affection and genuine desire, and the gown, she believed, was a necessary beginning. She must light the spark of passion in Mr. Ridley before it was too late.

"Signora Ricci is a genius." Lily kept her voice low out of respect for Mama, who sat across from her, arms tightly crossed and twin lines furrowing her handsome brow.

"She understands color and form superior to other modistes. I was fortunate that Richard sent me to her."

Sophia's reply was unapologetic, each word polished and deliberate.

Mama gave another indignant cry.

"Hugh! Why would the earl know a modiste?"

This time Lord Moreland appeared rather uncomfortable. He shifted slightly in his seat and shot a glance at Sophia, who met it with a serene smile and a raised brow.

She shrugged slightly. "My husband was a rogue. Thankfully, he has excellent taste, and I have the advantage of his past in my present. Signora Ricci is a veritable artiste who makes her customers look like the subjects of great art."

Lily giggled. "Lady Slight would agree with you."

"Lady Slight!" Mama's voice rang out, shrill in the confined space of the carriage.

Sophia colored, her cheeks blooming pink as she turned to look out the window at the passing traffic. "The viscountess frequents the dress rooms."

"Dash it, Hugh! We must turn this carriage around."

Papa cast another pained glance at Sophia, who remained studiously engaged with the view beyond the glass.

"Be that as it may, Lily's gown is modest compared to Lady Slight. She is embarking into marriage, and she deserves to feel beautiful, Christiana. And she is. Beautiful. I have never seen her look lovelier than she does at this moment."

Lily peered at her reflection in the carriage window, the distorted surface bending her features. She could scarcely credit the transformation. Her image shimmered back at her, an elegant stranger who resembled herself, yet finer, brighter, more assured.

She had always suspected that the modest colors and

virginal flounces she had been assigned did her no favors. The pale muslins and forgettable trims drained her complexion, leaving her to appear younger and more insipid than she truly was. It was no wonder that only the oldest bachelors and widowers ever showed interest. Their eyes skimmed past her, as if she were the wallpaper.

The fashionable shades touted for debutantes—powder blue, washed-out lilac—rendered her wan and unimpressive. It had been a match made in sartorial hell. But now? Now, in the rich burgundy folds of this gown, with a tulle overskirt that shimmered like mist in candlelight, she might, at last, be considered pretty.

Sophia had brought her abigail to style Lily's hair, twisting her chocolate brown locks into soft curls and pinning them with gilded combs. It was the perfect finishing touch. An entire wardrobe was being prepared in her trousseau, but Signora Ricci had worked miracles to deliver several gowns in time for the ceremony.

This one—perhaps more suited to the theater than the church, true—was her favorite. It gave her confidence, and Sophia had insisted she wear it. Lily wanted to walk into the church with her head held high, not as a meek offering but as a woman worthy of notice. She wanted to ignite Mr. Ridley's interest, even if just a flicker. She would need every weapon she could summon to distract her groom from the alluring paramour he had left behind.

"Mama, I love you dearly. But this is my wedding day, and I barely know Mr. Ridley. It is imperative that I do everything in my power to set our marriage on the path to success. I wish to enjoy the companionship that you and Papa share, and to do that, my groom must view me as a grown woman and not as a charitable gesture. This will be a happy marriage if I make it so."

Her family, barring Aidan, who had left for the church earlier, turned to gaze at her. Mama's face crumpled into an expression of tearful adoration.

"Oh, Lily! My little girl is all grown up."

Zooks! I hope Mr. Ridley agrees!

The gentleman was masculine elegance in his perfectly tailored clothing, the sort of man whose cravat could probably intimidate lesser men. What would he think now that Lily, at last, had a competent modiste on her side?

BRENDAN STOOD at the altar with the vicar, awaiting the arrival of his bride. The faint scent of polish clung to the wooden pews, mingling with the musty hush of the stone chapel. Near him, Richard fiddled with his cravat and checked his timepiece, the fob chain catching a sliver of colored light that streamed from the high stained-glass windows. From the pews, Annabel watched with her hands folded over her rounded belly, while the duke stretched his broad shoulders, the tension in his frame belying his composed exterior.

Brendan's friend, Lord Julius Trafford, sat behind them in the next pew. Trafford had been indignant at the news he was to marry and had expressed as much in dramatic terms, but had begrudgingly shown up for the ceremony dressed to the nines in the latest fashion. Frankly, Brendan thought the elaborately embroidered coat and waistcoat looked rather uncomfortable, not to mention the intricate knot of his cravat, which tilted Trafford's chin to a haughty angle and gave him the appearance of a man prepared to duel rather than witness a wedding.

Across the aisle sat Miss Abbott's family, including her

brother and Mr. and Mrs. Thompson, kin to Richard. Their expressions were carefully neutral, but Brendan felt their scrutiny like the press of heat through a frock coat.

"My lord, I have services soon." The vicar shuffled on his feet, a pained expression on his dour face. "I need to prepare."

"They will be here any minute." Brendan's assurance was thin, thinner than he wished it to sound. He did not know his bride. Not truly. It had been his assumption that the wedding was imperative to mitigating their scandal, a formality to preserve reputations. But how well did he truly know the Abbott family?

What if they do not come?

Brendan shifted, raising a hand to knead his temple and shield his eyes from the vivid shaft of sunlight pouring through the stained-glass window above the altar. The light scattered in jewel tones across the flagstones, falling like a benediction he did not feel he had earned.

The thought that Miss Abbott might not appear carried more sting than logic could explain. That sting required examination. She had struck him as a genuine person. When he had imagined his future marriage, it had always been to someone sincere and enlivened. Someone with grace like his late mother, someone with courage like his sister, and someone capable of strategic insight like Richard's wife—or the indomitable woman who had chosen Perry.

It seems Miss Abbott fits the bill.

The young lady was everything he admired in a person. She possessed sincerity, a quiet intelligence, and a refreshing absence of affectation. His only objection—if it could even be called that—was the absence of romantic spark. Yet surely that was a trifling concern in the face of something as enduring as a lifetime partnership. He was, after all, a man of the world. With time, mutual respect would bridge any such gap.

Confound it!

The thought slipped sideways, turning to the expectations of the evening ahead. Duty would require him to consummate a union with a girl who, in her sweetness and softness, reminded him somewhat of a younger sister— playful, innocent, even childlike in her manner and manner of dress.

Brendan pressed his thumb to the ache blooming at his temple, attempting to relieve the mounting pressure behind his eyes. It was no use. The discomfort only grew sharper.

The vicar shuffled again in agitation, a quiet clearing of the throat reminding Brendan that their ceremony was running increasingly late.

Just then, a burst of movement at the chapel doors drew every head around, including his own.

The countess entered with Lady Moreland, gliding swiftly down the aisle to take a seat near the Abbott family. Brendan blinked, registering their presence with only half his mind, for at that moment, Lord Moreland followed, escorting a woman he did not recognize.

Brendan's breath caught.

For the span of one stunned heartbeat, he could do nothing but stare.

My word. If only I were marrying her.

The young woman was arresting. Her rich brown hair had been swept into an elegant coiffure, several curls escaping to frame her face in soft, artless spirals. She wore a deep crimson gown veiled with gossamer tulle threaded with gold, which shimmered faintly with each step. The color brought a luminous warmth to her complexion. The modest cut of her bodice did little to obscure the refined grace of her figure—poised, confident, composed.

A strange yearning swept over him, unbidden and unwanted.

He shut his eyes. *This is your wedding day, and you are admiring another woman?* He might as well be a schoolboy again, ruled by fancy and impression rather than principle. Had he no discipline?

Opening his eyes, he saw that Lord Moreland and the young woman had progressed to the front pews. She released his lordship's arm and stepped forward, pausing near Brendan with an elegant nod.

He returned the smile automatically, though his expression was still puzzled. Where was Miss Abbott?

Turning his head to glance at the chapel doors again, he could see no sign of her arrival.

When he looked back, the woman gave him a curious smile, her brows rising ever so slightly.

"Shall we begin? The vicar surely needs to prepare for service."

"Miss Abbott?"

Her smile widened, tinged by gentle amusement. "Were you expecting someone else?"

Brendan hesitated, his eyes surveying her quickly. She was undeniably petite, the approximate size of the young woman he had visited at the Abbott home. She had a heart-shaped face, wide brown eyes framed by thick lashes, a pointed chin, and delicate ears that peeked from beneath her coiffure. If he imagined her in ringlets and ruffles, he supposed these might indeed be the same elfin features with which he had spoken only days before.

Drat! Do I not even know what my bride looks like?

A slow wave of mortification crept up his neck. Perhaps he had never truly seen her, not as an assemblage of lace and decorum, but as a living, breathing person. A woman with her own strength, choices, and presence. His only defense was that the whirlwind of the past week—negotiating the marriage contracts, conferring with Briggs about the murder, and rushing through plans for the license and ceremony—had left him with little clarity or time to reflect.

Still, it was a poor excuse.

Feeling foolish, he refrained from shaking his head and instead moved to his place beside the vicar, whose expression had grown markedly impatient. As he adjusted his stance, a soft fragrance teased his senses, something warm and sweet, like honey, and he found himself glancing sidelong at his bride, wondering whether the scent belonged to her.

The strangeness of the week showed no signs of abating. Each time he believed he had grasped who Miss Abbott was, a new facet emerged unexpectedly, quietly inviting his admiration. He felt a scoundrel for failing to recognize her, for being momentarily distracted by someone he believed to be another. How had he been so blind?

It was high time to open his eyes ... and his mind. The events of the past fortnight had been jarring, but perhaps they were precisely what he needed to chart a better course.

Fancy that! She is gorgeous under all that childish adornment.

THE WEDDING BREAKFAST had been a success. Despite the aged state of the room, the guests were largely acquainted and their easy conversation filled the space. Hothouse flowers added bursts of color, their blooms providing bright spots against the gleam of crystal and the soft glint of silver. Lily's groom had expressed his doubts about hosting the breakfast at Ridley House, but Sophia had insisted that the Abbotts must feel welcome in Lily's new home, to set their minds at ease from the very start.

Privately, Lily preferred the location. Ridley House, situated on a side street close to the square, offered the discreet breakfast she favored, unlike the Abbotts' grander home, which stood directly across from Lady Slight's townhouse and would draw the widow's curiosity.

She thanked each guest as they departed, enduring her mother's suffocating embrace and the trail of damp handkerchiefs left in her wake. Papa, ever a man of few words, had gently taken Mama by the arm and escorted her to the door with quiet solemnity.

Brendan's odd-fish friend, Lord Trafford, approached next, cutting a striking figure. His hair was a strange combination—wheat-hued atop and distinctive brown beneath—and Lily could not help wondering whether it was a misguided affectation or merely a mishap of nature. If the former, she suspected the heir to Lord Stirling had far too much leisure on his hands.

The gentleman bowed deeply, his frothy cuffs fluttering at his wrists, every inch the image of a man who had stepped from the pages of *La Belle Assemblée*.

"Congratulations, Lady Filminster. Ridley is a good chap. Take care of him, you hear?"

Lily smiled tentatively, uncertain how one ought to respond to such a peculiar declaration. Lord Trafford strolled away without awaiting an answer, heading toward the duke and her groom, who stood conversing quietly in the dim hall.

That left the duchess and Lily alone in the breakfast room. Like the other rooms she had seen in the townhouse, this one bore the weight of time—its ebony wood paneling darkened by age, its carpet worn thin in places, and its wallpaper gently fading. The furniture, heavy and brooding, loomed as if it remembered a dozen generations. The house yearned for renovation.

My townhouse!

The duchess rose from a heavy hardwood chair and made her way to where Lily was standing.

"Your Grace." Lily dipped into a curtsy, her voice soft. "Thank you for attending."

The duchess shook her head, smiling down at Lily, whose head barely reached her chin. "We are sisters now, Lily. You may address me as Annabel."

Lily's jaw dropped. She quickly shut it.

"You will catch flies if you allow your mouth to hang open like that." Mama's voice echoed in her mind from long ago, while Lily's thoughts scrambled at the idea that a duchess —a *duchess!*—viewed her as a sister. "Thank you, Your— Annabel."

"It is I who must thank you. I appreciate what you have done for my brother. It was a remarkable sacrifice, and I am pleased to welcome you to the family. Sophia regards you very highly, and it is a wonderful day for the Ridley family to welcome such an exceptional young woman into our midst."

"Um—I—thank ... you." Lily was rarely speechless, but she had always been somewhat in awe of the duchess. It would take time to accustom herself to being on such familiar terms.

Annabel smiled, then leaned in to press a sisterly kiss upon Lily's cheek. "Welcome to the family, Lily Ridley."

Lily Ridley!

Lily Beatrice Anne Ridley!

Lady Filminster!

She was a married woman. And she had found herself a young, handsome gentleman, one with steady eyes and a quiet strength, whom Sophia and Richard both well liked. Now all that remained was to kindle something tender between them, and she would have achieved the future she had planned for herself. Even after the recent debacle, she had managed to chart her course.

Lily watched the duchess glide toward her husband, the butler opening the front door with an air of inherited hauteur. The couple soon took their leave, and Lord Filmi—*bosh!*—Brendan returned from the hall, striding into the breakfast room to find her lingering in the doorway.

"Miss Ab—" Brendan winced slightly. "Lily, you are … radiant today."

A warm flush crept into her cheeks, and she stared down at her slippers in bashful pleasure. She had not failed to notice the shift in his demeanor. At the church, he had looked rather as though he had been struck by lightning upon seeing her. During breakfast, he had cast frequent glances her way, some lingering as though attempting to reconcile the spirited companion he had wed with the figure she had become today.

Her gown, selected by Signora Ricci with tasteful precision, offered her an elegance she was not accustomed to. Aware of the impression she had made, Lily could only hope that the woman Brendan saw before him was compelling enough to cast shadows over his past infatuation.

But is it enough to make him forget the voluptuous Lady Slight?

Brendan escorted Miss Ab—his bride—to a drawing room just down the hall. It was a modest sitting area overlooking the garden and the mews at the rear of the property, a space he had always preferred to the grander one upstairs. The light was better in this room, his chief reason for favoring it over the more stately chamber above. That, and the room's quietude, which he found soothing.

Lily stood framed in the early afternoon light, the sun painting faint gold across the polished floorboards. The transformation in her appearance—her gown, her coiffure, the quiet assurance in her bearing—had unveiled not a stranger, but a revelation. A lovely young woman had emerged from behind the girlish veneer, and she had lingered in his thoughts from the moment he had glimpsed her in church that morning.

She might be petite, yes, but she possessed an ethereal beauty that drew his attention again and again. That such musings, monumental ones at that, should occupy his mind was a turn of events for which he had not been prepared.

Burn my buttons! Was there truth to this matchmaking notion, this idea that one might be steered, gently and with good sense, toward an appropriate companion?

His only previous attempt at joining the marriage mart had been swiftly and unpleasantly curtailed, due to the baron's interference, delivered by way of the Royal Mail. The memory still left a sour taste. Disillusioned, he had drifted into the company of merry widows, embracing a life of careless charm and consequence-free gallantries.

But recent days had revealed the cracks in that carefree philosophy. When he had most needed a companion—not a mistress, not a distraction, but a partner, it had been Lily who had appeared, unexpected and steadfast.

He had admired his friends' matches from afar—Philip with his luminous duchess, Richard with his gentle yet iron-willed countess—and thought himself unfit for such a connection. Yet somehow, despite his checkered path and impulsive decisions, he now stood beside a wife of his own, one whose presence was beginning to stir thoughts of permanence.

However, the weight of responsibilities was a new burden to bear, and before he could begin to build a life with his bride, he needed to secure her safety. Lily was a virtuous and kind-hearted woman, one who may very well have saved his neck from the hangman's noose. He must do everything in his power to ensure a long and peaceful future for her.

"I have some news to impart, I am afraid. It is our wedding day, and I wish to focus on the celebration of it, but there is a ... situation ... that I must inform you of. For your safety."

Lily sat, somewhat engulfed by the red timeworn settee. She leaned forward slightly, her gaze trained on him with such directness that it pulled him taut. Brendan remained standing, shifting his weight as he studied the polish on his boots, momentarily seeking the right words.

How to broach the subject? His bride had already risked much on his behalf, and now he must tell her that further shadows lingered beyond the door?

His gaze lifted and caught upon her, her face earnest, her posture attentive, her hands folded with quiet resolve. The sunlight softened the edges of her features, and in that moment, she looked so entirely unlike the girl he had once dismissed. She was no longer simply a brave young lady in unfortunate gowns. She was a fully-grown woman. His wife.

Deuce it, she scarcely resembled the childish figure from their earlier encounters. Her complexion glowed with health, her eyes shone with intelligence and sincerity, and her gown, chosen with such care, seemed to underscore the grace that had always been within her, now revealed to the world.

"What is it? Is there something wrong? Are the duke and Richard aware?"

Her voice broke into his reverie, and Brendan jolted back into focus, realizing with embarrassment that he had been lost in admiration. *Pull yourself together, man*, he silently rebuked himself. He was not some green youth dazzled by his first dance partner.

How could she affect him so strongly? There was a quiet fortitude in her that stirred something he had long dismissed, a belief that beauty could exist alongside goodness.

"It is regarding the matter of the baron's murder. Halmesbury and Richard are well informed. We have discussed the matter, along with the countess, and I do not wish to alarm you, but I feel it is imperative you know what has happened, so you might be alert and take measures to protect yourself."

Lily's eyes rounded slightly, but she maintained her composure, her calmness belying the gravity of their conversation. Brendan hesitated. Before he could stop himself, the question tumbling around in his mind escaped.

"Exactly how old are you, Miss Ab—Lily?"

When he had first encountered her, she had seemed no more than seventeen, perhaps due to the demure gowns and youthful styling so often imposed upon debutantes.

Later, he had recalled a vague memory of seeing her at a previous Season's ball, which placed her a little older. But now, attired as a married woman with graceful poise and a quiet confidence, she seemed altogether more grown, and the disparity between his earlier assumptions and present reality unsettled him.

She leaned back, her brow lifting in surprise. Ladies did not often declare their ages, and he knew full well he could have consulted *Debrett's Peerage* or asked Lady Saunton discreetly. Yet here he was, married, and only now realizing how little he knew of his bride's particulars.

At last, she grinned, and the expression transformed her features. The soft curve of her smile, paired with the sparkle of amusement in her large, expressive eyes, caught him utterly off guard. Her playfulness and warmth had a disarming quality, one he had not expected, but welcomed all the same.

By Jingo, what spell is this?

"I am older than I appear, twenty years of age, and this was my third Season. Another Season or two and I would have been on the shelf, so I suppose this was a strange but fortuitous turn of events." She paused, her mirth giving way to alarm. Her hand rose to her cheek as color flooded her face. "Oh, no! I swear I was not attempting to take advantage of your situation to trap you!"

Brendan shook his head, lifting a hand to rub the back of his neck in rueful embarrassment. Yet inwardly, he was reassured. She was just seven years his junior, far closer in age than he had feared, and with far more candor than he was accustomed to from society beauties.

"I am still deeply embarrassed about that accusation," he said honestly. "Lady Saunton made the quality of your character clear to me, and Richard certainly seconded her opinion."

Lily's shoulders relaxed as the flush receded from her cheeks. Her expression softened with profound relief, and in that moment, Brendan was struck anew by the sincerity in her eyes. Eyes that held both courage and kindness.

"What is the concern regarding my safety?" she asked gently.

The shift back to his earlier allusions stirred anxiety in Brendan's gut. He had been contending with a rising sense of inadequacy, a small voice inside whispering that he was ill-prepared to shoulder the burden of those now depending on him. Lily's honor, as far as he could see, far outshone his own. He scarcely deserved the vows she had spoken that very morning.

It was time—past time—for him to become a man he could respect. The days of idle carousing and self-indulgence were over.

Crossing to the sideboard, he reached for the decanter. A bit of claret would not go amiss to steady his nerves. "Claret?"

"No, thank you."

Brendan froze, glancing down at the decanter poised in his grasp. In his experience, young ladies, when afforded the opportunity, were not usually inclined to refuse a sip of something stronger. He turned, brows raised in surprise.

Lily's gaze darted away from his, and her expression softened with apology. "My family does not imbibe. After Sophia lost both her parents and came to live with us, Papa removed spirits from the household out of respect for her and her brother. And after what her brother did to her last year … and because Richard was nearly killed by that drunken lord who broke into their home, I made a promise to Sophia that I would never drink spirits. She has seen too many loved ones destroyed by it. It was the least I could do."

Brendan winced and turned back to the decanter with a grimace. He had forgotten the sordid string of events that had shadowed Sophia's past—violence, betrayal, trauma wrapped in the lingering scent of brandy. *I am a bacon-brain.*

"But you are welcome to enjoy one, if you wish."

He let out a short, humorless huff and placed the decanter back with deliberate care. "I should probably reduce my drinking. There will not be much time for it now that I am to manage the baronial estates."

"What was the problem you wished to share?"

Brendan wandered the room for a few paces, his steps muffled by the threadbare rug, before returning to sit beside her on the settee, leaving several feet of polite distance between them. The air between them, however, felt taut with unspoken weight.

"It is possible the baron allowed his killer entry. However ..."

His pause was heavy, and when Lily drew in a breath, it was sharp with realization. "One of the servants might be involved?"

Brendan was impressed. She had reached the conclusion faster than he had. "It is a possibility. The runner we hired—Briggs—has questioned the servants. There are only five in ... our ... home who attend to the front door."

Lily leaned toward him, her expression sharpening with curiosity. "Who?"

"There is Michaels, the butler. And the two footmen—Wesley, whom you have met, and Stephen. In addition, the baron brought two footmen with him, Stanley and David.

And there is a coachman who brought them to London, but he did not have access to the house. The baron's valet was away that night and did not return until the next day. My valet assisted the baron but had been sent to retrieve an item that the baron had misplaced earlier in the day and was absent for several hours."

"And whom does the runner suspect?"

"He ruled out Wesley because he was not on duty that night. Stephen was sent out on an errand by the baron, which kept him away overnight with the baron's coachman. The other footmen deny attending to anyone that evening, but it is Michaels whom he is most concerned about."

"Michaels? The butler? What motive would he have?"

Brendan sat up slightly. He had not known what to expect when he shared the potential danger, but Lily did not shrink from it. She leaned in with unfeigned interest, her brows drawn in concentration, her hands gently folded in her lap—composed, but attentive. She was asking intelligent questions and absorbing the details with unflinching clarity.

"I did not know, but Michaels has been with us since his youth. His father was the gamekeeper at our country seat, Baydon Hall. The father was killed in the woods, perhaps by poachers, and apparently his mother blamed my grandfather for his death. It is a long time ago—"

"But Briggs thinks it might be a motive for Michaels to either have lost his temper with your father or assisted someone else to cover up the murder?"

"There is no evidence, and Briggs is still investigating Stanley and David, but I need you to be vigilant until this matter is cleared up."

Lily nodded, seemingly lost in thought as she considered all he had just revealed. Then she turned back to him with those wide, steady brown eyes.

How had he never noticed the sweep of her lashes? They fanned downward as she blinked, drawing attention to the soft roundness of her cheek. There was something delicate about her, a softness that stirred a deep ache within him. His hand itched to reach out, to trace the graceful curve of her jaw in a simple, wordless connection.

"I am sorry for your loss," she whispered the words, her voice low and warm with sympathy. The soft, throaty murmur pulled him toward her almost unconsciously, and before he knew it, he had shifted closer on the settee.

Seated beside her now, he caught the faintest trace of something sweet in the air, like honey warmed by the sun. Perhaps it was a skin cream or perhaps simply her. Whatever the source, it tugged at his senses in a way that left him strangely off balance. But this time, he mastered the urge to lean further. He would not startle his bride, not now, when something so much more important needed to be said.

"I suppose I must confess a secret. The others are already aware, and you might hear about it amidst the gossip making the rounds." He sighed and leaned back, giving her space, though her closeness still filled the air between them. "The baron was not my father."

Lily drew in a sharp breath, sitting back with visible surprise. Brendan's pulse ticked upward, wary now. Was she horrified? Would this revelation undo the tentative trust they had begun to build?

CHAPTER
ELEVEN

"Supreme excellence consists in breaking the enemy's resistance without fighting."

Sun Tzu, *L'Art de la Guerre* (*The Art of War*)

~

L ily had thought that her new husband might have been thinking about kissing her. His gaze had lingered on her mouth, and his brandy-colored eyes had grown warm—heavy-lidded with unspoken thought—until he made the most unexpected confession.

She had wanted the kiss. To feel what it was like to be chosen in that way, not with politeness or duty, but with yearning. And not by just any gentleman, but by her own husband.

His admission swept those thoughts aside like a dropped fan tumbling across a polished floor.

Lily blinked at him, aghast. "What?"

"My mother was betrothed to his older brother, Lord

John Ridley, who died just weeks before their wedding. My uncle stepped in and married her to deflect the scandal."

Lily's brow furrowed in dismay, despite Mama's frequent admonitions about expressions aging the face. "That is awful. Your father died before you were born?"

Brendan was studying his hands, long-fingered and motionless against the brocade-covered cushion. His profile betrayed little, but the silence hung like fog.

"I did not know. I only learned the truth a few years ago, so I believed the baron was my father for my entire youth."

The stillness around them sharpened. The heavy tick of the longcase clock in the corner marked the seconds like a measured heartbeat. The scent of wax polish lingered faintly in the air.

Lily had only recently begun to grasp the weight of adulthood, of learning how many things one's elders had shielded from view. Their conversation felt momentous, more meaningful than the simpering chatter that occupied her days. This was real. This was the beginning of something honest. How she responded would set the tone for their union.

Shifting ever so slightly, she laid her hand atop his, her fingers brushing against his knuckles. The warmth of him seeped into her skin, grounding her.

"Thank you for sharing these things with me. You said we should be friends, and this feels like friendship in its truest form."

Brendan turned to look at her then, and there was something unguarded in his expression.

"I am committed. We must make the best of this situation."

"As am I," Lily replied, her voice hushed.

His eyes returned to her mouth.

The moment seemed to stretch, suspended like a drop of water at the edge of a leaf.

He leaned forward and brushed his lips gently across hers. The contact was so brief she might have imagined it, but then he returned, with a firmer touch, a question rather than a demand. One of his arms curved around her waist, drawing her into the space between them, the warmth of his body radiating through the layers of her muslin gown. His other hand rose, steady and reverent, to cradle the back of her head.

Her breath caught. She had read of moments like this, spoken of in whispers between girls or found within the pages of well-thumbed novels. But no words could prepare her for the hush in her chest, the stillness between heartbeats.

Her fingertips curled lightly into the fabric of his coat. His mouth did not press with urgency. The kiss deepened not in fervor, but in meaning—a shared hush, a lingering pause that meant more than words could ever carry.

She sighed against him, and in that sigh was every unspoken hope she had not dared name aloud.

He murmured something. She thought it might have been *honey*, as his lips drifted along her jawline. When he reached her ear, his breath stirred the loose tendrils at her temple. She leaned into the sensation.

And then, as if an invisible hand had severed the moment, they pulled apart in the same instant, staring at one another with wide eyes and parted lips.

"Did you hear that?"

Brendan nodded and rose to his feet in one swift movement, the floor creaking softly beneath his boots. He strode to the door and threw it open, the charged stillness of the moment giving way to a world abruptly intruding.

Lily craned her neck, heart fluttering. Beyond the doorway, there was only shadow, long and restless. Ridley House stood like a relic of gothic tale, the kind whispered about in drawing rooms and brooding novels. The murder from the week before lingered like fog at the edge of thought, the echo of tragedy seeping through stone.

From the shadows emerged Michaels, composed as ever. His gaze slid to her new husband, cool and appraising, and offered his declaration in that dry, unwavering tone.

"Lady Filminster's room is ready."

Michaels had summoned Wesley, who was now leading her up the steep staircase of Ridley House. The thick runner beneath their feet muffled each step, though its edges were worn and fraying. Apparently, the townhouse had been operating with a reduced staff, just enough to maintain the premises and attend to her husband, who had likely not entertained in years. That meant there was currently no housekeeper in residence, and Michaels himself was overseeing the maids.

They reached a landing on the second floor, and the footman veered into a narrow corridor lit only by an aging wall sconce and the gloom beyond. Dour portraits of Ridley ancestors loomed on either side of the hall, their powdered faces and oil-darkened eyes watching Lily in eternal judgment. It was absurd, but she could not shake the feeling that their painted gazes followed her, tallying her missteps.

Wesley must have noticed her hurried gait, for he

slowed his pace to match her smaller stride. She smiled up at him, grateful.

"Ridley House is much bigger than it appears from the outside."

"I believe the darkness exaggerates the size, milady."

"It is very dark in here. The place has not been used much, by its appearance."

"Until now, Mr. Rid—Lord Filminster is the only one who has lived here in years. Many of the rooms have been shrouded, but Mr. Michaels directed us to open them up when we received word the baron was coming to London for the coronation."

Lily listened with interest. Her curiosity itched with questions. Had Brendan entertained visitors? Had Lady Slight ever crossed its threshold? But she was a newcomer in the household and could hardly interrogate poor Wesley like a character from one of those gothic novels she and her cousin liked to read.

Lud. Her need to know was difficult to ignore.

"And my room?"

"Lord Filminster has been moved into the baronial bedroom, and your room connects. It had not been occupied in many years, but Mr. Michaels replaced the bedding, and we have cleaned the rooms thoroughly in anticipation of your arrival."

They reached the end of the corridor, where a tall window let in a reluctant sliver of gray light. The glass panes were dulled with age and time, warped ever so slightly. The faded drapes framing the window bore the wear of decades, and the air was tinged faintly with dust, polish, and something older, like time itself had steeped into the walls.

The footman opened a heavy door and stepped aside for

her. Lily entered cautiously, her slippers brushing against the well-worn rug that stretched across the floor. A wide stone fireplace yawned at one end of the room, flanked by windows that peered out with their cloudy stare. The drapes there were of the same ancient fabric, their folds stiff and reluctant to sway. A massive four-poster bed, carved with climbing vines and crowned with a cheerful new coverlet, drew her gaze at once. Beside the bed sat a chest, atop which lay her French dictionary and her book on military strategy.

But it was the door across the room that truly captured her attention, the connecting door to Brendan's chambers.

"The maids have unpacked your trunks," Wesley said, gesturing toward a tall ebony wardrobe. "And there is a dressing table and washstand over here. The bell is here, should you need anything."

She nodded, though her eyes remained on the bed. "Wesley, is there a bed step?"

The top of the mattress rose to her waist. It looked fit for a duchess—or a circus performer.

Wesley frowned and walked over, peering beneath the bed. His features creased slowly into an expression of dismay, and he rubbed his jaw with clear regret. "I don't believe I have ever seen one in the house, now that you mention it."

Lily sighed and considered. "Is there a spare chair I can use while steps are ordered?"

"Of course. I shall fetch one from another room and inform Mr. Michaels of the issue."

"That would be excellent." She offered him a bright smile.

He disappeared and, within a few minutes returned

with a sturdy armchair, which he positioned at the foot of the bed before excusing himself with a polite bow.

Exhaling heavily, she paced the room with growing familiarity. She opened the wardrobe to find her new gowns—sleek, well-fitted, and undeniably adult—hanging alongside a few of her older frocks. The latter would be donated at once. She had no intention of donning anything that made her resemble a schoolroom miss.

Her fingers drifted unconsciously to her lower lip. She could still feel the ghost of Brendan's mouth there. That her wedding gown had kindled interest in her husband's eyes was no small triumph. If it gave her even a slender chance of banishing Lady Slight's memory, then she would not risk being mistaken for a child ever again.

Sophia's abigail had taught her how to arrange her hair simply, and her cousin was already interviewing prospective lady's maids on her behalf. If fortune smiled, she would have one within the week. She only wondered who was to attend her until then.

Climbing onto the bed using the chair, Lily flopped back against the pillows and stared up at the ceiling. Ornate plasterwork in the shape of interlacing vines twined above her. The room had once been grand but it needed life breathed back into it. She would have to speak with Brendan about restoring Ridley House. Not to mention hiring a proper housekeeper. Would he bring one from Baydon Hall?

She sighed again. There was still so much she did not know about her new life.

~

BRENDAN PACED THE LIBRARY, uncertain what to do with himself. He had a bride upstairs. The thought still startled him, as though some stranger had married in his stead and left him with the consequences. It was something he would need to grow accustomed to.

Michaels had informed Lily earlier that there was no housekeeper currently in residence, and the revelation had mortified Brendan more than he liked to admit. He had not taken the time to assess the state of Ridley House beyond his own needs. It had simply not occurred to him. And now, was there even a maid assigned to attend her?

The house had stood empty for the better part of two decades, with only Michaels and a handful of servants to take care of it until the day that Brendan had shown up and taken residence. Michaels had then added additional servants, and they had an acceptable cook, but the staff were not accustomed to having a young lady in residence. Or a lady of any age, for that matter. The staff had been merely maintaining the home and taking care of its solitary resident these past six or seven years.

What did he know of such matters? He had managed no one, simply being an heir who came and went as he pleased. He was going to need to ask questions of Halmesbury and Richard. For all intents and purposes, he might as well have been an orphan for his entire adulthood, for the amount of interaction he had had with the late baron.

Perhaps he should set a meeting with his man of business. Perhaps he should discover if he had a man of business and who that might be.

Once a quarter, he had visited the baron's solicitors to receive his allowance, so truly he did not know. If someone specifically handled the finances, he would need to find out who that was. What did a man of business do, as opposed to the solicitors? And should he write to the incumbent steward at Baydon Hall?

Brendan groaned aloud and dragged his hands through his hair, fingers tightening at his temples.

He strode to the library table, its surface scattered with correspondence that had gone unanswered for months. Sitting down, he reached for a sheet of paper and dipped a quill into the inkwell. He needed to make a list. A long one. And once that was complete, he would seek out Halmesbury or Richard to gain some clarity on how to proceed.

It was time to pick up the scattered pieces of his inheritance and understand what it meant to be Baron of Filminster. He had people depending on him now. What that meant in definable terms he had yet to discover, but the discovery could wait no longer.

LILY CAME DOWN for dinner wearing the same gown she had donned that morning, deciding it was entirely acceptable and not yet ready to relinquish it after such a triumphant debut earlier in the day. The rich red silk still carried a faint warmth of pride and possibility, and she drew confidence from the memory of Brendan's gaze.

She had spent the afternoon exploring her new residence, her slippers whispering across faded carpets and creaking floorboards as she moved from room to room. Every chamber seemed filled with imposing furniture far too large for modern taste, heavy drapes dulled with age, wallpaper curling away in neglected corners, and the occasional moth-eaten tapestry sagging like a forgotten memory. Her footsteps echoed down long halls punctuated by stiff-shouldered portraits in gilded frames, their stony expressions giving her the distinct impression that none of them approved of her presence.

Of her husband or his sister, the duchess, there was no trace, not a single recent likeness. The youngest portrait appeared to have been painted before the turn of the century.

Their home, she concluded with certainty, was in need of care. And she would see to it.

After opening and closing a dozen wrong doors, she finally discovered the dining room, only to find it empty. Wandering back down the corridor, she noticed a sliver of light beneath one door. The library.

She entered to find Brendan seated at the library table, his shirtsleeves rolled and the surface scattered with books and ledgers. A glass oil lamp flickered nearby, casting amber shadows across the leather bindings and illuminating the thoughtful lines of his face.

"What are you doing?"

Brendan started slightly, straightening up. "I am not precisely sure. These are the household account books, and I thought I might get familiar with … well … anything. I know nothing about how the Filminster barony is managed, so I have made a list of questions to pursue. This was the first afternoon I have not been consumed with other matters."

Lily grimaced sympathetically, then slid into the chair beside him. "We are both rather new at this, are we not? I just explored the house to get some notion of the state of it. Most of it appears untouched. Only the breakfast room, the small drawing room, and your"—she faltered, heat creeping into her cheeks—"your bedchamber seem to be in use."

Brendan tilted his head, a slow smile spreading. "Did you enter my room, Lily Ridley?"

Her new name in his husky tone made her heart flutter. She dropped her gaze to her folded hands. "I may have."

"Hmm ... You did, or you did not. Which is it?"

"I did," she admitted quickly. "I wanted to see what it looked like. I went in nearly every room, except the study. I think I found your old room, too."

Brendan reached across the table, his movement gentle. With one gloved finger, he tilted her chin so their eyes met. His touch was featherlight, yet commanding. "I hope to visit your room, too."

Lily froze, caught in the moment. The air between them shifted, as though the room itself held its breath. His gaze was steady, brandy-colored and warm, and she saw in it curiosity, affection, and something quietly reverent. Her breath came slower, the edges of the world softening.

Her lips parted slightly as if to speak, but no words came. She sensed, more than saw, his eyes drop briefly to her mouth before he drew back, the intimacy of the moment receding like the tide.

"We should eat some dinner, I suppose."

She nodded, though her mind remained on the kiss they had shared earlier that day and the silent question of when the next might come.

CHAPTER

TWELVE

"The art of war is of vital importance to the state. It is a matter of life and death, a road either to safety or to ruin. Hence it is a subject of inquiry which can on no account be neglected."

Sun Tzu, *L'Art de la Guerre* (*The Art of War*)

They dined in the breakfast room, a smaller and more inviting chamber than the formal dining room, which felt better suited to ancestral portraits and awkward silences than pleasant conversation. Brendan had always preferred its cozy dimensions and the warmth offered by the smaller hearth.

To his surprise, he found that he was enjoying Lily's company. He had never spent much time with a woman, excluding his mother and sister in his youth, when he was not pursuing an agenda of seduction.

The widows he had courted had been lively and alluring, but their charms had eventually paled. Once desire was spent, all that remained was a weariness he could never quite explain. Lady Slight, for instance, was undeniably attractive, yet ultimately empty of meaningful discourse. Her conversations revolved entirely around the peerage, dressmakers, and social scheming. He could scarcely recall anything she had said that was not rooted in self-importance.

Lily, on the other hand, was wholly unexpected. She was curious, candid, and animated by genuine interest in the world around her. At first, her tendency to prattle had overwhelmed him, but now he recognized the intelligence beneath her chatter, her words weaving through ideas and questions with unselfconscious delight.

Across the candlelit table, her face glowed with good humor as she recounted her afternoon adventures through the draughty halls of Ridley House. He listened as she described faded tapestries, uneven carpets, and portraits that seemed determined to glower at every passerby. Her eyes sparkled when she described discovering a hidden linen closet, as though she had stumbled upon a secret room in a novel. The flicker of candlelight caught the golden tones in her hair and the soft curve of her cheek.

She seemed to grow more at ease with him as they talked, and he found himself leaning forward, engaged and wholly attentive. Her conversation carried more weight than one might expect when met with the rapid stream of words. It was thoughtful, sincere, and, increasingly endearing.

He thought fleetingly of their kiss earlier that day. The shared stillness, the connection. The way she had looked at him afterward. There was something deeply appealing about her openness, her eagerness to engage with life, and her unexpected courage. He wondered what it might be like to share a future with someone so spirited.

He realized with a start that she had gone quiet and was watching him expectantly.

"I ... am sorry. What did you say?"

Lily's brows drew together slightly, her expression puzzled. "I asked if you would like dessert?"

He smiled, the tension in his shoulders easing. Reaching across the table, he gently covered her ungloved hand with his own, the gesture warm and deliberate.

"I would, indeed," he said softly.

Her head tilted, her lips parting slightly as she processed the tone of his voice. "What ... oh." A flush bloomed across her cheeks and crept along her throat. She waved a hand as if to dispel the moment.

He was utterly charmed.

Brendan found himself beginning to understand why Richard had so willingly given up his freedoms to marry Lady Saunton, a woman of intelligence and formidable spirit. There was something remarkably grounding about forming a partnership with a woman of depth and heart. He had never thought to look so close to home. His wife was, after all, Lady Saunton's cousin. If he had not dragged his heels for so long over the notion of matrimony, he might have discovered this delightful companion sooner.

She was far more engaging than any of the young ladies who had ever vied for his attention, and he looked forward to their wedding night together despite his earlier reservations.

∾

JULY 30, 1821

Brendan awoke with a start. A sharp crash had pierced the silence of night, and now the sound of racing footsteps echoed beyond his chamber. It had not been a dream.

Lily lay nestled against him, warm and serene in the crook of his arm, her breath teasing against his chest in a slow, contented rhythm. Careful not to wake her, he gently eased her onto her side, drawing the coverlet up over her shoulder as he slipped from the bed.

The air was still and faintly perfumed with honey. Brendan pulled on his trousers, then reached for the nearest object with weight, an ornate brass candlestick resting on a nearby commode. Its polished surface felt cold in his hand.

Crossing the room in bare feet, he eased open the connecting door. Even now, after days in residence, it still felt unnatural to be sleeping here, in the late Viscount Ridley's rooms. But Brendan had claimed the suite in preparation for Lily's arrival, determined to move forward.

The corridor beyond was cloaked in darkness, but a faint draft stirred the hairs on his forearms. Standing in the adjoining chamber, he noted that the door to the hall stood ajar. His pulse quickened.

Then, a sudden flare of light caught his eye. His valet, Peterson, had entered and lit the oil lamp on the escritoire. The light flickered unevenly, casting elongated shadows across the chamber's paneled walls.

Both men blinked against the sudden glare before turning to take in the damage, a broken ceramic jug lay in jagged fragments near the washstand, glistening with spilled water. Beside it, a chest of drawers hung open, its contents half-spilled in disarray—undershirts, cravats, and one of Brendan's cravat pins glinting in the lamplight.

Brendan stepped back and quietly pulled Lily's door closed behind him. "Someone took advantage of my wedding night to search my room," he said, his voice pitched low with fury.

Peterson, a meticulous man in his fifties, rubbed the back of his neck, eyes scanning the wreckage. "It would appear so, milord."

Brendan exhaled heavily, massaging his temples as a dull throb flared once more behind his eyes. "I must have forgotten to lock the door when I came up."

"I apologize, sir. I ought to have checked after you ..." Peterson's eyes flicked toward the closed door to Lily's room.

"We shall need to take more care, Peterson."

His valet nodded grimly, his mouth a thin, tight line.

Briggs's suspicions that either a murderer or a traitor had entered Brendan's household now rang with grim truth. Someone had been here. Someone with purpose. And the threat was no longer abstract.

Lily had brought light and laughter into Ridley House, scattering the old gloom like morning sun upon shuttered rooms. She had become everything he had not known he was missing, an embodiment of hope.

If she were harmed because of his failure to protect her, Brendan would never forgive himself.

It was time to act.

Deliberately. Without delay. Before the shadows crept any closer to the one person who now mattered more than his own life.

❧

Lily gradually awakened, a soft smile playing on her lips as she stretched her limbs beneath the fine linen sheets. Her entire body hummed with contentment. Her plans to distract Brendan from Lady Slight had gone rather better than expected. In fact, if she were any judge, they were well on their way to falling in love and making their union a genuine match.

She rolled to her side, reaching for him, only to meet cool, empty bedding. The spot beside her was long vacated.

He had left?

A spark of unease flickered to life in her belly as she sat up. Pale morning light filtered through the drawn curtains, casting softened gold across the room's muted furnishings. Judging by the angle of the sun and the hush in the corridor beyond, it was still quite early. Perhaps he had simply gone to his chamber to prepare for the day?

Slipping from the bed, her bare feet met the plush pile of the Aubusson carpet with a muffled thud. She found her night rail discarded over the back of a chair, the silk now cool to the touch. Pulling it on, she padded quickly across the room and knocked once at the connecting door before pushing it open.

Brendan's room was dim, the curtains only partially drawn. It was tidy and undisturbed, bed made, clothing hung—no indication of recent use. Lily bit her lip. It was the first morning of their marriage. After such a night, she had envisioned a long, languorous morning with her husband by her side.

Perhaps he is eating breakfast?

Sighing, she returned to her room and rang for the maid. The soft tinkle of the bell was followed by quick footsteps in the corridor. Her ablutions were brief, and soon, her hair had been arranged in a loose knot, her morning gown of soft muslin fitted over her stays. Within a quarter-hour, she was ready to seek out her errant husband.

She flung open the door and promptly stumbled back with a yelp. A hulking figure stood in the hallway, half shrouded in gloom.

"Do not be concerned, milady. I am here to protect you."

Her heart pounded, but she steadied herself and squinted into the shadowed corridor. The man was large and broad-shouldered, clad in a battered overcoat with frayed cuffs. He bore the air of someone more accustomed to alleyways than drawing rooms, and his expression, though lacking menace, resembled a grotesque leering from a gothic arch, intended to ward off mischief.

"Who are you?"

The man cleared his throat, as though unused to conversation. "You may call me John."

Lily raised a brow. "John?"

"That is correct, milady."

Something in his tone, or perhaps the sight of him, dislodged a distant memory. She tilted her head, studying him. "One of the Johns who protected Lady Saunton last year?"

"Uh ... yes."

"You are not pretending to be a footman this time?"

"No, milady."

She clasped her hands before her, the muslin tight at her wrists as she tapped her fingers thoughtfully. "Lord Filminster hired you to protect me?"

"Aye, 'e had Lord Saunton 'ire us in this mornin' an' told us to make sure you was safe."

"Us?"

"Me mate ... John ... 'e's downstairs. We'll be takin' turns watchin'."

"And you are to follow me around? In my own home?"

"Aye, m'lady."

"Why? Did something happen?"

He dropped his gaze to his scuffed boots. "I wouldna know, milady."

Lily clenched her jaw, inhaling through her nose. With no answers forthcoming, she swept past him, the hem of her morning gown brushing the floor as she marched toward the staircase. The old treads creaked beneath her hurried steps, steps that would no doubt have earned her a reprimand from Mama had she been present.

John followed at a respectful but ever-present distance. He moved with surprising grace for a man of his bulk, though the weight of his tread and the faint rasp of his breath made it impossible to forget his proximity.

She checked the breakfast room, the blue salon, and the morning room. Each stood silent and empty. When she reached the study, she paused and placed her ear against the heavy wood. Not a sound. The room was not in use.

Behind her, John waited silently, arms folded across his chest like a sentinel carved in flesh and bone.

Where the blast is my husband?

She turned sharply. "Did Lord Filminster leave me a note to explain?"

"I wouldna know, milady."

A huff of frustration escaped her lips. It was not even nine o'clock, and Brendan was gone. No note. No word. Just this rough-edged stranger and his promise of protection. Lily wrapped her arms around herself and turned toward the grand entrance hall. The hush in the house was absolute. Without Brendan's presence, Ridley House felt bleak once more, a grand, echoing shell draped in memories and dust.

Yet the presence of John, silent and solid, reminded her that Brendan had not left her wholly unguarded. Perhaps, in his own frustrating way, this was a gesture of care.

Even so, the ache of his absence had settled in her chest.

BRENDAN alighted from his carriage to stand at the edge of the teeming road. Pulling out his timepiece, he confirmed the hour to be a few minutes past nine o'clock. He was late. His meeting with Halmesbury, Richard, and Briggs at the club had been set precisely for nine, but the unruly snarl of London traffic had conspired to delay him. The capital was thoroughly awake. Horses jostled in their harnesses, wheels clattered over cobblestones, and the morning rush turned St. James's Street into a river of motion.

"Brendan?" The dulcet voice halted him mid-step. He turned sharply to find Harriet peering at him from several feet away, one hand poised delicately on the open door of her waiting carriage.

His spine stiffened.

The widow looked striking in striped muslin and a feather-tipped bonnet, her gloved fingers raised to conceal a coy smile. Brendan forced himself to lift his beaver and bow.

"Lady Slight."

"So formal," she teased, stepping down lightly from the carriage.

He did not have time for this.

Suppressing a sigh, Brendan offered a polite, measured smile, even as every instinct urged him to make for the door of the club. There were too many eyes upon them, and he had no wish to be entangled in street gossip. That she had dared approach him in public, knowing he was recently wed, betrayed either foolishness or an unsettling boldness.

Still, he was a gentleman. And a gentleman did not walk away from a titled lady on a bustling street.

Harriet approached, her presence wrapped in rosewater and memory. Her gaze swept over him as if appraising the man she might have claimed. That she had once considered him beneath her was a truth that left ashes in his mouth. And now?

"Is it true that you wed the silly chit from my street?"

It was a crude question, asked with the softness of velvet and the sting of vinegar. Brendan's smile did not waver.

"I married Miss Abbott yesterday. I have found her mind to be remarkably lively." He paused. "Not so silly, after all."

"My commiserations," Harriet murmured.

His smile faded.

Brendan had no desire to discuss his wife—his warm, thoughtful, intelligent wife—with a woman who had stepped aside rather than stand beside him when he had needed her most.

He would have left it there, but Harriet stepped closer. Too close.

The cloying sweetness of her perfume reached him, evoking no warmth, only the jarring sense that she belonged to another time, another self he had shed.

She raised one gloved hand and, with calculated ease, traced her fingers down the edge of his lapel.

He stepped back, discomfited by the familiarity. The gesture, once welcome, now struck him as absurd. How had he ever thought her touch beguiling? Honey and cheerful conversation and soft kisses, those were the scents that lingered in his thoughts now.

"Feel free to visit, Brendan," she said lightly. "There is no need to be a stranger. Now that you are respectable again."

Her tone was light, but the insinuation struck like a whip. He narrowed his eyes.

"That will not be happening."

Harriet's mouth curved into a smile both coy and cruel. "We shall see. The little debutante is bound to bore you. And now that you are a married man ... Why, it is all rather perfect, is it not?"

Before he could respond, she turned with practiced grace and mounted the carriage steps, vanishing behind the velvet curtains as the footman shut the door.

He stared after her for a moment, not with longing but with grim clarity. He would not chase her. To do so would draw attention, and he refused to create a scene in the middle of St. James's Street. Let her have her games.

Brendan turned and strode toward the club, jaw tight. He would be better prepared next time they crossed paths. But right now, he had far more urgent matters at hand— namely, the safety and happiness of the only woman who had chosen him for all that he was, and not what he could give.

Brendan made his way inside, quickly spotting his party seated at a corner table set a modest distance apart from the other patrons. As he crossed the floor, he became aware of conversations pausing. Several gentlemen turned in their seats to track his progress, eyes narrowing with unspoken curiosity. He kept his gaze ahead and his expression unreadable, pretending not to notice.

Upon reaching the table, he pulled out a chair and sat

with a little too much force, exhaling as he settled. The low hum of conversation resumed cautiously, as if the room itself were deciding whether to treat his presence as scandalous or simply noteworthy. Brendan suspected that, in several corners, he and Lily were already being discussed.

"Thank you for meeting me."

Briggs inclined his head. Richard, seated beside him, was fiddling with his snow-white cravat, an unmistakable sign of agitation. Halmesbury remained the most composed of the trio, leaning back with his arms crossed over his chest, the navy sleeves of his coat stretched taut over his broad shoulders.

"Is Lily in danger?" The question shot from Richard like an arrow, his emerald eyes sharp with concern as he leaned forward on the table.

Brendan answered with quiet urgency. "Something happened last night that confirms Briggs's suspicions. I judged it wiser not to discuss the matter where servants might overhear. There is no direct threat against Lily, but I am grateful you arranged for the Johns to be present. Until we know more, caution is essential."

Richard exhaled heavily and slumped back in his chair, his brows drawn tight with worry. "We should have taken steps sooner. If anything happens to her ..." He trailed off, waving a hand as if swatting at the dreadful possibilities. "Sophia would be beside herself."

Briggs cleared his throat gently. "If I may, your lordship, what occurred?"

Brendan rubbed at his temple, then recounted the events of the early morning hours with precise brevity. As he finished, a stillness settled over the group.

Halmesbury rubbed his jaw, his gray eyes narrowing in thought.

Richard clenched his fists against the table, then abruptly raised a hand to summon a server. "I need a drink."

"It is barely past nine." Halmesbury arched one brow.

"A small one. But a drink nonetheless." Richard's tone was dry, laced with fatigue. "This feels far too reminiscent of the mess Sophia and I endured last year. I would like to settle my nerves before facing her with this."

"Your wife will have opinions about you imbibing," the duke murmured with some amusement.

Richard sighed, lifting a hand to dismiss the server before placing an order. "She usually prefers that I maintain a clear head. And rightly so. These past two weeks have been unrelenting. Still ..." He drew a long breath. "Clarity is vital now."

Brendan turned to the runner. "Where do things stand with the servants?"

Briggs appeared to be chewing over the question. "I am still investigating Stanley and David, but as of now, Michaels is the only one with any discernible motive. The baron has not set foot in Town in two decades. It complicates matters. If something has been stirred up, the roots may be older than we can estimate."

"Are there others to consider? Visitors to Somerset, those with homes in the area?"

Briggs gave a slow nod. "Perhaps a handful. But it is unclear if any would have cause to act."

Halmesbury leaned forward slightly, lowering his voice. "What if this is not recent at all? What if the cause lies buried in the past? Briggs suspects Michaels because of decades-old grievances, but what do we know of the baron's history here in London? Could he have made enemies ... ones who might hold a grudge these many years?"

The table fell into contemplative silence again, the soft clink murmur of conversation around them a contrast to the weighty thoughts now threading between them.

Brendan cocked his head, considering whom the baron might have encountered during the brief window he had spent in London prior to his death. "He might have visited the tailor for a final fitting. His coronation garments were made in Somerset, but his valet could not say with certainty if he had any final alterations completed here in London. Naturally, he would have spoken with the household staff and the coachman, which Briggs has already been investigating. Beyond that, the only setting where he might have mingled was at the coronation itself. The lords were seated together at Westminster Abbey, were they not?"

"Like a gaggle of fops in our ridiculous trunk hose," Richard replied dryly. "I was practically naked, with that much leg on display."

"So every lord in London is a suspect, then." Brendan lifted both hands, half in jest, half in dismay.

Halmesbury shook his head. "Not every lord. We could begin with those seated in his immediate vicinity, his row and perhaps the rows just in front and behind. It would have been difficult to exchange words with anyone farther off. That seems a logical starting point."

Brendan cast him a questioning look.

"He was seated with the barons," the duke clarified. "Some of them may have been school or university acquaintances. He would not have known the rest. He had not visited in London for over twenty years. So the only men he would have recognized, or who might have recognized him, are those he knew from Oxford or Eton. And boys at school tend to band together by rank. That narrows the field somewhat. Many barons will be either too old or too young to have known him."

Brendan nodded slowly. "Agreed. We need more information. If I could get a list of the men seated near him, I could make inquiries. They might recall something from that day. Briggs will not gain admittance to their homes, but they will not shut the door in my face."

Halmesbury inclined his head. "I can obtain that list."

"I will help you interview them." Richard's offer was quietly spoken but decisive.

Brendan's shoulders loosened with relief. The thought of tracking down two dozen barons had seemed a formidable undertaking, but with Richard's help, the task no longer felt so impossible. And far preferable to waiting in helpless uncertainty.

Lily had assumed that her husband would return home at some point during the day to explain, perhaps, why she was now being followed from room to room or, at the very least, send word to shed light on the matter. But the day had passed in its entirety without a word from him.

She had dressed for dinner and made her way downstairs, but still there was no sign of Brendan's return.

Now, seated stiffly in the somber library, with the second John standing sentry by the door like some silent wraith, Lily felt tense with repressed frustration. The sensation of being shadowed, no matter how discreetly, left her unsettled. The indignity of visiting the necessary while a man lingered outside the corridor had been mortifying. She could not help but wonder, did the first John never require such human necessities himself?

It was fruitless to stew over the situation, yet she found herself doing just that with increasing frequency. If protection was truly warranted, she would accept it. But the absence of explanation from her husband ... that was what rankled most.

His absence from their gloomy residence only compounded her unease. She had harbored such hopeful plans to foster a tender bond during the first days of their marriage, to build something genuine and lasting. She had believed they had made progress the evening before. That their laughter, their quiet communion, and their kisses had marked the start of something fragile and rare.

And then there had been the intimacy. Lily blushed at the memory, heat blooming in her cheeks, before forcibly steadying herself. That moment had meant something to her. Had it not meant something to him?

Now, she did not know where he was or when he intended to return. All that had sustained her throughout the long day was the belief that he would come home in time for dinner.

Out in the entry hall, the grand casement clock chimed the hour.

Lily's shoulders sagged, the sound tolling like a judgment. She was lonely, wretchedly so. She had roamed the house, hoping to distract herself. Even a good book had failed to hold her attention. A visit to the kitchen to acquaint herself with the cook and maids had passed a single hour, nothing more. All the while, the women had cast wary glances toward the towering man who lingered like an ominous statue by the door.

From somewhere deeper in the house, she heard the

soft opening and closing of a door, followed by the faint cadence of footsteps in the corridor.

Heart leaping, Lily sprang to her feet. She rushed to the doorway, ignoring the silent presence of the second John, her breath catching in her throat.

Was it Brendan?

As she reached the threshold, Michaels emerged from the shadows like a well-timed specter in a Drury Lane production.

"Dinner is ready, milady." The simple announcement struck her like a slap. It was only the butler. Brendan had not returned.

Lily nodded and exited when Michaels stepped silently aside, his manner as unreadable as ever. She walked with composed grace toward the breakfast room, though inside, her composure frayed with every step. A tide of emotion threatened to crest into despair.

What could Brendan possibly be doing that was more important than returning home to dine with his wife?

As she crossed the threshold, the first patter of rain began against the windows. The soft drumming of water on glass mirrored her mood with uncanny accuracy, each droplet echoing the loneliness pressing in on her heart.

She took her seat at the long table, where the vase of flowers at its center offered the only burst of brightness in an otherwise joyless room. She stared at them, unseeing. Their vivid colors felt like an intrusion—unwelcome cheer in the midst of her rising sense of abandonment.

Until now, she had convinced herself Brendan must be engaged in some pressing matter, perhaps visiting a solicitor or tending to estate business. Something rational. Respectable.

But now, with dinner being served, his absence narrowed the possibilities.

The number of places he might be.

The people he might be with.

Stanley, one of the footmen Brendan had mentioned, approached to place a plate before her. He withdrew without a word, but his presence was a subtle reminder of everything unsettled in the house. She supposed his role was one reason the second John still stood at the door, silent and immovable.

Lily raised a trembling hand to her brow, her fingers cool against skin too warm with suppressed feeling. Tears pricked at the corners of her eyes. She fought to master them.

She would not—could not—allow herself to break in front of the servants.

But the thought rose, unbidden and merciless. Was it possible that Brendan was with Lady Slight?

THIRTEEN

"Prohibit the taking of omens, and do away with superstitious doubts. Then, until death itself comes, no calamity need be feared."

Sun Tzu, *L'Art de la Guerre* (*The Art of War*)

JULY 31, 1821

Twelve hours had passed, and Lily once again found herself seated in the breakfast room.

Alone.

Outside, the rain battered the windows, the heavens still weeping as they had done through the night. The sound was relentless—sometimes a steady rhythm, some-times a sudden lash—as if the sky itself shared her unrest.

It took much to dim her generally buoyant spirits, but Lily had discovered that being startled by the sudden pres-ence of the two Johns, coupled with her husband's complete silence since she had fallen asleep in his arms on their wedding night, was quite enough to accomplish the task. Add to that the dreary weather, and her hopeful mood had been entirely vanquished.

Sleep had evaded her, vanishing every time a floorboard creaked or the windowpanes rattled. Each unfamiliar sound had startled her awake, heart pounding, despite knowing that Second John stood vigil nearby. His muted pacing along the corridor did nothing to soothe her; rather, the soft, rhythmic footfalls added to the haunted quality of the night. It was as though she had wandered into a ghost story, one in which she herself was the abandoned heroine.

Their first evening together had been perfect. A promise. A beginning.

And now her heart ached with disappointment.

She had enjoyed Brendan's company more than she had dared to expect. She had enjoyed their tender intimacy. She had hoped—foolishly, perhaps—that it marked the start of something meaningful, something shared.

But now?

She could not rid herself of the suspicion that he had left her to seek out someone else. Someone he had known before her. Someone polished. Sophisticated. Intimate with him in ways Lily could only imagine.

Perhaps their night together, which had felt magical to her, had merely been forgettable to him. Perhaps she was dull by comparison. She was unschooled in seduction, lacking the practiced confidence of a certain widow.

Perhaps she was being a ninny.

It has been a day and a half since I last saw my husband. Surely, I am permitted a touch of melodrama.

Lily let out a soft groan and leaned her head against one hand. A dull ache throbbed behind her eyes. At this point, even the presence of First John no longer moved her. Her distress was plain, and she no longer cared who witnessed it. It was exhausting to be observed, to live beneath constant surveillance like some sort of prisoner.

Last night, she had retreated to her room and shut the door against Second John. She had tiptoed about her chamber, afraid to make noise, as though he might hear through the door. This morning, she had risen beyond caring. She could not pretend to composure forever, not while being ignored by her husband and shadowed by strangers.

She reached across the table and drew the small stack of news sheets toward her. Wesley had presented them when he showed her in, and Lily suspected it had been an act of sympathy. A thoughtful gesture, and one that had made her feel, if only for a moment, seen.

She sipped her tea and scanned the pages, willing her thoughts elsewhere. There was coverage of Town affairs, still abuzz with commentary on the coronation and King George IV's latest appearances. A few items of political import followed, none of which held her attention for long.

Moving the top sheet aside, Lily reached for another. This one was of a more frivolous sort, one of those gossipy broadsheets she rarely read. She began to discard it when a single line caught her eye, halting her movement and nearly causing her to drop her tea.

Her hand trembled.

Setting the cup carefully onto its saucer, she pushed it away and bent over the page once more, reading the line again—slowly this time, though her heart was already racing.

Just yesterday, Lord F. and Lady S. were seen conversing inti-

mately on a public street. Has the notorious widow taken back up with him, despite his recent vows to Miss A.?

Pain squeezed through her chest like a vise.

She released the sheet, letting it fall from her fingers, and dropped her head into her hands. The tears she had been determined to contain rose fast and hot, escaping despite her best efforts. Brendan had assured her that their marriage would be faithful. What did the word *intimately* even mean in this context? What had the observer seen? A touch? A smile?

How was she meant to interpret this?

"Lily?"

The voice, low and familiar, startled her. She gasped, spinning in her chair and hastily wiping her cheeks. Brendan stood in the doorway, rain-damp and travel-worn. His cravat was wrinkled, his coat rumpled and speckled with mud. His dark hair clung to his forehead, and water glistened on the shoulders of his coat.

"Brendan!"

"I must speak with you."

He stepped inside, closing the door firmly behind him and leaving First John in the hall. Without waiting for an invitation, he crossed the room and sank into a chair at the opposite end of the table. His eyes alighted on the covered plate, and with clear relief, he yanked off his gloves and drew it toward him.

Soon, he was eating like a man who had not seen food in days, while Lily watched in silence, taut with emotion. She longed to demand answers. The urge to knock the fork from his hand and force him to speak was almost overwhelming. But she held herself still. Just barely.

"Where have you been?"

Her voice rang sharply in the sudden hush, for just then the rain outside had eased, leaving only the sound of her own breath and the clink of cutlery. But she welcomed the fire that surged through her. Anger, at least, gave her strength.

Brendan sipped his tea, his plate now clean. "I was questioning the other barons who attended the coronation."

Lily blinked. That was not the answer she had expected. "What?"

"I was running down the lords who sat near my uncle to learn what they recalled. Lord Simmons was about to leave for his country seat, so I rode out to Chiswick to catch him. We started back late, but we were caught in the rain and stuck in the mud within an hour. With the horses too exhausted to continue, and no fresh ones to be found at such an hour, we slept in the carriage until dawn." He yawned, covering his mouth with the back of his hand. "Though I would not call it restful. Not with Stephen as my companion."

Lily stilled. Stephen, the footman whose intentions remained uncertain. So Brendan had not only been delayed, but he had been wary, perhaps even in danger.

"Oh," she breathed.

Brendan reached across the table and laid his hand gently over hers. His fingers were cool against her skin, and the gesture sent a shiver down her spine, as she reached a sudden understanding.

"My deepest apologies," he said, voice low and sincere. "Believe me, Lily, I would have far preferred to spend the night at your side."

She stared at his hand, her heart still uncertain even as her mind began to calm. When her eyes lifted to his, she found him watching her with that warm, quiet look that had undone her the first time he had used it. His brandy eyes were lit with something deeper than amusement, something close to tenderness.

"Oh," she whispered again, this time with less pain and more wonder.

The anger that had sustained her all morning faded, replaced by the bashful warmth of remembered closeness.

Brendan brushed his thumb across her knuckles before reluctantly withdrawing his hand, leaning back with a sigh.

"UNFORTUNATELY, I do not think we shall be sharing evenings for the foreseeable future."

Lily straightened, her expression sharpening like cut glass. "What does that mean?"

"It means ..." Brendan hesitated, then drew a breath. "I want nothing more than to be with you. But I have been thinking that perhaps, for a little while, you should stay with your parents."

"What?" She sprang to her feet, her voice rising in disbelief. "Are you trying to send me away?"

He shook his head quickly. "Certainly not. This is about protecting you. Until we know who killed the baron, I do not believe Ridley House is safe. After all you have done, I cannot risk something happening to you."

She threw up her hands in exasperation. "I refuse to leave! I am not some helpless child. I can take care of myself."

Brendan stood as well. In two strides, he was beside her. Gently, he drew her into his arms. At first, she remained stiff, unyielding. But he held her close, his face buried in her hair, drawing comfort from her nearness after such a long and wearisome night. Her scent, warm and familiar, washed over him. A balm to a frayed spirit.

He leaned close and whispered, "If anything were to happen to you, Lily Ridley ... I do not know what I would do."

She softened. Slowly, her arms encircled his waist. She rested her cheek against his chest, and he felt the tension ease from her frame.

"Did something happen?" she asked quietly. "I was ... I expected to see you when I awoke, but then you were gone. No one said a word, and I had two strangers trailing me all day."

Brendan lifted his head. "You did not receive my note?"

She pulled back, looking up at him with narrowed eyes. "There was no note. I searched the house. I looked in every room."

"I left it on the pillow beside you. Perhaps it slipped onto the floor?"

Lily let out a low, frustrated sound. "I thought you had vanished. I thought you had simply ..." She broke off, collecting herself. "What did the note say?"

Brendan released her and gestured toward her chair. She resumed her seat, watching him closely. He returned to his own and lifted his tea, sipping slowly before responding.

"I was sleeping beside you when I awoke to a crash. Someone had been rifling through my room and overturned the water jug in their haste. That moment confirmed it. One of the servants is involved. My first thought was for your safety. That is why I sent for the Johns. Then, after speaking with Briggs, Halmesbury, and Richard, I was compelled to seek out more answers."

Lily's shoulders sagged slightly. "So ... all this was about keeping me safe? Not ..."

Her gaze flickered to the gossip sheets still strewn across the table.

Brendan tilted his head, confused. "Yes, of course. What else would it be?"

She shrugged faintly, her voice low. "Nothing. I ... was not sure what to think."

LILY DID NOT AGREE to leave Ridley House, but she consented to consider it and to accept the continued presence of the Johns. She could not, in good conscience, argue against the reality that a woman of her petite stature might struggle to fend off a desperate or frenzied attacker. And someone had been killed. The threat, however shadowy, could not be dismissed.

Still, the conversation had left her ill at ease. She reassured herself that Brendan—athletic, alert, and strong— would be capable of defending himself should danger come his way. At least, she hoped that was true. He certainly seemed tense enough to react quickly, his entire manner imbued with vigilance beneath the surface.

Despite her reluctance to part so early in their marriage, especially when her most urgent hope was to transform it into a love match, Brendan's logic held merit. If she returned to her parents' home for a time, he could pursue the investigation without the added burden of worrying for her safety. And she, in turn, could go about her days unburdened by the silent scrutiny of two large men trailing her through every corridor.

Leaving the breakfast room, with First John falling into

step behind her, Lily noticed that the rain had ceased altogether. The sudden stillness within Ridley House felt eerie, too quiet after the relentless rhythm that had dominated the past day.

As she rounded a corner, she nearly collided with Michaels in the dimly lit passage. She gave a slight gasp, more startled than she cared to admit. Ordinarily, one could hear the butler approaching. His heavy step echoed with predictable rhythm upon the wooden floors. But this time, there had been no sound.

Had he been standing in the shadows?

Lily stiffened, unease prickling her skin. She disliked the thought, but Brendan's revelations had seeded mistrust. She hated to admit it, but Ridley House no longer felt entirely her own.

Perhaps Brendan was right. Perhaps she should go home. It was no good leaping like a frightened ninny every time a servant appeared without warning.

"Is the carriage ready?"

Michaels pursed his lips ever so slightly, as though the question wounded his professional pride.

"Of course, milady. You requested it for ten o'clock, so—"

From the entry hall, the deep toll of the casement clock cut through his words. Michaels raised a single eyebrow, letting the chimes answer her more pointedly than he had.

"May I have my pelisse and bonnet?"

He gave a short bow and disappeared into the gloomy hallway to fetch her things, leaving Lily alone with her thoughts.

Her conversation with Brendan lingered in her mind. To learn that he had been running about Town on her behalf, to protect her, had stolen the fire from her indignation. It was rather sweet. Unsettling, yes, but undeniably sweet.

She had meant to ask him about the broadsheet. About Lady Slight. But the moment had not felt right.

Or perhaps, a small voice whispered within her, *you are simply afraid of the answer.*

She would address the matter at dinner, Lily resolved.

The thought of visiting Sophia offered a welcome reprieve. Brendan had made it clear that First John must accompany her, given that the footman and coachman might pose a risk, but within Sophia's home, she would be free to move without her silent shadow dogging her every step. Brendan had agreed that John could wait with the servants in the mews behind the Saunton townhouse until she was ready to return.

Brendan, meanwhile, would spend the day speaking with more lords who might have conversed with the late baron. With arrangements in place, Lily left Ridley House with a sense of relief. She had grown weary of the silence, the uncertainty, and the unrelenting suspicions about the staff.

When she arrived at Balfour Terrace, the earl's London townhouse, her spirits lifted immediately. To her delight, Miles was in the drawing room with his mother. Lily scarcely paused to greet Sophia before sweeping the infant into her arms, cooing over his round face and bright eyes.

Miles gurgled and grinned, reaching for a strand of her hair with an eager, tiny hand.

"Oh, Sophia! I want a little angel of my own."

Sophia laughed. "Give it a moment. Perhaps let the menfolk solve this murder before introducing a child."

Lily sighed and took a seat, settling Miles on her knees

to face her. She pulled silly faces, delighted when his eyes sparkled and he gave a delighted chuckle.

"Brendan has informed me I am in danger," she said softly.

"I know," Sophia replied. "Richard told me he arranged for the Johns. Where is …" She trailed off, then added a bit awkwardly, "One of them?"

"In the mews. Brendan and I agreed that I only need protection when I am near our own servants. We even spoke of pensioning Michaels and letting the footmen go, but it felt unfair to dismiss all of them on the suspicion that one may be at fault. Besides, if we do not know which man poses the danger, then removing only one solves nothing."

Sophia's brow furrowed. "So what happens now?"

"Brendan wants me to return home." Lily's shoulders slumped. "But I want to stay. Things were beginning to go so well between us. I was so sure we could fall in love. Now it is all murder and mystery, and I cannot bear the thought of Mama interfering. If she finds out I am in danger, she will never let me hear the end of it."

Sophia pulled a sympathetic face. "We are returning to Saunton Park in a few days. If the matter is not resolved, you might come with us. Or even stay here at Balfour Terrace until we leave."

Lily tickled Miles, who squirmed and laughed, his little body wiggling with joy. "It is not ideal, but perhaps I shall. I would much rather spend the summer with you and Richard than endure Mama's commentary on my marriage."

"I think you are fortunate to have a mother, especially one like Aunty, who cares so deeply, but I understand the need to shape your own life now that you are wed. The invitation remains open."

Lily spent the rest of the day with Sophia and Miles, grateful for the warmth and comfort they provided. For a few blessed hours, the shadow of Ridley House faded.

It was only as she departed that evening, her carriage rolling quietly through the streets, that she realized she had forgotten to ask Sophia about the *on-dit* in the gossip sheets.

But what could Sophia truly say, other than to encourage her to ask Brendan directly?

Lily's stomach knotted as she tried to plan how to broach the subject.

Perhaps it was not simply the how that troubled her. Perhaps it was that she feared the answer.

BRIGGS SHOOK HIS HEAD. "I can find no other suspects among the servants. Michaels is the only one with any apparent grievance against your family."

Brendan cleared his throat. "Even so, we cannot dismiss the possibility that one of them has been bribed, or threatened, into silence by the killer."

"Indeed. And given that both the study and your chamber have been searched, it is difficult to believe Michaels murdered the baron in pursuit of some long-forgotten revenge. The accidental death of a gamekeeper over thirty years ago does not explain his interest in your belongings."

The air in the library hung still and musty, tinged faintly with the pungent tang of leather-bound tomes. A faint ticking from the mantel clock underscored the conversation, its rhythmic beat marking time like a metronome to their speculation.

"In summary, then ... we know very little of value." Brendan exhaled, his voice edged with frustration. "The barons I interviewed could only recall idle conversation before and after the coronation. The baron did not attend any gatherings that followed. According to Michaels, he returned home for dinner, gave his valet the night off to visit family in London, and dined alone in the formal dining room. Afterward, he secluded himself in the study and instructed the staff not to disturb him. At some point between ten o'clock and dawn, he was struck from behind with a marble sculpture taken from the mantel."

"He was killed well before dawn," Briggs added. "The coroner was clear that he had been dead for several hours by the time we arrived."

Brendan nodded. "Then we presume he was murdered between ten o'clock and midnight. By that hour, most of the male servants would have been belowstairs in the servants' hall."

The chair creaked as Briggs shifted his weight. "Which means one of them may be lying about their whereabouts. They would have had both opportunity and, possibly, motive."

"Or," Brendan added, "Michaels or one of the footmen answered the door and allowed the killer in. Whether out of fear or for a price, they might be keeping silent."

"And now," Briggs continued, folding his arms as he leaned against the edge of the table, "that same person may be searching for something in the house. Some item that links the baron to the killer ..."

"Or something entirely unrelated," Brendan finished, sweeping a hand across the clutter of correspondence on the writing desk. "Either way, we are still in the dark."

A quiet pause settled between them. Outside, a faint clatter of hooves echoed down the distant street, softened by the thick stone walls of Ridley House. Brendan rubbed at the back of his neck.

"The difficulty is that the baron has spent the last two decades at his country estate," Briggs said, his voice lower, more measured. "There are no known connections here in Town. I questioned his solicitors, unremarkable fellows, but they had nothing to offer. The baron's world was Filminster, not London. If answers exist, they may lie there."

Brendan glanced toward the window, where gauzy curtains stirred slightly in the evening draft. Dust motes drifted in the fading summer light, which cast a pale glow across the floorboards.

"Perhaps the truth lies in Filminster," he murmured. "The baron despised travel, enough to shirk his duties at Westminster entirely after inheriting the title, preferring to remain cloistered at Baydon Hall. I could travel there and search for anything that might cast light on this matter."

He glanced once more toward the window, where the summer clouds cast large shadows upon his view. "And if I go without any of the servants from this household, I could remove Lady Filminster from danger at the same time."

Briggs stroked his mustache, deep in thought. "There might be merit to that. I shall continue the investigation here in Town. Meanwhile, I can recommend a discreet and experienced runner, whom you might take with you. He would be of use in Filminster."

Brendan stood and began pacing the length of the library. His boots made muffled sounds upon the old rug, worn smooth by generations before him. The plan made sense. Not for reasons of strategy, but because of sentiment.

He did not wish to be parted from Lily. These past few days, brief though they had been, had shifted something within him.

She was a revelation. Her optimism, her intelligence, her refusal to bend before convention had brought an unexpected lightness into his otherwise grim affairs. She had not only saved him from a protracted trial, but made him feel less alone. In her presence, burdens seemed a little lighter.

"I shall do it," he said firmly. "Lady Filminster and I will leave for Baydon Hall as soon as I can make arrangements for travel. Perhaps the duke might lend me a carriage and men."

Briggs inclined his head. "Then I shall send word to the runner and bring him to you in the morning."

After Briggs departed, Brendan glanced at the longcase clock by the hearth. The day had slipped past unnoticed, the hours marked only by the subtle shift of light in the room and the scent of cooling ashes from the earlier fire. Despite the season, the house retained a damp chill that settled in the bones.

The list of tasks for departure would need to wait until morning, as Briggs had suggested. But already Brendan felt a sense of direction. If he could take Lily with him, he could keep her safe … and perhaps use the quiet of the countryside to better understand this new bond between them.

He had barely seated himself at the desk when a sharp rap sounded at the door. He looked up, startled.

Michaels entered, his expression as flat and disinterested as ever. "Lady Slight to see you, milord," he intoned, as if announcing the arrival of the footman with tea.

Brendan rose at once, his face tightening in disbelief as

Harriet swept into the library unbidden. He turned a furious look on Michaels, unable to fathom how she had been allowed past the threshold without his express permission.

"What are you doing here?"

CHAPTER
FOURTEEN

"Now, when your weapons are dulled, your ardor damped, your strength exhausted and your treasure spent, other chieftains will spring up to take advantage of your extremity. Then no man, however wise, will be able to avert the consequences that must ensue."

Sun Tzu, *L'Art de la Guerre* (*The Art of War*)

～

Michaels withdrew in haste, the door shutting with a decisive click. Brendan stood rigid, fury rising like a tide. Perhaps it was time to pension off that wretched butler after all. A man who accepted his coin ought to extend a modicum of respect. Brendan had never mistreated a servant, but the continued insolence was unacceptable.

He drew a slow breath, willing his voice to remain calm. Composure, not outrage, would rid him of this unwanted guest.

He turned back to her, voice clipped. "Harriet. What are you doing here?"

The viscountess smiled, her expression syrupy and self-satisfied. Her red curls bounced as she tilted her head, and Brendan detected the pleased gleam in her eyes.

"This is my first visit to Ridley House, Brendan," she said, as though that explained everything.

She stepped toward him, and once more, the overpowering scent of rosewater and wine reached his nose, cloying and artificial. The fragrance did not complement the space. It invaded it, masking the faint scent of aged paper and wood polish that normally brought him comfort.

"I realized that now you are a married man, it is perfectly respectable for me to call upon your wife," she continued, the smirk curling her painted lips betraying any pretense of civility. "I could always claim I came to see that little featherbrain you married."

Brendan's jaw tensed. How had he once found her enticing? Her décolletage was aggressively on display, her corset pressing her gown to the edge of impropriety. He could not understand how he had ever mistaken this theatrical parade for elegance.

Not since Lily.

Lily, with her open laughter and quick wit. With her scent of honey and her bright, intelligent eyes that shone even in a dimly lit room. There was no comparison.

"I do not wish to receive a visit," he said sharply, his tone resolute.

Harriet arched a brow and took in the chamber with a mocking gaze. "Your home is ... quaintly Gothic."

He fought the flush rising in his neck, determined to see her out before further damage could be done. "Be that as it may," he said coldly, striding across the room to throw open the door Michaels had so thoughtlessly closed, "I do not receive visitors without invitation."

Before he could call for a footman, Harriet advanced again, lifting her hand slightly, her fingers brushing the air near his coat in a gesture that hovered ... too familiar, too bold. Brendan took a measured step back, spine straightening, his presence hardening like a shuttered door. The impropriety of the moment hung in the air between them, unmistakable and uninvited.

"You cannot prefer that silly debutante to me," she murmured, her voice dropping into an insinuating hush.

Brendan stared at her, astonished. "It is time for you to go," he said, voice low with tightly controlled anger.

Harriet swayed slightly, the boldness in her face flickering into uncertainty. "You would not discard me the way Perry Balfour did last year, would you? I am ... fashionable. Admired. Most gentlemen are honored to spend time with me."

Brendan shut his eyes in horror. Was Harriet having a sodding crisis of the soul? And was he not a thorough idiot for picking up with her after Perry had left Town to marry little Emma Davis? Perry had warned him to stay away from the widow, but Brendan had thought he could handle her.

"I beg of you. You must leave at once."

It would seem he was now going to pay for his error in judgment involving Lady Slight yet again. His association with this particular widow was proving to be a very poor choice.

Somehow, he needed to get the viscountess out of his home before Lily returned. It would be the height of disrespect for his bride to find his former paramour in her new home. But how to remove the viscountess expediently, without wounding her dignity?

He did not know how to march a woman out, and his skills of diplomacy were failing him in such an unprecedented situation.

Brendan had never had an overlap with the women he was pursuing. He had always been a one-woman kind of man, so there had never been any jealous lovers or unseemly displays of emotion. His affairs had always ended naturally, both parties happy to move on. He did not seek drama in his life, an unfortunate hindrance now, as he had no relevant experience in disentangling himself from someone like Harriet.

I must get her out before Lily returns.

Carefully, he lifted his hands and placed them with deliberate restraint near her arms, an unmistakable signal to create distance, not contact.

"Harriet," he said in a quiet, unyielding tone, "please step back."

She did not. Instead, her posture shifted forward, the fabric of her gown brushing his coat as she closed the space between them, her face far too near.

It felt all wrong. Every inch of him recoiled. He wanted his little chatterbox with her quick wit and luminous smile, not this forced intimacy, not this painful shadow of a past mistake.

Brendan took another step back, but Harriet leaned in again, her presence oppressive. He shifted, attempting to guide her back without insult, but she clung to him like a woman desperate to reclaim something already lost.

~

"Good evening, Wesley. Do you happen to know where Lord Filminster is at the moment?"

Lily had decided to find Brendan forthwith to discuss the gossip in the news sheet that morning. She ought to have spoken to him earlier, when the opportunity had presented itself, because her anxiety over it had grown exponentially on the way home from Sophia.

Ordinarily, Lily preferred to tackle worrying issues as quickly as possible. She hated having thoughts fester in her head, and there could be no more poisonous fear than the notion of her husband being unfaithful with the voluptuous widow. Brendan had done nothing to deserve mistrust, so she must simply speak with him.

"His lordship is ... in the ... library." Wesley's pleasant face was stiff, and he was clearly reluctant to impart Brendan's whereabouts. Lily's brows drew together in query, but the footman merely turned a ruddy shade before darting off to put away her bonnet and pelisse.

Heading down the dim hall in the opposite direction the servant had taken, with First John trailing a few feet behind, Lily saw the library door standing open and moved to walk through it.

She stopped in shock.

Her gaze collided with the unwelcome sight of Lady Slight far too close to Brendan in the doorway, her arms wrapped around him in a way that made Lily's stomach twist. Her head began to swim. She realized she had stopped breathing.

Inhaling a reedy breath, her eyes flickered to Brendan, who appeared ... appalled.

Appalled he has been caught?

"Lady Slight! What an unexpected ... Has anyone

offered you any tea? I must apologize for not being here to receive ... I do hope that Lord Filminster has been ..."

From a great distance, Lily heard herself speaking and wished she could slap herself into silence.

Shut up, Lily!

She had never hated her propensity to babble more than she did in that moment. Her nerves were speaking for her, when what she really wanted was to scream at the widow to remove herself from Brendan's person. It was pure drama, a scene from a Drury Lane production, complete with the three of them and First John standing in the wings.

And, suddenly, Lily did not have the strength to deal with it.

She just wanted to disappear into one of the many gloomy rooms of Ridley House and cry. All her worst fears had been realized, and her hopes of finding love with Brendan Ridley were for naught.

"I shall leave you to your visit, then."

Spinning away, Lily ran down the hall, passing First John as she hurried to the little drawing room where she and Brendan had shared their first kiss ... the day she had believed their marriage stood a chance. The wonderful, perfect day when she had fallen in love with her new husband.

"Lily!" Brendan's strangled voice called after her, but she did not stop.

Running inside, she slammed the door behind her and fumbled to lock it with trembling hands. First John was not a welcome visitor just now.

Hurling herself onto a settee, Lily curled into a ball and wept in the empty room.

She had thought that, after what she had done for him

and the way he had looked at her on their wedding day, they could build something real. That she had made progress in her campaign to compel Brendan to fall in love with her.

How had she ever thought she could compete with all that feminine sophistication on display?

Most men of the peerage would give their eyeteeth for Lady Slight's attention, and foolish little Lily had thought she could convince a worldly man like Brendan to fall in love with her ... by being honest and cheerful and changing her wardrobe.

What a farce.

"Oh, dear! Your wife seems a trifle upset."

Harriet's voice lilted with mockery, but her posture betrayed something more grasping. She leaned in toward him, far too close for comfort, her chin tilted up as though she might collapse against him again. Brendan growled in fury, barely tempering his impulse as he stepped back and raised a hand, not to touch, but to signal distance.

Enough.

His restraint held firm as he moved decisively, leading her back into the library with a stiff arm extended to indicate the path, careful to avoid even the semblance of further intimacy. The cloying cloud of rosewater and wine made him gag once more as she finally took a stumbling step away, her blue eyes widening in surprise.

This time Brendan was not brooking any argument. He was going to make his stance clear, rid his home of her once and for all, and then find Lily to straighten this travesty out.

To think that minutes earlier he had been planning to

take Lily away from Ridley House and the lurking danger within, to give her the attention she deserved as his bride, only to have the vexing viscountess wreak havoc.

He gestured toward a chair. "Please, sit."

When she hesitated, Brendan gave her a pointed look. She lowered herself into the seat with the reluctant grace of a performer asked to leave the stage. He circled the room and deliberately chose a chair across the library table from her, ensuring a safe, impersonal distance. Let there be no mistaking his resolve.

"Lady Slight, you are not welcome in my home."

Harriet's cheeks flamed, her narrowed gaze landing on him like a blade. Brendan considered his options. If he were cruel or scolded her mercilessly, the viscountess would have endless opportunities to seek revenge by belittling Lily or spreading gossip among the *ton*. Worse, she could attempt mischief like this again if he pushed her too far, which would only wound his wife again.

If his mother were here, she would advise him to be kind. She would point out that each person carries their own burden. That life could be crushing, and one cannot know the trials a person has endured. And when it was possible, one should attempt to lighten their load and disengage without fighting.

Deuce it. He would far rather berate her and throw her out of his home in a rage after such ignominious behavior, but . . .

I do not know the burdens that Harriet might carry. Or what vengeance she might seek against Lily.

"I delighted in our time together." Brendan struggled to find cajoling words to persuade her to leave his home and never return. "We enjoyed those days. But this was always to be a temporary arrangement. You have no wish for permanent ties, and I ... I find that I do. Because of circumstances beyond our control, Lady Filminster is my wife, and I am not a man to dally with multiple women."

"You no longer want me?"

Brendan raised a hand to the pulse beating in his temple and applied pressure while he tried to think how to convince Harriet to walk away.

And never return!

"It does not signify. You are a beautiful woman, and you are quite aware I sought your companionship with great fervor for several months, but that chapter has closed. I believe, if you think on it for a moment, that you grew weary of me. You made excuses not to see me in recent times, made arrangements that kept us apart."

Inspiration struck while he was talking, and Brendan realized the best strategy would be to persuade Harriet that their parting of ways was, in fact, her idea. He permitted a regretful expression to settle upon his features to complete his argument.

"I think, perhaps, I knew you would end things with me soon, and it seemed wise to move on rather than have to experience the pain of being sent away."

He watched her closely, in breathless suspense, as he waited for her response. He had come to realize since spending time with Lily that Harriet was essentially a selfish woman who only thought of her own wants and needs. Appealing to her basic nature might convince her to lose all interest in him if he could just—

"That is true."

He almost straightened in relief but carefully maintained the expression of regret. Slowly, he lowered his eyes to stare at the table, offering the appearance of melancholy, even allowing his shoulders to sag just a fraction, as if devastated at her declaration.

"I thought it might be. When you forgot our appointment that night of the coronation ..." He shook his head as if overcome, hoping his performance was natural but not daring to look up at her in case he broke the illusion he was attempting to cast. The illusion of an enamored man attempting to protect himself from pain.

"I decided it was time to see to my duty before you ..." He waited with bated breath to see if she would respond to his cue.

"Brendan, I am afraid that our time has come to an end. Your circumstances have become too complicated for a woman in my situation, so I think it would be best if we no longer meet."

He exhaled in a puff, dropping his head as if hearing the worst news. When he sorted out this muddle with Lily, he would confess to her how he had addressed the widow's lingering hopes, but right now, he stood on the precipice of a resolution, and it was imperative he remove this troublesome distraction. There were matters of life and death to contend with.

"I ... understand. And I thank you for your company." *I shall always remember our time fondly.* He could not bring himself to say the words aloud, which would have been untrue and an assault on his integrity, regardless of how perfectly they would conclude their scene together.

A rustle of skirts informed him that Harriet had risen, but he dared not glance up in case his deception was revealed upon his face. The widow walked around and paused beside him, resting her hand lightly on the back of his chair, a final, theatrical gesture of closure more than comfort.

"Do not despair, Brendan. I shall always remember our time fondly."

He nearly burst into incredulous laughter when Harriet echoed his unspoken thought from seconds earlier. Instead, he bobbed his head in acknowledgment, keeping his eyes fixed on the grain of the mahogany table. "Thank you."

With that, Harriet walked away. Finally able to look up, he watched her, noting she was unsteady on her feet. He could only hope she was not too soused to recollect that she had ended things with him.

He waited in the library, playing out his tragic air until he was certain she had left. It would ruin everything if he sprang to his feet too soon, determined to find his bride and explain this invasion of their home.

LILY HAD BEEN WEEPING in the dismal drawing room, while outside the bright sunlight of a summer afternoon mocked her. She would have her trunks packed as soon as she could master the storm of tears.

"Milady?"

She screeched in fright, jumping up to swipe her eyes dry before slowly turning around the room to find the source of the voice. As she swiveled toward the fireplace, she was utterly astonished to find Wesley standing by an open, previously concealed door with a tea tray.

There was so much to comprehend.

First, there was a door next to the fireplace she had never noticed before. It was covered in oak paneling and wallpaper to blend in with the rest of the wall. Under normal circumstances, she would be fascinated to discover what was ostensibly a secret entrance, the sort that wealthy homeowners had a penchant for, but with other matters pressing, she concluded she would inspect it later.

If there is a later.

Wesley stood with a pained expression on his face, raising the tray as if to remind her he was there. Lily shifted her gaze back to him. The footmen hired in noble residences were part of the presentation of the household's wealth and status, an extension of the grand houses they served in. The footmen of Ridley House were no different, Wesley and the others being tall, lean men who were distinguished even in the dated style of livery they wore.

He had a pleasant countenance, as did the other footmen, with a spattering of freckles across his cheeks and nose that spoke to the reddish tint of his brown hair. The servants wore the customary white stockings and shining buckled shoes expected of household livery, but the cut of the navy breeches and coat was faded and of a bygone era.

"I do not wish to be impertinent, milady, but ... I thought perhaps you would like some tea?"

Lily blinked in surprise. Given all that had happened in the past few minutes, this mundane conversation was completely unexpected. She recollected that Wesley had seemed uncomfortable earlier—reluctant, even—when he had directed her to her husband. And now he had taken pains to find her and offer tea? It was almost unbearably kind.

She realized she had no desire to carry on with the tension and distress she had endured this past week.

She thought about how she had always been friends with many of the servants in her parents' home. How their footman, Thomas, had once caught an intruder when Sophia had convinced him to lay a trap for a man seeking to abduct her. How Nancy had been her constant companion since Sophia had married. Suddenly, Lily wanted nothing more than an ordinary interlude with another person.

No murders, no enforced courtships, no hasty weddings, no reluctant or unfaithful husbands, no fear. Just a normal conversation between two normal people.

"Only if you join me," she replied, gesturing to the tray.

"Oh no, milady! It is not permitted."

"Wesley, I ... order you to sit down and have a cup of tea with me."

Wesley stared at her, his eyes wide as he thought about it. "Very well, milady. If that is what you wish."

"It is."

He nodded, moving forward to place the tea tray on the table by the settee. Then he glanced about the room before walking over to collect a tumbler from the drinks cabinet. Returning, he sat across from her, perched awkwardly on the edge of the armchair as though ready to spring to his feet at any moment.

Lily straightened up on the settee, lowering her feet to the floor, and leaned forward. Placing the strainer over the cup on the tray, she poured her tea and then raised the teapot toward the footman. Wesley placed the tumbler down.

"I hope it is acceptable for me to use this? I only brought the one cup."

She could not care two pennies about what became of her husband's crystal tumblers after what she had witnessed in the library. "It is suitable."

Moving the strainer to the glass, she poured his tea for him. The orange-brown tint made her mouth water in anticipation, and for the first time in days, Lily felt a genuine moment of peace. These past weeks had been a kind of slow torment, and it felt so wonderfully common-place to sit quietly and take tea.

Sitting back, she sipped the hot liquid, and the tension slowly began to melt away. Soon, she would have to confront Brendan with the remnants of their marriage and decide how to piece together her shattered hopes, but that moment was not now.

Wesley raised his glass and sipped, visibly ill at ease. Lily supposed it was fortunate he wore the gloves of his livery, as the glass must have grown quite warm from its contents.

"How long have you worked at Ridley House, Wesley?"

The footman lowered his glass and cleared his throat. "A few years, milady."

"So you never met the baron before the coronation, I suppose."

"No, milady. But I did not meet his lordship even then. I was away for several days. My brother married in Yorkshire. Mr. Michaels generously allowed me the time off, and I returned the morning the baron was found."

Lily vaguely recollected that Brendan had mentioned this on the afternoon of their wedding. "I never met the late baron either. His death certainly created a pickle for those of us left behind."

Wesley appeared unsure how to respond. "Yes, milady." He raised his glass to sip his tea again, and Lily suspected it was to avoid further conversation.

She sipped her own tea, flinching slightly and spilling a few drops when a distinctive knock sounded on the door she had locked.

"Lily, we must speak."

Sighing, Lily set her cup down and offered Wesley an apologetic glance. The footman looked positively relieved to rise. Bowing, he walked away, tumbler in hand, and exited through the concealed door, which he quietly pulled shut behind him.

She crossed the room. Drawing in a deep breath, she turned the key and stepped aside.

Brendan must have heard the click of the lock, for the handle turned, and her rogue of a husband entered.

BRENDAN WAS RATHER proud of how he had handled Harriet, but he had not the faintest notion how to explain the matter to Lily, who sat stiffly upon the settee, her arms folded across her chest and her expression mutinous in the golden rays of sunlight slanting through the drawing room windows.

The amber light played across her features, illuminating the fine tension in her jaw and the dull sheen of unshed tears. The sharp line of her shoulders warned him against attempting any tender overture.

He could hardly blame her, not after what she believed she had witnessed in the library.

"I did not invite Lady Slight into our home," he said at last, his voice lower than he intended.

"That did not seem to be a problem."

Her tone was cool, flat as a pane of glass. It sliced through the awkward silence between them. He shook his head, resisting the urge to pace.

"It was most certainly a problem. I had no desire to see her, and I was doing my best to send her away when she flung herself into my arms, mere seconds before you arrived. The door was open … purposefully so. I knew you were expected for dinner, and I would have to be a halfwit to think I could conceal her presence."

Lily's face softened by degrees as she weighed his words. Her arms slowly unfurled, and she let her hands settle upon the edge of the settee. She turned away from him, gazing out at the muted green of the garden, where the last remnants of daylight caught the leaves in silver.

She did not look at him as she finally replied. "Be that as it may, it does not explain the gossip in the news sheets."

Brendan frowned, caught off guard by the turn in conversation. "What gossip?"

"You and Lady Slight were mentioned." Her voice was quiet, but steady. "They claimed you were seen conversing with her intimately on the street."

He ran a hand down the side of his cheek, the rasp of stubble under his fingers a small irritation compared to the one blooming behind his eyes. "So that is what started this."

He exhaled slowly. "Harri—Lady Slight—approached me in Bond Street yesterday, before I met with Halmesbury, Richard, and Briggs. She suggested we might resume our former arrangement. I declined. Emphatically. She took offense—plainly. She had been drinking and, I suspect, brooding over why I would prefer the company of my wife to her own."

Lily rose so quickly he took a step back.

"There is no need to coddle me, Brendan Ridley!" Her voice was bright with fury. "I am not some wide-eyed child. I am a grown woman, and I can endure the truth!"

He lifted his hands in confusion, utterly at a loss. "What truth?"

"That you were forced to marry me!" she cried. "That

had the baron not been murdered, you would even now be sharing Lady Slight's bed! That you never chose me!"

Her voice cracked, and the anger wavered at its edge, revealing the sharp glint of hurt beneath. "So do not stand there and pretend you would rather spend time with me than that ... than that trollop!"

Brendan dropped into a nearby chair, his gaze turning upward to the ceiling with unfocused weariness. The ornate plasterwork overhead might as well have been a blank expanse of sky. Apparently, Lily believed him regarding the incident with Lady Slight, a trait he admired in her. It was part of her general impulse toward honesty and sincerity, and he valued it deeply even as he grappled with what to say next.

But how to address her envy of the attentions he had once paid to another? That was far less straightforward.

His feelings for Lily were growing at a pace that unsettled him. There was a kind of fondness budding between them, rooted in shared moments and her relentless authenticity, but he was not ready to unravel the matter of how their marriage had come about, not yet. That conversation required time. Intimacy. A sense of foundation. It was not a subject for raw hours like this one, clouded by gossip and misunderstanding.

They needed, above all, time together to build the affinity that was quietly forming between them. He hoped it might grow into something enduring. But this was not the moment to rush it.

With a sigh, he rose to his feet and crossed to where she stood. Her back was to the window now, and the last light of day haloed her figure in soft hues. He reached for her hands and enclosed them in his own, his fingers lightly brushing the edge of her sleeve. Her palms were icy through the gloves, but she did not pull away.

"I am here with you now," he said softly. "The past is inconsequential to our present. I have spent every waking moment since you agreed to marry me ensuring your safety, taking steps to end this danger and to care for you."

"So you do not deny you would be with Lady Slight tonight if I were not here?"

He suppressed a curse. Lily was warm-hearted, quick-witted, and generous, but Harriet's appearance had kindled her jealousy. Now they were quarreling, when only an hour ago, he had been looking forward to dinner and the possibility of closing the distance between them ... of drawing her into his arms and beginning the next chapter of their marriage in earnest.

"I cannot say where I would be," he replied, trying to keep his tone even. "I can only state that I am here with you. And I have ensured the viscountess will never set foot in Ridley House again."

Lily drew back slightly, her jaw tight. "And how many times has she been here?" she demanded, her voice taut with outrage. Her spine was straight, her chin lifted, and he hated the sight of her so guarded. His Lily was soft and quick with her thoughts, restless, inquisitive. She filled a room with life. He did not like this cold-eyed stranger glaring at him with fury.

"Never," he said, the word ringing in the hush between them. "I have never invited her to my home. You are the only woman I have ever brought into this house or allowed into my bedchamber."

Her eyes narrowed, and she bit down on her lower lip. "Pshaw!"

Brendan wanted to tell her what she needed to hear,

but he wanted to be honest, too. And honesty, at least the sort that meant something, could not be conjured like a parlor trick. He was not entirely clear on what his feelings for Lily were, only that she made him feel something new. Hope, perhaps.

Hope that they might build a life that did not merely fulfill obligation. Hope that their growing familiarity might blossom into something deeper. Hope that, given time, he might know a genuine meeting of the minds with the woman fate had thrust into his path.

But until he gained clarity, he did not wish to speak promises he could not yet uphold. Since the morning of their wedding, they had been honest with one another, painfully so at times, and he would not toss empty words at her now simply to mend a quarrel. That sort of balm was fleeting, and he had learned from experience that it never healed properly.

They had only been wed three days, blast it. The ink on the registry was barely dry.

Lily rose abruptly, her skirts whispering against the carpet as she stalked back to the settee. She flung herself down with careless grace and stared at her slippers peeking out from beneath the hem of her emerald dress. That color, vivid and rich, suited her remarkably well.

But that was neither here nor there whilst they were quarreling.

Brendan lowered himself onto the chair across from her again, the old leather sighing beneath his weight. He folded his hands between his knees and waited, the silence taut between them like a line of thread stretched to snapping.

"I wish ... you had chosen me," Lily said at last, her voice small and tight. She did not look at him. "All my life, I just wanted someone like you to notice me. To choose to wed me. To ..."

She pressed her lips together, swallowing the rest. Then, with a sudden rush, she added, "I cannot even walk the halls of my home without one of the Johns, and now that ... viper ... has invaded ..."

Her eyes filled with tears, and Brendan's breath caught at the sight. She looked so young just then, so heartachingly burdened for one who should be basking in the glow of a new marriage. He felt the ache in his chest like a bruise being pressed from the inside. She had done so much for him, borne so much. He could not deny that she had every reason to feel wronged.

And that made everything more complicated.

Do I feel genuine affection for Lily or is it simply gratitude?

Certainly, such a truth could not be uncovered in a matter of days. He needed time. He needed to breathe. But if he could have said the right words, if he could have offered her comfort without the burden of false hope, he would have done so gladly.

"I am sorry for everything you have had to deal with," he offered quietly.

At once, Lily's features hardened. She looked away. Brendan realized, with a twist of dismay, that he had said the wrong thing. Perhaps she had hoped for different words he did not yet have the certainty to give.

"Sophia has invited me to Saunton Park, so I need not live with my parents," she said, her voice brittle. "She said I could stay with them at Balfour Terrace until they leave London, so I believe ... I shall accept her offer."

Brendan felt a quiet thud of disappointment. He did not want her to go. But after everything she had endured—

Harriet's intrusion, the ever-present danger, the gossip—it was not his place to protest.

He had asked too much of her already. She deserved sanctuary.

"That would be wise," he said, his voice even.

A flicker of something—hurt? Or was it disbelief?—passed across Lily's face. She seemed surprised by his swift agreement. And unhappy. He sensed it, but could not name it. He had no notion what words might reach her now.

When the time was right, when the danger had passed and he had made sense of what was blooming inside him, they could speak again. Perhaps then, he would be worthy of her honesty.

FIFTEEN

"The general who advances without coveting fame and retreats without fear of disgrace, whose only thought is to protect his country and to do good service to his sovereign, is the jewel of the kingdom."

Sun Tzu, *L'Art de la Guerre* (*The Art of War*)

AUGUST 1, 1821

Michaels directed the maids to pack Lily's trunks, a sour expression carved deep into his lined face. His mouth was pinched, his eyes full of judgment as he oversaw the proceedings with the sort of officious gloom that now seemed the prevailing atmosphere of Ridley House.

What a blessed relief it would be to quit the place. She longed to escape the constant weight of unease, the need to glance over her shoulder every few minutes, wondering whether Michaels or one of the identically suited Johns would emerge from some dim alcove with hostile intent.

After providing her instructions to the staff, Lily left them to their tasks and descended the main staircase to take breakfast, the toe of her slipper tapping softly on each polished tread. First John followed a pace behind like an echo, his breath audible in the hushed stillness, a heavy-breathing shadow cloaked in ill-fitting livery.

She and Brendan had parted ways the previous night without so much as a proper farewell. After agreeing she would remove to Sophia's home, Lily had penned a short note to her cousin and then taken her dinner upstairs on a tray. She had eaten alone, her food grown cold from neglect while she sat cross-legged in her nightdress, staring into the fire. Brendan had remained downstairs, and if he had come up at all, it was sometime after she had finally drifted into an uneasy sleep just before dawn. She had stirred once to the muffled creak of Second John pacing outside her chamber door, the sound constant and dull.

It had been a miserable night. Her mind had turned in relentless circles, berating her for allowing herself to fall in love with a man who had been compelled into marriage with her. How foolish she had been—how utterly naïve—to believe she could wage a campaign for his affection without sacrificing her heart in the process.

Entering the breakfast room, Lily halted briefly on the threshold, letting her eyes sweep the space with muted hope. The tall windows were unshuttered, letting in the pale spill of morning light across the polished floor, but Brendan was nowhere to be seen.

A quiet disappointment unfurled inside her. She had wished, absurdly, that he might be here. That perhaps, with the light of day, things might have softened between them.

But it seemed that even parting would be conducted at a distance.

She crossed to the table, her slippered feet soundless on the Aubusson carpet. They had not discussed when or where they might reunite, but she supposed it must wait until this wretched murder business was behind them at last.

I am not admitting defeat, she reminded herself, straightening her shoulders as she pulled out her usual chair.

This was merely a retreat. A pause. A chance to plan for the future without fear dogging every step or wicked widows turning up in her home uninvited.

But even as she mounted the defense in her mind, it did little to fend off the ache that lingered since the moment she had found Lady Slight clinging to her husband like ivy to a stone wall. She could not rid herself of the image or the certainty it confirmed. How could she hope to compete?

Brendan was the very embodiment of sartorial elegance. He was handsome, commanding, and always composed. Lady Slight was a practiced coquette, voluptuous and dripping confidence. And Lily—Lily Billy—was none of those things. She might be cheerful and loyal and honest, but she was hardly the sort of woman who turned heads in a crowded ballroom.

He was likely keeping to his vows out of duty, nothing more. Her intervention had altered the course of his life, and though he was determined to do right by her, she had never been chosen. Not truly. No one had ever chosen her.

And now, married to a man bound to her by necessity, she would never know what it felt like to be the center of someone's world.

She had always believed, somehow, that things would work out for the best. It was a trait that set her apart. Her boundless optimism, her trust in fate. But now, sitting in the heavy silence of a house cloaked in secrets, she could think of no tidy path through the tangled mess she found herself in.

With a small sigh, she sat down and uncovered her meal. The scent of hot bread and coddled eggs met her nose, familiar, but unappetizing. She picked up her fork and pushed the eggs to one side.

Perhaps a respite at Saunton Park will restore me, she thought, raising a bite of toast to her lips. *And with rest, perhaps clarity will come. Inspiration.*

At the very least, she would be free from the creeping dread that haunted every corridor of Ridley House.

BRENDAN HAD WANTED nothing more than to join Lily in her bed the night before. The desire had gnawed at him while he sat alone in the drawing room, staring into the decaying coals. He had remained downstairs to master the urge, knowing full well he would not be welcome. Still, the memory of their one night together clung to his senses, whispering of what could be. The warmth of her skin. The sweetness of her kiss.

It haunted him now. Tormented him.

He wanted to know her. To become a proper husband in truth, not only in name. Which was precisely why he now found himself wandering the quieter streets of Mayfair in the early morning light like a man pursued by ghosts.

Had he shared breakfast with her, he would have said too much. Or worse, begged her not to leave. And that, he could not bear to do.

He had never expected marriage to mean so much, so

swiftly. Never expected Lily—chattering, unfiltered, endlessly sincere Lily—to slip into the corners of his heart with such stealth. But she had. Somehow, she had.

Brendan had not realized how profoundly lonely he had become until she arrived.

Since his mother's death thirteen years earlier, that void had deepened, carved out slowly by silence. His mother, Annabel, and he had been close, bound not merely by blood but by a shared understanding. Then came Richard at Eton, that first true friend who filled the empty spaces left behind.

But the baron had sent him to Cambridge, away from Richard, and when Brendan had finally come of age, his uncle had cast him out of Baydon Hall altogether, severing him not only from the house but from his sister.

He had lived in London ever since. Surrounded by acquaintances, but close to no one.

When Annabel had returned to his life, newly married to Halmesbury, there had been a kind of healing. Observing their domestic contentment, watching the way Halmesbury adored his sister and their child, Brendan had been reminded of something he thought long gone—the comfort of family. Of belonging.

Then had come Lily.

The night of their wedding, as she lay beside him snoring ever so faintly in sleep, her arm draped across his chest, he had felt something he had not known in years. Peace. The kind of peace that only comes when one is seen and accepted.

That night, he had dared to believe in something more. That this might not be a marriage of convenience or necessity alone. That Lily, who chattered her thoughts like birdsong and defended others with the courage of a lion, might become his partner in every sense.

The summer morning should have buoyed his spirits. The sky overhead was a brilliant wash of blue, unmarred by cloud. The leaves in the square danced in a gentle breeze, casting shifting shadows on the cobblestones. A thrush chirped from the branch of a tree, and the scent of roses lingered on the air.

It was an idyllic morning.

But Brendan felt nothing but the slow, aching pressure of regret.

He stopped beside the large iron gates of the private square, resting one gloved hand atop the cool railing. Within, the riot of blooms—lavender, foxglove, nasturtiums—blurred before his eyes. He stared, unseeing.

His wife was leaving.

And he did not know when, or if, he would see her again.

After everything he had done, after everything he had failed to say, what right had he to ask anything of her?

Will she be gone when I return home?

The thought was a stone in his chest, pulling him down, back into the tedious gray ennui he had only just begun to escape since Lily came into his life. Since Sunday morning, when they had wed and he had glimpsed, for the first time in years, the possibility of joy.

LILY WAS WAITING in the little drawing room down the hall, while First John stood guard at the door.

Soon, she would be leaving. But she refused to dwell on that fact, instead keeping her focus on the news sheets that had been brought in. As she turned a page, a print slipped loose and drifted like a falling leaf, coming to rest on the carpet.

Setting the papers aside, Lily leaned forward to retrieve it just as Wesley entered, carrying a tea tray with careful dignity.

"Wesley! You read my mind."

The footman's face creased into a warm smile. "I wanted to serve you tea before you left, milady. I ..." He stopped short, and Lily sensed the farewell hovering unsaid, as if it had proven too personal to utter aloud.

She smiled at him gently. "You brew excellent tea. When the new housekeeper begins work at the end of the week, you must ensure she learns how to do it correctly for when I return."

"Thank you, milady."

He stepped forward and set the tray on the nearby table. Lily sat back on the settee, still holding the print she had picked up. One glance at it and a laugh escaped her lips. It was a caricature of the peers in their coronation attire, absurd striped trunk hose and ballooning breeches rendered in the most unflattering light. A gaggle of spindly legs marched awkwardly across the scene like marionettes in a farce.

Wesley paused, uncertain whether she was laughing or had gone quite mad.

"It is the coronation attire," she explained, holding up the image for him to see. "My family was thoroughly entertained when my father descended the stairs dressed just like this. Lord Saunton insists the King orchestrated the whole affair as an elaborate jest to make the entire peerage look ridiculous."

Wesley tilted his head to better view the print, the

corners of his mouth twitching. "It was difficult not to react when I saw the baron."

Her heart stuttered mid-beat, and her breath stalled. But outwardly, Lily allowed no reaction to break across her features.

When I saw the baron?

She gave another light laugh—too quick—and shifted her gaze toward the door, eyes flicking to where John remained posted.

"Quite absurd!" she said, rising in one graceful motion. She moved toward the door, her steps measured though her nerves prickled beneath the surface. From the corner of her eye, she caught Wesley's sudden tension—his attention fixed, not on the caricature, but on her.

Time seemed to slow. He realized what he had said. And he realized he had just revealed far too much.

She stepped faster.

Wesley darted forward.

"JO—"

It was too late. He had seized her by the waist, dragging her backward against his body. One arm crossed her chest and rose higher, pressing uncomfortably beneath her chin as he lifted her off the ground. The strength in Wesley's hold was shocking, coiled like iron beneath his livery, unforgiving and cold.

First John had spun at her shout of alarm, charging into the small drawing room.

"STOP!"

The command rang out with the force of a musket blast, echoing through the tension like the crack of thunder. First John froze at the threshold.

"I will break her neck like kindling if you take another step."

Lily gasped, her hands flying up to claw at the crushing pressure beneath her jaw.

"Cannot ... breathe," she rasped, vision beginning to narrow. Her lungs screamed for air, her limbs flailing in protest. The pressure eased, just slightly, and she drew in a shuddering gasp as her toes brushed the ground. He was lowering her, but the threat remained. His arm held firm, angled tight across her, his breath grazing the crown of her head.

She felt him leaning forward, and the dread deepened in her stomach.

First John stood braced at the ready, his body coiled to act, but he could not.

"Back up. Out the door," Wesley commanded, his tone void of warmth.

Whatever First John read in his eyes must have convinced him, because he slowly stepped back into the hall.

Lily's throat ached beneath the unyielding restraint.

This. This was what Brendan had warned her of. Wesley, frightened and desperate, had reached the edge and taken her with him. She might not walk away from this. And in the silence that stretched between moments, her heart spoke louder than fear.

She wished—oh, how she wished—she had spent the night in Brendan's arms.

She wished she had told him that their wedding day had been the most precious of her life. That though circumstance had entangled them, she had never doubted that he was her heart's true choice. That she loved him.

She had not said it. She had not said any of it.

And now, teetering on the brink of a terrible unknown, Lily wanted to live. Not just to escape, not just to survive, but to love fully. Fiercely. Foolishly, even. To feel the highs and lows, the aching beauty of loving someone who made the world feel whole again.

BRENDAN HAD BEEN STANDING at the wrought iron gates to the square for some time. Finally, he straightened his shoulders with resolve. He could not allow Lily to leave without him. That was not his desire—not now, not ever—and it was time he proved it. He would no longer let silence speak for him.

He supposed he ought to be tracking down more names from his ever-growing list of potential conspirators, but this —*she*—came first. His wife deserved more than evasions and half-measures. With new determination, he set off for Ridley House. He would take Lily to Baydon Hall, where they belonged. Together. He would settle the misunderstanding between them and send for his trunks, as he had intended before Harriet's sudden arrival had torn the moment apart.

When he reached home, Michaels answered the door at once.

"Where is Lady Filminster?"

"I believe she is in the small drawing room, milord."

Brendan nodded and strode past him, crossing the foyer with urgency that bordered on haste. His heart thudded as he turned down the corridor. He would speak his heart. He would not lose her.

But as he neared the doorway, he faltered.

First John was stationed just outside the drawing room, his hands raised, palms outward in a placating gesture. His posture was tense, eyes fixed on something within.

"I assure you I will not enter!" the guard called out.

Something was terribly wrong.

Brendan rushed forward, boots slipping slightly on the polished floor as he reached the threshold—and froze.

Inside, Wesley held Lily against him, his arm braced tightly beneath her chin. Her chest rose and fell in rapid bursts, and fear radiated from her like a storm wind. Her wide brown eyes locked with his, luminous with desperation. In that instant, she looked straight into him, as if she had always known he would come.

"Do not enter, milord! I will kill her if you do!" the footman cried, wild-eyed.

Brendan's instincts roared, but he held them back with iron restraint. Raising his hands slowly, he mirrored John's posture. "Do not panic, Wesley. We can speak as men. There is no need for rashness."

From the corridor behind him, the sound of approaching footsteps echoed—Michaels. They halted abruptly just out of sight, and Brendan knew the butler had assessed the tension in the air.

"What is the meaning of this, Wesley?" came his deep, steady voice. "Has something happened?"

"She saw," Wesley snapped. "She noticed something ... a slip. She knows I was involved in the baron's murder. I am afraid she must be my leverage now."

Brendan's pulse thundered at the sight of Lily in such peril, but he registered, dimly, that some of the wild panic had faded from Wesley's face the moment Brendan had stepped back from the room.

Heaven have mercy! He should have sent Lily away the morning he had discovered his chambers ransacked. If anything happened to her now, he would carry the guilt for the rest of his days. And worse, he would lose the woman he loved.

Love.

The word resounded through him with painful clarity. He had fallen irrevocably, helplessly, in love with his wife. It had happened the night of their wedding, though perhaps the seed had been planted even before. There had been no stopping it, no slowing its bloom.

And if she were harmed, even the smallest, most beloved inch of her, it would shatter him.

Brendan dragged a hand through his hair, trying to push the storm of panic aside. He had to think. He had to talk, to keep Wesley engaged, and find a way to free Lily before it was too late.

"Did you kill the baron?" he asked, voice tight but calm.

Wesley's face twisted with fury. "Of course not!"

"But you know who did?"

Hesitation. Then, a stiff, sullen nod.

"Was it someone in this household?"

Wesley scowled, clearly offended by the question. "Why would a servant wish the baron dead?"

Brendan pressed on. "Then someone outside the household paid you to remain silent?"

Another reluctant nod.

"Then why are you still here?"

"I was promised more coin if I could find a letter the baron had written. They needed someone within the house to search for it."

Brendan inclined his head, heart pounding as he tried to devise a plan. "I will pay you double."

"I am not a fool!" Wesley snapped. "My only chance now is to flee ... and take the baroness with me. That way, you won't risk apprehending me."

Brendan shook his head, lowering his voice to a coaxing tone, though it cost him dearly to speak so evenly. The mere thought of Lily being taken away twisted something sharp and primal in his chest. He wanted to roar, to tear down the walls. Instead, he reasoned.

"If you take her, we will pursue you without rest or mercy. Perhaps …" He swallowed, wincing at the idea even as he voiced it. "Perhaps I could pay you what I have now, and you could … tie us up. To make your escape."

It was a wretched suggestion. If they gave up their freedom, Wesley could do anything he pleased. And if the man was lying, if he was not desperate but deranged, then Lily might be in even greater danger.

His wife must have had the same fears. Though she stood captive and terrified, Lily shifted slightly, trembling against Wesley's hold. Her eyes—those vast, brown eyes—met his with a spark of fierce clarity.

"No!" she choked out, her voice barely more than breath, yet unflinchingly firm. "You will not risk your safety for me. Do you hear, Brendan Ridley? If he must take me, then you must allow it … so long as you remain unharmed!"

Wesley glanced down at her, clearly startled by the sudden burst of resolve from the fragile form he held. But Brendan was not surprised.

Of course she would say such a thing.

That was who Lily was. Brave. Selfless. Infuriatingly noble.

But he could no more let Wesley leave with her than he could stop breathing.

If something happened to Lily, if she were lost to him because of his misjudgment, then Wesley need not strike a blow. Brendan would already be destroyed.

"Take me instead!"

"No!" Lily cried out at once.

Wesley scowled. "Are you jesting? I should take a grown man rather than this small girl as my hostage?"

Grudgingly, Brendan conceded the point. The reprobate had the upper hand ... for now. He prayed Michaels might summon a Bow Street Runner or some other aid, because he was fast running out of options. All he could do was keep the footman talking. Keep him thinking. Because desperate men made rash choices, and Lily's life was a thread stretched to snapping.

"I will give you everything I have in the house," Brendan said, voice tight with desperation. "You may lock us in any room you please. But I beg you ... do not harm the baroness."

As if conjured by thought, the concealed door behind Wesley inched open. A shadowed figure slipped into view—Michaels. The butler's eyes scanned the room, and Brendan's mind whirled.

What was he planning?

Michaels was older, smaller, and certainly not a soldier. But still, he moved with the quiet purpose of someone unshaken by fear. Brendan knew he must not look toward him—any shift in attention could alert Wesley even as every impulse in him screamed at him to stop the butler.

He focused instead on Wesley's face, speaking to keep him distracted.

"Who killed the baron?"

The question dropped like a stone into still water.

"That ... is my secret. The killer will have to pay me. I will demand passage from England, and they will arrange it to hide their identity." Wesley's voice was hesitant when he finally responded. He was not certain he would receive help, Brendan realized. There was an opportunity to negotiate and strike a deal.

In the background, where Brendan resolutely refused to look in the event he alerted Wesley to Michaels's proximity, the butler stepped out from behind the door.

"I do not care about the baron's murder as much as I care about my wife. I will pay you to release her and allow you to leave without hindrance, Wesley. On my word."

That was the moment when Brendan noticed Michaels was raising a rifle to his shoulder. Brendan wanted to shout out for him to stop, that Lily could be hit, but before he could react, the butler cocked the hammer and then pulled the trigger.

It was as if time stood still, the musketball firing from the barrel with a loud bang and belting of smoke, and Wesley crumpled to the floor, dragging Lily down under him.

"Lily!" Brendan ran into the room, dropping to his knees to pull the large footman off his wife. He wrenched Wesley aside with brute force, breath ragged with dread as he reached for his wife.

CHAPTER
SIXTEEN

"100 soldiers who are in a desperate situation lose the feeling of fear. If there is no refuge, they will stand firm. If they are in a hostile country, they will show a stubborn front. If there is no help for this, they will fight hard."

Sun Tzu, *L'Art de la Guerre* (*The Art of War*)

∾

L ily lay curled beneath Wesley's heavy form, dazed and trembling. A deafening blast had sounded, but her mind refused to place it. The footman was motionless above her, and she could scarcely think, let alone move.

With effort, she pushed against his weight, trying to dislodge him.

Moments later, the burden was lifted away, and a rush of cool air touched her skin. She fell back with a soft gasp, grateful for the release.

"Lily, are you hurt?"

It was Brendan. He hovered above her, his hands brushing over her arms and shoulders with urgent care.

"My throat is sore, and my knees are rather battered," she whispered. "And I may have twisted my wrist. I ... I cannot seem to catch my breath, and I have never felt such terror, but I am rather thrilled that ..." She lifted her hands slightly before letting them fall again, adrift in the shock of it all. *Now is not the time to ramble, Lily Billy.*

"What happened?" she breathed, her voice shaking.

Brendan gathered her gently into his arms, enveloping her in warmth and strength. The embrace undid her. After the cruel grip of Wesley, Brendan's presence felt like sanctuary.

"And what are you doing here?" she murmured.

He said nothing at first, only buried his face against her shoulder and held her as if he never intended to let go.

Then, at last, he raised his head.

"What the devil, Michaels?"

The butler replied in his usual dry fashion. "I was protecting the baroness."

"With a rifle?" Brendan asked, incredulous. "What if you had missed?"

Lily heard Michaels click his tongue. Still cradled in Brendan's arms, she did not look around. She had no desire to leave the safety of him. Not yet.

"I imagine your runner informed you that my father was a gamekeeper," Michaels replied. "I know my way around a rifle. Besides, her ladyship is nearly a head shorter than the footman. My odds were solid."

There was a soft thud behind her. Perhaps he had nudged something aside.

Rifle. Her thoughts reeled. Michaels had shot Wesley.

Brendan's cheek came to rest once more against her temple.

"Thank you," he said quietly.

"It is my pleasure, milord. Shall I send someone for Briggs?"

"Yes." Brendan's arms tightened around her again, not with panic, but possessive relief. And this time, Lily leaned into it freely. His grip no longer frightened her. Her hand slid around his waist, fingers curling into the fabric of his coat.

She became aware of his breath at her temple, then the light press of his lips in her hair. Gentle. Reverent.

He tipped her chin and kissed her—soft, slow, as though promising he would never let her come to harm again.

Lily sighed, all her fear dissolving into stillness. Her heart fluttered like petals caught in spring wind.

When he rose, he carried her as if she weighed nothing, striding from the small drawing room with careful purpose.

"John," Brendan said over his shoulder, "find a sheet to cover the body until the coroner arrives. Then meet us in the drawing room at the top of the stairs."

Ridley House was rapidly running out of suitable rooms, Lily mused in a hazy sort of way as she nestled into her husband's chest, his familiar warmth anchoring her to the present.

Brendan carried her down the corridor, up the stairs, and into the larger drawing room on the next floor. Without a word, he crossed to the windows overlooking the quiet street and sank into the faded navy settee, keeping her gathered close against him. His cheek came to rest atop her head, and he simply held her.

Lily did not mind the silence. Not in the least.

She floated somewhere between exhaustion and wonder, her mind too muddled to piece together all that had just occurred. Perhaps it was the shock of the assault, the breathless terror of nearly being strangled, or the dizzying relief that she was still here, in Brendan's arms. Whatever the cause, she refused to dwell on the horror. For now, she let herself simply feel the miracle of being alive, safe, and cherished.

They sat without speaking while her pulse slowed and her chest eased, her thoughts gradually aligning into order. At last, she stirred.

"Michaels shot Wesley?" she asked softly.

"He did."

"Is he ... ?" She trailed off, uncertain how to phrase the question.

Brendan nodded once.

Lily stilled. A ripple of revulsion passed through her, her stomach twisting. She had been beneath the footman, beneath the lifeless weight of the man who had threatened her life. The lassitude that had dulled her mind since the moment she hit the floor began to fade.

"That is ... horrifying."

"I have never been so afraid," Brendan said, his voice low. "I thought I was going to lose you."

She pressed her cheek to his chest again, comforted by the steady rhythm of his heartbeat. "Would that have been such a terrible thing?"

His arms tightened around her. "A very terrible thing, Lily Ridley."

"Why—?"

A discreet cough from the doorway interrupted her.

"I have sent for Briggs," Michaels said calmly, "and I have arranged to notify her ladyship's family of what has occurred. Shall I bring a restorative for Lady Filminster? Perhaps a cordial for the nerves?"

Brendan did not move, still wrapped around her protectively. "No. Lady Filminster does not imbibe."

"Some sweetened tea, then? Or coffee, perhaps?"

Lily stirred slightly. "Coffee? I have never tried it. Is it truly any good? It costs a fortune. I remember seeing the accounts at home. Papa pays an outrageous sum for it. He is not one to spend frivolously."

Brendan chuckled and raised his head. "Coffee, then. But, Michaels, with plenty of milk and sugar."

The butler's steps receded down the hall.

"I would not advise developing a taste for it," Brendan said, his tone warm with affection. "You are spirited enough as it is."

Lily smiled, then gave a small squirm. "I believe I should like to sit up now."

Brendan shifted carefully, easing her from his lap and settling her beside him. She smoothed her dress, straightening folds and tugs, trying to collect her thoughts. Brendan said nothing. He only reached for her hand and held it gently between both of his.

Michaels returned with the tray before Lily had quite gathered her wits. Brendan poured a cup, adding the generous amount of milk and sugar he had requested.

Lily blinked as he stirred the contents. "So much sugar?"

"To help clear the fog after your shock. And coffee is terribly bitter." He extended the cup to her with a reassuring look.

Leaning forward, she accepted it, lifting the delicate porcelain to her lips for a tentative sip. "How strange it tastes."

"It might be wiser to take tea," he said with a faint smile. "Coffee can have peculiar effects on one's energy."

Lily nodded, uncertain whether that was a gentle jest at her expense. She certainly did not wish to chatter any more than she already had.

"Why did you come ba—"

"Lily!"

She turned to see her brother entering the drawing room at a run. His face was flushed, glistening with perspiration, his hair disheveled and cravat half undone.

"Aidan? How did you arrive so quickly?"

"Ran here … as soon as we heard the news … Left our parents … to take the carriage … Terrifying … to hear you had been attacked. I …" Her brother raked his hands through his damp hair before crossing the room to drop on a knee by her side. Taking her hands up in his, and shaking his head as he sought words, he exhaled sharply. "This is my fault! If I had taken care of you that night, instead of abandoning you to carouse with my friends …"

Lily frowned, pulling him closer and lifting her arms to hug him. "It is not, Aidan. I am well. Gracious! You must have run like the wind to arrive here so quickly."

"I should never have left you alone."

"But you did, and now I am married. Life goes on."

Aidan groaned. "Until it does not."

"I am safe. See, you are speaking with me at this very moment. The entire matter is settled."

Aidan pulled away. Her brother was so tall that even lowered to one knee, they were practically eye level. From this close, she could see his pupils were dilated. "Is it over? Was the footman the one who committed the murder?"

Brendan cleared his throat. "No, I am afraid not. He

claims he was paid to conceal the identity of the killer. At least we know now that it was nobody in the household."

Aidan jumped to his feet. "How do we know it is true?"

Her husband must have felt uncomfortable with her brother towering over them. He rose up, walking into the cleared space in the middle of the room. The drawing room had plenty of the large, wooden furnishings of the rest of Ridley House, carefully placed around the perimeter of the room. They were surrounded by the exceptional strapwork of very fine pieces, even if their home was as gloomy as a cave. But Lily had heard that the King preferred to arrange his furniture in a different manner. Perhaps when they renovated Ridley House, they would rearrange the furniture into the informal groupings of the royal household.

Brendan's voice called her back to the more pressing subject at hand. "I suppose we shall search his things to find evidence of the payoff."

Aidan's nostrils flared. "If it is true, then there is still a killer out there. Someone who might harm my sister!"

"We will keep our guards to patrol the house—"

"What?"

Brendan glanced over at Lily, who had straightened in dismay. She did not want to be followed around the house now that they knew Wesley had been the one on their staff working in collaboration with the true perpetrator.

"They do not need to shadow you. Simply take care of our home until we know we are safe. In addition to that, we will have a new housekeeper and maids at the end of the week, so Ridley House will be properly staffed, along with a new lady's maid. It will be far more difficult for any attempt at intrusion once there is a full staff on duty."

Lily turned her gaze to her brother, who appeared mollified by Brendan's assertions.

"See that you do, Filminster. My sister is irreplaceable."

∾

BRENDAN WISHED he could speak with Lily, and communicate to her all the thoughts simmering in his head, but after allaying Abbott's fears, more family arrived.

Lord and Lady Moreland were first. The latter swept into the room with visible agitation, her expression strained with maternal panic. At the sight of her daughter, she let out a soft cry and rushed forward, gathering Lily into a fierce embrace that all but overwhelmed her.

Brendan watched as Lily all but disappeared in her mother's arms, her slight frame nearly vanishing beneath the taller woman's protective hold.

Then Lord Moreland pulled his daughter into his own embrace, shaking his head and murmuring something Brendan could not hear. Cradled against her father's chest, Lily looked more diminutive than he had ever seen her, still so composed, yet achingly fragile.

He had just begun to make his way toward the Abbots, intending to ease their understandable alarm, when the next announcement came, the arrival of Richard and his wife.

That was the moment Brendan fully comprehended the extent to which his familial circle had expanded in the past week. Though distantly connected to Richard through Annabel's marriage to the duke, the earl and the duke being cousins, he had never thought of the connection as meaningful. Now, things were different.

Now he was wed to someone the earl viewed as under his personal protection. A faint ache in Brendan's jaw reminded him precisely how fiercely Richard defended those he loved. Brendan doubted he would ever forget the force of that punch.

And now he had a new brother-in-law as well. Aidan stood at a slight remove, watching him with a gaze still taut with tension. Brendan suspected the younger man's vigilance would not lessen any time soon.

And of course, Lord and Lady Moreland. After confirming their daughter's well-being, their attention turned to him.

Lord Moreland gestured him over.

"This is a fine tangle, son," he murmured. "I thank God no true harm came to anyone. Is the matter concluded?"

"Not entirely, my lord. We have reason to believe the footman was acting under instruction, or at the very least, in someone's employ. The household itself is secure now, but we must still uncover the identity of the person who hired him."

"Wesley confessed, then?" Richard asked, his voice sharper.

"He did. According to him, he was paid to suppress the truth ... to conceal the identity of the baron's killer."

"Wesley confessed to his involvement?" Richard demanded.

"He did. The killer paid him, according to what he told us."

"If he was paid, why was he still here? Do you think he was waiting to quit in order not to raise suspicion?"

"That, and he had been promised additional blunt if he could find a letter that the baron had written."

"A letter?"

"I was going to task Briggs and Michaels with searching the house to see if they could locate it. It might reveal the identity of the murderer."

Richard exhaled hard, shaking his head. "That would be a wonderful thing, if we could find it. This situation this morning with Lily could have turned lethal. Sophia would be devastated if ..."

The earl turned his gaze across the room where Lily and the countess were seated together, Lady Saunton's arm around Brendan's wife as they both sat in relieved silence across the room.

"There are no words to describe how devastated I would be right now if something had happened to Lily."

When Brendan turned back, he found Richard contemplating him thoughtfully, his emerald eyes glimmering. "There is something special about these Abbott girls. Have you informed your wife that you are in love with her?"

Brendan felt heat rise along the back of his neck. "Not yet."

A hand landed warmly on his shoulder, and Brendan turned to see Lord Moreland, whom he had momentarily forgotten was standing behind him.

"Splendid news," the older man said, his voice rough with emotion. "There is nothing in the world quite so rewarding as loving one's wife. Is that not so, Saunton?"

At that moment, the duke and Annabel entered the room. His sister moved with no concern for formality, her composure undone by anxiety. She rushed forward without hesitation and threw her arms around him, holding him tightly, as if to be certain he was truly there.

"You wretched, wonderful man," she whispered through tears as she clung to him again. Brendan had no notion what she was scolding him for, but he understood the depth of her relief and accepted it in silence.

Halmesbury followed more slowly, clapping him on the shoulder with a solemn nod. His lips parted as if to speak, but no words came. Instead, he gave another firm clap to Brendan's back, twice, and simply stood beside him.

Then Briggs appeared on the threshold.

Brendan disentangled himself gently from the embrace and turned toward the runner, motioning to him before glancing back once more to ensure Lily remained surrounded by those who loved her.

She was safe.

He descended the stairs, leading Briggs to the library, where Richard and the duke had already gathered. The door clicked softly shut behind him.

Only then did he notice he was not alone.

Lily's brother stood just behind him.

"I need to help," Lily's brother said quietly, his voice steady with purpose.

"What of Lord Moreland?" Brendan asked.

"My father preferred to remain upstairs with Lily. He asked that I gather the details and report back."

Brendan studied him for a moment, then nodded and stepped aside, allowing him to enter.

SEVENTEEN

"For it is precisely when a force has fallen in danger that it is able to strike a blow for victory."

Sun Tzu, *L'Art de la Guerre* (*The Art of War*)

∽

"Where did you acquire the rifle?" Briggs asked, poised over his notebook, a stub of pencil balanced between calloused fingers.

Michaels sniffed with open disdain. "From the study. There is a collection of flintlock rifles mounted upon the wall, which I believe you have observed."

Briggs continued his notes without responding to the subtle rebuke.

"Those rifles are decades old. How did you know they would prove serviceable?"

The butler's irritation was no longer veiled. "I am responsible for their upkeep. As you are aware, my father served as gamekeeper at Baydon Hall. I was taught the proper care of such weapons from the time I could walk."

Briggs's pencil scratched faintly. "And yet, you had fresh powder at the ready? It would not have been advisable to fire a musket with powder that had sat undisturbed for thirty years."

Michaels's gaze turned stony. "I requisitioned a modest quantity through the household accounts shortly after Lord Filminster's death."

Briggs paused. "Why?"

"Because I concluded that someone within the household must have aided the killer ... or perhaps was the killer. I deemed it my duty to safeguard this house, and those within it."

"Did you suspect Wesley?"

Michaels sat straighter, his expression glacial. "Indeed. And while I understand you chose to investigate me, despite over three decades of loyal service, I could not help but notice that Wesley's account of his return from Yorkshire did not align with the mail coach timetables. It seemed entirely possible that he reached London the very evening of the murder." He gestured toward the room, the events of the morning implicit in his sweeping motion. "And so, I prepared."

Brendan grimaced. "I regret that you must endure this questioning, Michaels. Please know that we are indebted to you for your swift and courageous action."

The butler drew in a slow breath and gave a brief, dignified nod. "I was raised alongside Master Josiah. The notion that I could ever have harmed him—" His voice caught. He shook his head, and Brendan saw past the stern veneer of the man who had served him faithfully for nearly seven years.

Michaels had known the late baron as a boy at Baydon Hall, and it was evident he still thought of him that way. His gruffness had always masked a deep loyalty to the memory of the boy he had grown up with.

"I grieve with you for Lord Filminster's death," Brendan said gently. "And I am sorry you were placed in a position where you were forced to take a man's life to protect another. You are a valued member of this household, and we shall speak further about recognition and recompense for your service and your foresight."

A flicker of emotion passed across Michaels's lined features before he inclined his head in quiet acceptance.

Brendan, watching him, could only be grateful that he had not taken rash action earlier and forced the butler into retirement out of misdirected suspicion. Had Michaels not acted when he did, Lily could have been lost. Injured. Or worse.

Briggs cleared his throat. "I mean no offense, Mr. Michaels. My questions are necessary only so I might present a complete account to the coroner's office and ensure the inquiry proceeds swiftly. It is my view that this household has suffered enough of late and that your actions were both justified and commendable. The protection of a nobleman's wife is no small matter."

Michaels allowed his shoulders to ease, the frost in his tone beginning to thaw. "I appreciate that, Mr. Briggs. I have no wish to prolong this matter."

"I shall definitely put in a good word and ask the Home Secretary to have this matter closed as quickly as possible. There are certainly sufficient witnesses to what transpired with Wesley to settle it." The duke spoke from across the library, where he had been listening from the window facing the street.

Brendan thought how welcome it would be to draw a line beneath this grim chapter. Two dead men within the walls of Ridley House in scarcely more than a fortnight was more than enough. At that moment, all he truly desired was to send every visitor on their way and return to Lily. There was so much he had yet to say to her.

"I suppose that leaves us with the matter of the missing letter," Richard said from within the gloom of the bookcases.

Brendan shook his head. "I fear we should temper our expectations. Wesley searched the house for nearly a fortnight without success. It is entirely possible the letter never existed. Or, if it did, that it has long since been destroyed."

When Briggs had completed his interview, Brendan dismissed the gathering with quiet efficiency. As the others filed from the room, he motioned for Michaels to remain.

They stood side by side at the window, Brendan with his hands clasped neatly behind his back, his gaze following a lone carriage as it rattled along the street below.

"I am deeply grateful for what you did … for my wife and for me. I should be pleased to offer you a generous pension, should you wish it."

The butler's frame stiffened. "Do you wish me gone, milord?"

Brendan turned slightly. "Not in the least. I merely thought you might welcome retirement. I could arrange a cottage for you in Somerset."

Michaels scowled. "I am not ready to stumble into old age, milord. Ridley House is stirring after a long slumber, and I would like to remain to see it flourish."

Brendan considered this, then gave a slight nod. "Very well. I shall see to it that your wages are increased, and I shall speak with my solicitors to formalize arrangements for the cottage and pension for whenever you deem the time right."

Michaels inclined his head in acknowledgment. "Thank you, milord."

He withdrew with his usual composed efficiency, the heavy door whispering closed behind him.

IT HAD DISAPPOINTED Lily to glance up and discover that Brendan had gone. Her head still felt somewhat clouded, the aftermath of the morning's terror lingering in a haze of unreality. For one dreadful moment, when Wesley's weight had collapsed upon her, she had believed he meant to kill her. Her life had not precisely passed before her eyes, but rather, the life she had hoped to live, a future that had seemed poised to slip away forever.

As she sat amongst her family, Sophia's comforting arm about her waist, Lily gradually reoriented herself. Their gentle chatter grounded her, but her thoughts remained fixed on the revelations that had raced through her mind in those final seconds. No matter Brendan's feelings, she was now resolved that she would speak plainly from her own heart. She would not carry regrets.

When the gentlemen returned, the household quickly agreed to gather that evening for dinner. Halmesbury offered the use of their townhouse, and Lily was quietly grateful. The duke's residence was far better suited to a family gathering than Ridley House, especially now that the latter had seen two deaths in as many weeks.

Lily and Brendan accompanied their guests down to the entry hall, exchanging farewells as each carriage arrived in turn. At last, they stood alone, save for Michaels, who took his leave with quiet discretion.

Without a word, Brendan reached for her hand and led her to the staircase. "Come with me."

She followed, her smaller steps quickening to match his as they ascended. She noticed, with no small tenderness, how he adjusted his pace for her when he could. Yet once they reached the upper hall, he resumed his urgent stride, drawing her along beside him.

At her chamber door, he turned the handle and flung it open.

Inside, her maid gave a small shriek of surprise, nearly toppling the oil lamp she had just filled. Beth caught it in time and set it back down upon the low chest near the bed with a shaky hand.

Lily tamped down her impatience at yet another interruption. She longed for a quiet moment alone with her husband, and lingering downstairs had hardly been a welcome alternative, given the morning's grisly events.

"Would you leave us, Beth?" Brendan asked. His tone remained courteous, but there was a taut undercurrent to his voice, betraying his own urgency.

"Yes, milord." The maid bobbed a curtsy and began gathering her things, clutching them as she made her way to the door. At the threshold, she paused and turned.

"Is it true, milord? About Mr. Michaels and Mr. Wesley?"

Brendan nodded solemnly. "It is. I regret to say that today has been most grievous."

Beth inclined her head. "I am glad that her ladyship was not harmed."

"As are we both," he replied. "Thank you, Beth."

The maid offered a final nod before slipping quietly into the corridor, leaving them alone at last.

Lily nodded in fervent agreement. She was thrilled to be unharmed, even though a residue of unease lingered over Wesley's fate. Had his kindness been a ruse, or had he been a good man led astray? She supposed they would never know. The chamber was still, the scent of honey faintly rising from the linens on her bed.

Finally, Brendan closed the door behind them, his hand still warmly enclosing hers. As he led her deeper into the room, his grip was steady, reassuring in a way that made her chest ache. With a strength that felt both effortless and protective, he lifted her by the waist and set her gently atop the edge of her high featherbed, its damask coverlet cool to the touch beneath her fingers. Even as she sat upon the mattress, her muslin skirts pooling at her knees, he stood tall before her, broad-shouldered and solemn, his gaze fixed upon her as if she were a question he could not stop asking.

In the mellow afternoon light filtering through the casement windows, his eyes gleamed, flecks of amber catching in the brown, like sunlight through a cut-glass tumbler of fine brandy. They were warm, penetrating, and far too perceptive. Lily found herself breathless beneath the weight of his attention, as though he had placed her entire being under gentle scrutiny.

"I choose you."

"I love you."

They spoke in unison, and for a moment, time faltered, suspended by wonder.

"You love me?" Brendan asked, his voice rough with astonishment.

"You choose me?" Lily returned, her words no louder than a breath.

Again, they paused, two hearts speaking faster than their tongues.

Brendan opened his mouth just as she did, but this time, he lifted one finger to press gently against her lips. The touch, featherlight and reverent, made her pulse flutter.

"Allow me first."

Lily nodded, her voice caught in her throat, and pressed her lips closed around her smile.

"I choose you, Lily Ridley."

The words were spoken with such intention that they reverberated through her chest like a hymn. Her throat constricted, and her heart began to race.

"I choose your effervescent chatter."

"Some would say I talk too much."

"But I would say you speak just enough to bring color to the world."

Heat bloomed in her cheeks, rising until her ears tingled. She dared not look away.

"I choose your courage in doing what is right, even when it threatens your own safety."

"I could not watch you be arrested for something you were innocent of."

"It was the act of a truly noble heart. And I am not yet finished." His voice deepened, mellow as molasses. "I choose your beautiful face … and your glorious chocolate-brown hair."

Lily lifted her hand to tuck a loose curl behind her ear. "Chocolate brown?"

He reached out to gently retrieve the lock she had tucked away, coiling it around his finger with deliberate care. "The richest, most decadent chocolate available at Gunter's."

A smile curved her lips. "Oh," she whispered, dazed by the warmth in his gaze, a warmth that seemed to gather her up and carry her to safety.

"I choose your incandescent eyes," he said softly, brushing the silken strand down her cheek before letting it slip away.

She bit her lower lip, her pulse fluttering like a lark trapped beneath her stays.

"And I choose the boundless energy with which you greet the world."

He leaned forward slightly, his presence eclipsing everything else. But Lily, in a rare moment of mischief, lifted her hand to stay him.

"What about my bosom?"

Brendan halted mid-motion, eyebrows drawing together in bemusement. "Your ... bosom?"

She nodded toward her bodice. "My bodice is not as full as Lady Slight's."

His laugh was low and warm. "Perhaps not. But it is just the right size to suit the man who loves them ... and you. I require nothing else."

Her blush deepened, but she could not look away.

"I was hopelessly beguiled by you at our wedding. Such a relief it was to discover a strong-minded woman beneath those gauzy debutante gowns."

"Mama insisted I wear them," she replied, rolling her eyes. "I knew they were unsuitable."

He chuckled, and for a moment, the tension between them softened into shared understanding. His unflinching gaze held hers, full of promise.

"I love you, Lily Ridley."

This time, when he lowered his head, Lily did not protest. Her breath trembled on her lips, and when his mouth found hers, she met him with a quiet sigh of gladness, lifting her arms to encircle his neck. Their lips met in a kiss that was deep with promise yet restrained in action, his body drawn close in an embrace that melted the lingering chill of uncertainty from her limbs. His nearness wrapped around her like a cloak, but he made no attempt to deepen the kiss or rush the moment.

He drew back from the kiss, his lips brushing against her jaw in a gesture so tender it made her eyes sting.

His mouth lingered near her neck, not urgent, but reverent, as though memorizing her pulse with every breath. His hands, capable and sure, rose not to claim but to steady her as he held her close.

Lifting her hand, he pressed his lips to her palm, and she felt his mouth curve against her hand. "I love you," he murmured, his voice low and warm, "Lily Ridley."

He leaned in to kiss her cheek, her temple, her brow— each kiss a blessing, deliberate and tender. His affection wrapped around her like a quiet storm, not rushing, not claiming, only existing. Lily could hardly remain still, caught up in the overwhelming sense of being cherished. Her heart beat wildly in her chest as her hands clung to his shoulders.

He did not push for more. Instead, he settled beside her on the bed, drawing her close. The weight of his embrace was steady and grounding, and she melted into it as if into sunlight after rain. Her head rested against his chest, the strong rhythm of his heart an anchor in the swirling tide of her emotions.

"I love being married," she whispered, eyes fluttering closed, a slow smile curving her lips.

"As do I. You are an enchanting woman, Lady Filminster," he said, brushing a kiss across her brow. "I have not had you out of my thoughts since you walked into the church on Sunday."

Lily licked her lips, her mouth suddenly dry from the richness of his tone. "Truly?"

"Every single minute," he said, voice low and fervent. "I admired you long before that day. But then you walked into church and I saw you, not just as the woman I hoped to marry, but as someone who might change my life." He paused, his gaze locked with hers. "After everything that happened, I needed a breath. But since that night, I have wanted nothing more than to be here. With you."

He leaned down slowly, and the warmth of his breath sent a tremor through her. A soft gasp escaped as he pressed a kiss beneath her ear, and her eyes fluttered closed.

"I have been thinking of it, too," she whispered, shivering at the contact. "But this ... this is better. Because now I know you choose me."

"I do choose you, Lily," he murmured. "Every entrancing inch of you."

Their foreheads met, breaths mingling, hearts thudding in perfect rhythm. Lily felt the moment shift, not with haste, but with the quiet weight of certainty. Their hands intertwined, fingers locking as though anchoring them to the moment.

He kissed her again—slowly, deeply—a promise in every press of his lips. Her arms wrapped around him, and he gathered her close, holding her as though he never intended to let go.

"I choose you, Lily," he whispered again, fierce and reverent. "Every single moment of every single day."

His voice was a vow, etched not in paper but in the very air between them.

Lily smiled, tears prickling her eyes. Her campaign had succeeded, but it was not victory she felt. It was wonder. Peace.

General Tzu would be proud of her.

Their marriage was no longer a contract.

It was a love match.

CHAPTER
EIGHTEEN

"Therefore in chariot fighting, when ten or more chariots have been taken, those should be rewarded who took the first. Our own flags should be substituted for those of the enemy, and the chariots mingled and used in conjunction with ours. The captured soldiers should be kindly treated and kept."

Sun Tzu, *L'Art de la Guerre* (*The Art of War*)

AUGUST 2, 1821

L ord Aidan Abbott paced the library, the soles of his boots muffled by the thick Aubusson carpet as he gestured sharply, his voice clipped with frustration. "There is still a killer out there, Filminster. And if this man believes there is a letter connecting him to the crime, he might take it into his head that you or Lily know something. That means my sister is still in danger."

"Or a woman."

"What?"

"We do not know it was a man who committed the murder. It could have been a woman."

"Why would a woman kill the baron?"

"Why would a man kill the baron?"

"Faugh! I have quite forgotten my point."

"You were stating that Lily and I are still under threat, especially if the killer believes we might find this mysterious letter."

Abbott exhaled harshly, running a hand through his tousled hair before stalking across the floor to collapse into a well-worn leather armchair near the hearth. The scent of beeswax and ink hung in the air, mingling with the faint metallic tang from a nearby tray of untouched tea that had long since cooled. Brendan remained standing, hands clasped behind his back. He understood the protective urgency in Lily's older brother.

They sat in a charged silence for several moments, the heavy ticking of the longcase clock in the corner measuring time like a judicial metronome. Then came a disturbance from the hallway, shuffling footsteps and raised voices that immediately caught their attention.

"Lord Trafford, his lordship instructed me he was not to be disturbed. He is in a meeting!" Michaels's voice, usually placid and dry as sandpaper, now carried the unmistakable strain of impending panic.

"Unhand me immediately, you ... you serf!" came the indignant cry in reply, though there was a note of theatrical flourish that betrayed the speaker.

Brendan suppressed a sigh. "Lord Trafford!" Despite Michaels's typical restraint, the final exclamation bordered on a shriek, a most undignified sound from Ridley House's usually imperturbable butler.

Lord Julius Trafford, heir to a prosperous northern earldom and prone to bouts of insufferable boredom, had long made it his mission to cause gentle chaos wherever decorum threatened to reign too comfortably. Brendan feared this might be the day his friend finally sent Michaels into apoplexy.

"Just a jest, Michaels. You know what a rapscallion I am."

There was an unintelligible murmur from the butler, no doubt clipped and scathing.

"You see? Admit it. I am your favorite."

More mumbling ensued. A few seconds later, Michaels appeared, composed once more, as though his earlier outburst had been someone else's entirely. "Lord Trafford to see you," he announced coolly, executing a precise bow before retreating with upper servant efficiency.

Trafford came striding in as if entering a ballroom, his boots clicking confidently on the parquet flooring. He paused, sweeping the library with theatrical deliberation before his gaze landed on Abbott, whom he regarded with faint curiosity, then turned to Brendan.

"What is this I hear? A man was killed in your home yesterday? You did not think to summon me?"

Brendan was not certain whether Trafford's indignation was genuine or feigned, so he swallowed the chuckle rising in his throat. "Summon you?"

Trafford had a penchant for seasonal reinvention, a personal antidote to what he termed "the soul-crushing sameness of the high society." The previous year, he had penned abysmal verse while wrapped in black velvet à la Byron. This year, he had evidently embraced a flamboyant foppishness.

His polished buckled shoes gleamed beneath slim-fitting trousers, and his purple jacquard coat shimmered faintly in the lamplight. A gold-embroidered waistcoat completed the ensemble, startling against the contrast of his thick blond curls and the clipped, dark hair that framed the sides of his head in a fashionable undercut.

Brendan recognized the spectacle for what it was. Calculated theatricality.

With a sniff that spoke volumes, Trafford sauntered to the library table. He gave a perfunctory tug to his lace-edged cuffs, flicked an invisible speck of lint from his lapel, and then dropped into a carved mahogany armchair. Stretching out his legs in studied indifference, he folded his arms and turned his brown eyes once again on Brendan. "Am I not your friend? Should I not be informed when you are in mortal peril?"

This time, Brendan let the laugh escape. "Are you taking umbrage regarding the peril, or are you more outraged that something of intrigue took place and you were left out of it?"

Trafford surveyed him with a look of dignified disdain. "The intrigue, of course."

Abbott, who had been watching in open-mouthed disbelief, abruptly straightened and glowered. "Who is this ... this fool, Filminster?"

Trafford's face crumpled into unrepentant mirth.

Brendan gave an apologetic shrug. "Allow me to introduce Lord Julius Trafford, heir to the Earl of Stirling. And first-rate clown."

"Clown?" Trafford echoed, pulling a face of contemplation. "Like the performer Grimaldi? I am not fond of the garments, but I admire the slur. Well done, little Ridley."

Abbott sprang to his feet, his shoulders tense. "My sister was almost killed, you ridiculous fop!"

"Now you know who I am. Who are you?" Trafford asked with lazy amusement.

Brendan stepped forward before Abbott could do anything rash. "This is Lord Aidan Abbott, heir to Viscount Moreland. My wife's brother."

"Ah! Another token title like my own. Dear Papa holds a barony, I suppose? Or is it an Irish viscountcy?"

Abbott's eyes narrowed as he assessed Trafford with animosity. "You were at the wedding breakfast."

"I was. Which is why Filminster should have sent for me."

"A desperate criminal manhandled my sister. Your amusement was not foremost in our minds."

Trafford tilted his head and appeared to think deeply. "I concede your point."

"Dash it! Concede this—" Abbott stormed forward, and Brendan had to step between them.

"Trafford is attempting to get a rise out of you," Brendan said quickly. "He acts out when he finds himself excessively idle, but he is not the fool he appears to be."

Trafford beamed, clearly pleased with himself, even as Brendan worked to calm his brother-in-law. "Why, Ridley. I do believe you like me."

Brendan coaxed Abbott back into his seat, both exasperated and faintly amused by his friend's relentless provocation. Trafford was, at the best of times, insufferable, but there was no denying the wry charm threaded through his mischief. Beneath the irreverence beat a fiercely loyal heart, and for all his diabolical vagaries, Trafford enjoyed a surprising number of allies among both ladies and lords.

"Only in small doses, Julius."

Trafford placed a hand theatrically over his heart and pouted as if wounded by sentiment. "So how can I help?"

Brendan resumed his own seat, glancing between the two heirs, so opposite in bearing that one might mistake them for creatures from different realms entirely. "I have nothing to tell you, gentlemen. Ridley House is being searched, but beyond that, we have no new clues as to who paid the footman. All we can do is wait for something new to come to light."

"The murderer must be part of the peerage," Trafford said airily.

Abbott frowned, brows drawn. "Why do you say that?"

Trafford rolled his eyes. When he finally responded, he spoke slowly, as if explaining something to a child. "The baron never visited London, and the only event he attended was the coronation itself. And he sat with lords. So it can only be one of them or their connections who committed the crime."

Brendan's eyebrows lifted. "How would you know that?"

Trafford pulled a face that bespoke high insult, his tone dripping with disdain. "I asked around. What do you think I have been doing since the murder? Trimming my nails?"

Brendan snorted in amusement. "More like having your valet bleach your hair with lemon juice."

Trafford straightened in his seat, his face falling as his hand shot up to finger his blond hair. "It is not ..." He shook his head without finishing. Brendan felt a twist of guilt, realizing that he had touched on a nerve.

Trafford continued, "As you are aware, I have a wide circle of acquaintances. I asked around to confirm the late baron did not attend any social events within the few days he was in London."

Abbott snorted. "You cannot know that. There could

have been a small gathering at someone's home. A dinner, perhaps."

Trafford said nothing, but shot a look of long-suffering incredulity in Brendan's direction.

Brendan sighed. "Trafford means he checked with above and below stairs alike. He does not discriminate when it comes to seeking information. I should state that he is very thorough in gathering information about members of the *ton*."

"Why?" Abbott sounded honestly perplexed. "Why would he be an expert in such a thing?"

Trafford burst into laughter, the sound echoing against the carved paneling and high ceiling. "What a little breeches you have on your hands, Filminster. Is your brother-in-law truly so unsophisticated?"

Brendan soughed heavily. "Women, Abbott. Trafford is highly skilled in gathering information about women of the *ton*. I should have thought to request his help in learning about my ... father's ... movements." He hoped Abbott and Trafford did not notice his hesitation, or ascribed it to the pressure he had been under.

"Just so," Trafford said, flashing a knowing smirk.

Abbott shook his head, as though attempting to reorder his entire perception of the man seated before him. Brendan could hardly blame him. Trafford had that effect on people. It was difficult to imagine what, if anything, might one day tame the impudent showman. But until that day arrived, Brendan was grateful for his friendship, particularly in moments of crisis. Trafford had gone to considerable lengths to assist Perry Balfour the year prior, and that loyalty counted for more than eccentricities.

"So, what do we do now?" Abbott asked, his voice tight with frustration.

"I discussed it at length with Saunton and Halmesbury. There is not much to be done, I am afraid. We remain vigilant and continue our search for information." Brendan wished he had a better answer, but it was the only one he had.

IT WAS A GLORIOUS SUMMER DAY, the sun filtering gently through a haze of London soot, and the cobbles gleamed faintly from an earlier sweep of rain. The bustle of Piccadilly was tempered by a cooling breeze, carrying the scent of horse and cut hay from carts passing en route to the park.

Made even more glorious by the fact that her husband was accompanying her to Hatchards.

The bookshop, its large glass windows gleaming behind polished brass trim, was one of her favorite places in all the world. And now she could share it with one of her favorite people in all the world.

"I think we should order a number of novels for the library," she said, lightly brushing her gloved hand over the book spines as they stepped through the wide oak doors. The interior was cool and dust-scented, the tang of ink and old paper welcoming her like an old friend. "Most of the books in there are fusty old texts about agriculture. We should have some Byron, Wordsworth, and Keats. I also wish to order that *Frankenstein* book, along with Ann Radcliffe and Jane Austen."

Brendan nodded, already absorbed in the front stacks. He pulled several titles down with a discerning eye, the leather bindings creaking faintly beneath his fingers.

Lily leaned in to examine the one on top. "Coleridge's *Lyrical Ballads*! It did not cross my mind, but I love it!"

Their ongoing discussions about improving Ridley House had taken on a new dimension since the wedding. Brendan had proven surprisingly amenable to her taking charge of the estate's inner workings, and they had both agreed that the library should reflect the literary spirit of the age.

Soon, their new housekeeper would arrive, and Richard had recommended they consult his brother, Mr. Thompson, about more substantial renovations.

Barclay Thompson, a renowned architect, had attended their wedding. His firm had refurbished several Mayfair townhouses for the wealthiest members of society, and Lily was nearly giddy at the thought of what he might do for Ridley House. She looked forward to meeting with him and his assistant upon their return to Town.

It would be a wondrous thing if they could begin the process before departing for Baydon Hall in Somerset.

Soon, they stood at the shop counter, placing their order. The clerk's quill scratched softly over the parchment ledger as Lily listed her selections. She had never placed such a large order before, and her gloved hands trembled slightly from excitement. To bring Ridley House to its full potential, not merely functionally, but soulfully, felt like reclaiming something sacred.

Wiping away the remnants of the past would, she believed, be the surest way to banish the shadow of death that still lingered within its rooms.

"Have you read much?" she asked softly as Brendan handed over the final list. He had shown a canny eye while selecting their new acquisitions, and she was curious. The sad state of their inherited library had suggested otherwise.

"I have," he replied, holding the door open for her as the bell overhead gave a bright jangle. "But I mostly took advantage of the libraries of others. Annabel and the duke have an excellent selection, and I had access to Trafford's and several other friends'."

She paused at the threshold, turning back to question him with a glint of mischief. "Who is your favorite?"

But before he could answer, a familiar drawl cut through the hum of the street.

"Well, well. It is the scandalous Lily Ridley, if my eyes do not deceive."

Lily spun about to find Lady Slight, accompanied by a friend. The widow was resplendent in a striped blue walking dress, her bodice cut daringly low and her figure arranged for maximum display. Lily instinctively stepped back, half-convinced she might be knocked in the face by the other woman's prominently presented décolletage.

Lady Slight's companion, a fashionable blonde with a similarly plunging neckline and eyes like winter frost, giggled at the remark, clearly finding the widow's greeting devilishly amusing.

For a moment, Lily hesitated. The old Lily might have blushed and stammered. But the new Lily, Lady Filminster, could not afford apologies.

No, she would attack. With words.

"Oh, do you mean the scandalous night I spent with Lord Filminster while his father was being bludgeoned to death?" she asked lightly, turning and reaching for Brendan's arm. He responded without hesitation, stepping smoothly through the door and shutting it behind him with an elegant flick of the wrist before tucking her hand into the crook of his arm.

"Or do you mean when I stepped forward to speak to

the coroner in order to clear Lord Filminster's name of those dreadful accusations of murder?"

Lady Slight and her friend had drawn back, their expressions frozen in masks of wide-eyed horror.

"Or perhaps," Lily continued sweetly, "you mean our hasty marriage to protect my reputation?" She paused, arching a brow, but no response came.

"Perhaps you mean when our footman attempted to abduct me and my husband bravely offered to take my place? Before our butler shot the man dead, of course." Lily tapped a finger to her lip as if thinking. She tilted her head, eyes dancing with mischief. "But no, I think you must mean all of it."

With a sweeping gesture, she settled the matter. "If I think about it, I must confess that I am. I am scandalous. Scandalously happy, that is!"

Lady Slight's jaw had dropped unceremoniously. It appeared the widow had not anticipated being battered with the full brunt of Lily's irrepressible candor. Lily, after all, was not famed for subtle manners.

Beside her, Brendan raised a gloved hand to his mouth, his eyes glittering with barely restrained laughter.

Lily managed to keep her face composed, but her heart fluttered with delight as she watched both women visibly wilt under the weight of her unapologetic truth.

Turning toward her husband, she reached up and gently cupped the side of his neck. Rising onto the tips of her toes, she smiled as Brendan lowered his head to meet her. His mouth met hers in a kiss that was warm, firm, and reverent —an unmistakable public declaration. He wrapped his arm around her, steadying her, drawing her close. The embrace was secure and full of promise. Her breath caught from sheer happiness.

From behind her, Lady Slight gasped at the public display. It was not fashionable to like one's husband, nor to be seen enjoying his company, certainly not in broad daylight on Piccadilly. But Lily did not care a fig for what society considered appropriate. Let the gossips wag their tongues until they dropped from their jaws. She was deliriously joyful, and the entire world could go hang if they wished to complain.

Her dreams had come true, and she would not apologize for them.

Dropping back onto her heels, she drew a tremulous breath in an attempt to calm the riot of her pulse. Then, with composed dignity, she turned back to the widow.

"Whomever it was that my husband was with before me," she said softly, "I am ever so grateful that they set him free ... so that I could catch him."

Lily tilted her chin upward in challenge, daring the viscountess to speak.

But Lady Slight could only gape, opening and closing her mouth like a fish gasping for air. The deflation in her eyes, the flicker of exposed hurt, pierced Lily unexpectedly. Just for a moment, her heart twinged.

The widow must be a very unhappy woman deep down.

Her life seemed a hollow one. Married off to a decrepit lord who had died shortly after the vows were spoken, she had borne no children. Now she floated through drawing rooms and musicales, changing paramours as frequently as Lily changed her stays. These were not the actions of a contented soul.

General Tzu, she recalled, would advise mercy to the fallen foe.

Letting Brendan go, Lily stepped forward. With slow

grace, she reached out and touched the back of Lady Slight's hand. The woman flinched as though scorched.

"I wish you the boundless joy of truly connecting with another person," Lily said, her voice clear and gentle. "Of opening your heart to another, and finding that you care more for them than for your own self. I wish you a strong young husband and healthy children. And I wish you a long and full life filled with laughter, Lady Slight."

There was no mockery in her tone. Only sincerity.

Without waiting for a reply, she turned and returned to Brendan, slipping her gloved hand into the crook of his arm. Together, they strolled toward their waiting carriage, the wheels rattling softly on the cobbles as their driver readied the horses.

Brendan lowered his hand to rest over hers and smiled down at her with blazing, affectionate eyes. Leaning closer, he whispered into her ear, his breath brushing the curl at her temple.

"I choose you, Lily Ridley. Every kind, fiery, honorable inch of you."

She looked up at him and smiled, her chest glowing with contentment. "And I choose you, Brendan Ridley."

EPILOGUE

"Knowledge of the disposition of the enemy can only be obtained from other men."

Sun Tzu, *L'Art de la Guerre* (*The Art of War*)

After their afternoon spent selecting books, Brendan lingered in the entryway, watching Lily ascend the staircase to change for dinner. The fading light from the tall windows cast a golden sheen on the polished banister, and for a moment, he allowed himself the indulgence of watching her silhouette disappear around the landing.

So much had changed.

Turning to head toward the library, he was halted by the soft clearing of a throat behind him.

He pivoted on his heel. "What is it?"

Michaels, unusually hesitant, stood with his hands

folded. His usually impassive face bore a crease between the brows. "The study is ready, milord."

Brendan blinked. "The study?"

"We have ... managed to clean the floors," the butler said slowly. "And a new rug has been placed. I took the liberty of moving the furniture and rearranging the *objets d'art* to ..." He faltered, the final words lost in a vague motion of his hand.

Despite the uncharacteristic awkwardness, Brendan understood what was being conveyed. The traces of blood. The shattered statue. The final breath of the late baron. All had been erased or hidden beneath layers of polish and new fabric.

He lifted a hand to his temple, rubbing absently before catching himself. The old tension was back, coiling behind his eyes.

"I see." He had not stepped foot in the room since the night he had found the body. Perhaps it was time. Time to reclaim what was his.

"After you."

Michaels offered a short bow and turned toward the west wing. Brendan followed him down the corridor lined with gilt-framed portraits, the hush of the house swallowing their footsteps.

At the threshold, Michaels opened the door but did not enter, stepping aside with silent deference.

Brendan crossed the threshold alone.

The study was softly lit, the oil lamps casting a warm flicker over shadowed corners. The heavy damask drapes had been drawn back, allowing the last of the afternoon sun to brush over the furnishings. His mahogany writing desk, which once faced the east windows, now stood on the far wall, facing west. A new rug—Persian, from the look of it—had replaced the old one. Rich reds and deep indigos grounded the room in fresh color.

The arrangement atop the mantel had been altered. Bronze busts now flanked a clock he did not recognize, and the shelves between the tall windows had been restocked, their spines aligned with a precision only Michaels could muster.

Brendan stood still, taking it in.

"It was an excellent idea to rearrange the furnishings," he murmured. "I do not think I could have walked in to find everything ..." He hesitated. "To find it exactly as it was that night would be macabre, to say the least."

Michaels nodded. "It was a sad day for Ridley House, milord. I have no wish to think of it each time I enter the room."

Brendan turned slowly toward him. "Are you ... holding up? It must be difficult to take a man's life."

Michaels pressed his lips together, his gaze straying to the window. For several seconds, he stood in contemplative silence before replying.

"It would have been inconceivable to allow Lady Filminster to come to harm. Her ladyship is a vibrant mistress, one who will shape the next chapter of the Filminster title. I find myself quite looking forward to ... the progression of the Ridley family."

Brendan's lips twisted into a wry smile. The butler's oblique reference to Lily's future procreation stirred a warmth in him that he, too, anticipated with fondness.

With a discreet bow, Michaels turned and left, closing the door quietly behind him.

Brendan crossed the room and approached the desk—

his desk now. He ran a hand across its polished mahogany surface, his fingertips trailing the edge where delicate scrollwork had been carved into the wood. The shape was familiar. Solid. Steadying.

Dropping into the chair, he stretched his legs out, one boot tapping lightly against the rich wool of the rug. Deep reds and blues gave color to the otherwise somber room. Michaels had done well refreshing it. Even before renovations could begin, the space already felt less haunted.

Leaning back, Brendan's hand found the carving beneath the lip of the desk. He had always enjoyed journaling, though his thoughts had remained unwritten since the baron's arrival. His fingers moved along the groove with practiced ease, finding the hidden clasp. His mother had once shown him a similar drawer in the matching desk at Baydon Hall, so he had known what to look for.

With a muted click, the hidden compartment released.

Inside was his well-worn leather journal. But just beside it, half-tucked into the shadows, lay a loose page. His hand stilled.

Frowning, he carefully extracted the page and the quill that lay beside it, ink-stained and still slightly tacky at the tip. He placed them on the desk along with the journal, staring at the page as comprehension slowly dawned.

The scrawl was unmistakable—his uncle-father's angular hand, hastily looped and impatiently crossed. Brendan's pulse quickened. It appeared the old man had been interrupted while writing, for the page bore scattered droplets of ink that obscured sections of the text like black teardrops. The pen had spattered. In his panic, the baron must have swept the unfinished letter into the drawer and closed it, sealing it away, perhaps in his final moments.

A dreadful weight settled in Brendan's chest. This could be the answer. Or it could be something worse.

His breath grew shallow. For a long moment, he stared without truly seeing, his mind tightening around the implications.

The letter existed.

The mystery was not done.

A soft knock broke his trance, and he flinched.

The door opened, revealing Lily—now refreshed, her gown silken and her curls refreshed. She paused just inside the threshold, her gaze falling instantly to his face.

"What is it?" she asked, crossing the room in swift, graceful strides.

Brendan shook his head slowly. "I think I found the letter."

She gasped, rushing forward to his side. "What? How?"

"There is a secret drawer," he said quietly. "Where I keep my journal. When I opened it ... I found this."

He lifted the letter with fingers that trembled slightly.

He had never truly believed it would surface. Despite all their efforts—Briggs, Michaels, the endless search of Ridley House—he had considered it a rumor. A hope.

Lily wrapped her arm around his shoulders in a close, protective embrace.

"It will start everything up again," she said softly.

He nodded.

"But eventually," she whispered, "this story will end. And we shall have our lives ahead of us."

Brendan turned his head to look at her. "We shall see what the baron had to say, then."

Drawing a breath, he lifted the page and held it steady, her arm still draped across his back.

"It is addressed to the Home Secretary. Some of the words are obscured by the ink that soaked into the paper."

Sir Robert Peel

London, July 19, 1821

Sir,

It has come - - my attention that the true heir to Lord - - - - - - - - has not been acknowledged.

I was speaking with his lordship before the coronation, and he informed me of his recent bout of ill health. He spoke fondly of his youngest brother, informing - - of his strength, intelligence, and wit at great length. There was no mention of his lordship's middle brother, Peter, who you may be aware died near twenty years - - -.

Peter and I attended Oxford together, - - - his death was tragic - - - unexp- - - - -. I have thought of him often over the years, which is why I feel the need to pass this information - - - - - -u.

Before departing England, Peter married a wom- - of Catholic descent. She convert- - - - - - - - - were married - - - - - Church of England, before leaving our shores. I maintained correspondence with him until his death. He had written just months before his death to inform me of the birth of his son.

I cannot say for certain where the boy and his mother are - - - - - all these years, but he would be the true heir and I implore you to look into th- - matter. - - - - - - - - - is the true heir to the title of - - - - - and his father's legacy cannot be ignored.

I understand the trials of being a second son, and I cann- - allow this matter to stand. Whether - - - - - terrible injustice is a mistake due to ignorance of the child Peter sired, or a deliberate obfuscation of the facts, I must speak on my friend's

behalf. His son is the true heir and must be found immediately.
I will locate our shared correspondence when I return to
Somerset and have them forwarded to - - - - - - - - - - -

  J. Ridley, Baron of Filminster

Lily stood frozen, mouth parted in disbelief, as Brendan lowered the letter to the desk.

"This truly must be the reason the baron was killed!" she exclaimed. "Do you think the false heir is the one who did it?"

Brendan did not answer at once. His thoughts churned, slow and heavy.

Inheriting a title was not merely a matter of honor. It could involve estates, tenancies, seats in the Lords, and wealth beyond ordinary imagining. A hidden heir, a lost son —it all sounded like something from a dramatic novel, and yet here it was, spelled out in the scrawled hand of the late baron.

It could explain everything.

The late-night visit. The panic. The choice of weapon. The sudden violence.

It was a theory as logical as it was chilling.

"We do not know enough," he said finally.

Lily threw up her hands. "What are you saying? We have everything we need right here!"

Brendan shook his head. "We do not even know the identity of the lord he spoke with. Do you know how many peers have at least three sons? That the second son is named Peter narrows things only marginally."

"But we know Peter died about twenty years ago. He married a Catholic woman, she might have been from the Continent. And he left England before his death. That must reduce the number of possibilities by ... well ... quite a bit?"

Brendan reached up to cover her hand where it still rested lightly on his shoulder. "You are correct. It is simply ... a great deal to absorb."

He looked back at the letter, its smudges and blotches now imbued with cruel weight. "The baron's death suddenly seems almost trivial in light of this. It was a matter of chance. Someone must have come to silence him without even knowing this note would give them away."

"I suppose," Lily said, her voice low as she rested her chin against his hair, "you shall meet with Briggs and the others to discuss where this takes the investigation."

He nodded.

"The baron's murder was a tragic event," she continued softly, "but it led us to each other. It is dreadful to ponder the reason we are now married, but I cannot bring myself to regret that we are wed."

Brendan turned in his chair to look up at her. Her face was serene, yet her eyes sparkled with fierce conviction.

"No regrets," he said, his voice quiet but firm.

"None at all," she agreed and pressed her cheek gently to his temple.

Brendan felt a smile tug at his lips despite the unsettling revelation of the letter. Without thinking, he reached over and drew Lily gently into his lap, cupping her face as he pressed a kiss to her soft mouth.

"Despite how all this came to pass," he murmured, his forehead resting lightly against hers, "I regard myself as most fortunate to have married such a singular and intriguing woman."

"Intriguing?" Lily asked, her breath warm against his cheek.

"Absolutely captivating. Endlessly amusing. Ravishing in spirit and wit."

Her arms twined around his neck, and Brendan felt the lingering tension in his chest finally begin to ease.

"Thank you," he whispered. "For standing beside me. For helping me navigate this ordeal. For believing in me."

"For keeping you out of prison?" she teased, her tone light.

He chuckled. "Indeed. That, most especially."

Lily tilted her head, her eyes soft, and deepened their kiss in a way that was sweet and certain. Brendan lost himself in her affection, grateful beyond measure. Her presence anchored him more than any title, more than any inheritance.

Their closeness mounted like a slow-burning flame, and Brendan held her tightly, brushing a hand down her back in reverence. He thought, fleetingly, how much he would like to lift her into his arms and carry her upstairs, simply to hold her uninterrupted.

A knock at the door startled them both. They sprang apart slightly, laughter in their eyes as Brendan smoothed a curl behind her ear.

"Dinner is served, milord."

Michaels stood in the doorway, his expression serene and focused on a point somewhere beyond the far wall. His composure was exemplary, considering he had clearly interrupted a moment of newlywed intimacy.

"Thank you, Michaels," Brendan replied, mustering more dignity than he felt.

The butler nodded and withdrew, shutting the door with quiet efficiency.

Lily turned back to him with sparkling eyes before succumbing to a sudden, irrepressible fit of giggles. Brendan laughed in response, then drew her into his arms for one final embrace.

"Come now, Lady Filminster," he said with mock solemnity as he helped her to her feet. "It is time to dine."

~

Lord Aidan Abbott investigates Mr. Smythe but compromises his daughter, Gwen, at a ball in front of a crowd of important guests. Find out what happens next in *Miss Smythe and the Midnight Lord*!

DOWNLOAD A FREE BOOK

Enjoyed the story? The adventure isn't over yet ...

Subscribe to Jarrett's newsletter to receive a book—absolutely free!

The Meddling Duke: A determined duke. Three unforgettable women. And a meddling hand in each of their lives that may just lead to true love.

Join thousands of Regency romance readers who love exclusive content, behind-the-scenes peeks, giveaways, and early access to new releases. Your next favorite story is just one click away.

AFTERWORD

Napoleon was considered a brilliant military strategist, so it was no surprise when I discovered that *The Art of War* had been translated into French. In *Miss Hayward and the Earl*, you might recall Sophia's advice to Lily to improve her French so that she might study and apply Sun Tzu's strategies to the marriage mart of London.

Sophia was well familiar with the general's rules of battle, but Lily is still a novice in her story. She applies them energetically, but not always with finesse, which leads to some awkward situations.

By the Regency, there were just over three hundred coroners serving all England. They were always educated men of property, and it helped if they had both money and political connections to get appointed or elected.

One imagines a certain amount of cherry-picking of cases by the coroner for the assigned area, considering the workloads. And there would be a variety of reasons a man would seek the office in the first place, which leads us to Grimes and his political aspirations. Fortunately, Lily was there to thwart the ambitious coroner's campaign to raise his status by landing a peer in prison.

If you enjoyed this story, I would be incredibly grateful if you'd consider leaving an honest review. Your words help others discover the book and support future stories.

Now that Lily and Brendan have secured their household, Aidan Abbott is going to feel the pinch of culpability when danger continues to stalk Ridley House. Making it his mission to find the killer, a certain Miss Smythe is going to find herself in his arms at exactly the wrong moment, provoking a high society scandal.

When Aidan is forced to marry into the family he is investigating to protect his sister, is there any chance for these newlyweds to find a path to happiness? Or will Aidan's secrets ruin their love before it starts?

Find out in *Miss Smythe and the Midnight Lord*, the next chapter of the *Reluctant Reckonings* series!

About the Author

C. N. Jarrett started writing her own stories in elementary school but got distracted when she finished school and moved on to non-profit work with recovering drug addicts. There she worked with people from every walk of life from privileged neighborhoods to the shanty towns of urban and rural South Africa.

One day she met a real-life romantic hero. She instantly married her fellow bibliophile and moved to the USA where she enjoyed a career as a sales coaching executive at an Inc 500 company. She lives with her husband on the Florida Gulf Coast.

Jarrett believes in kindness and the indomitable power of the human spirit. She is fascinated by the amazing, funny people she has met across the world who dared to change their lives. She likes to tell mischievous tales of life-changing decisions and character transformations while drinking excellent coffee and avoiding cookies.

Stay in touch by signing up for the C. N. Jarrett newsletter!

ALSO BY C. N. JARRETT

DAZZLING DEBUTANTES

Book 1: Miss Ridley and the Duke

Book 2: Miss Hayward and the Earl

Book 3: Miss Davis and the Spare

Book 4: Miss Davis and the Architect

Book 5: Mrs. Brown and the Christmas Gift

The Meddling Duke: a Collection of Regency Romantic Short Stories

RELUCTANT RECKONINGS

Book 1: Miss Abbott and the Suspect Lord

Book 2: Miss Smythe and the Midnight Lord

Book 3: Miss Gideon and the Incident

Book 4: Miss Bigsby and the Aristocrat Next Door

Book 5: Miss Carter and the Baron's Heir

TREACHEROUS TREASURES

Book 1: Lady Slight and the Visitor

Book 2: Miss Bigsby and the Very Short Courtship

Book 3: Miss Fairfax and the Secret Symphony

Book 4: Miss Metcalfe and the Romantic Blunder

Book 5: Miss Caraway and the Encrypted Heart

www.ingramcontent.com/pod-product-compliance
Lightning Source LLC
Chambersburg PA
CBHW031336020726
47499CB00005B/1289